the
CRYSTAL
POOL

the CRYSTAL POOL

Thomas Bingham

TATE PUBLISHING
AND ENTERPRISES, LLC

Published by Tate Publishing & Enterprises, LLC
127 E. Trade Center Terrace | Mustang, Oklahoma 73064 USA
1.888.361.9473 | www.tatepublishing.com

Tate Publishing is committed to excellence in the publishing industry. The company reflects the philosophy established by the founders, based on Psalm 68:11,
"The Lord gave the word and great was the company of those who published it."

Book design copyright © 2011 by Tate Publishing, LLC. All rights reserved.
Cover design by Blake Brasor
Interior design by Chelsea Womble

Published in the United States of America

ISBN: 978-1-61346-419-9
Fiction / Fantasy / General
11.11.29

Dedication

To my grandchildren, who I hope will thoroughly enjoy this story and, through it, learn something of the One who loves them most

Acknowledgments

I would like to thank my five daughters, Tisha, Bonnie, Nikki, Ginger, and Christine, for providing the motivation for *The Crystal Pool*'s creation through our times of storytelling when they were young. As adults they continued to encourage the completion of this work, which was especially helpful during those times of writer's block.

A special thank you to Christine, who created one color painting and twenty-six pen and ink illustrations.

I would also express my great appreciation to my wife, Kay, who spent countless hours helping me examine the wording, character consistency and style, consistency of the story line, and applicability to the intended audience, as well as adding two additional chapter illustrations.

Thanks are in order to Jason Lund and Beth Faulkner, who listened to and read portions of the story's beginning when they were in elementary school, and who continued to remind me to finish the book for many years afterward.

Also for Roberta Scholz of Berkeley Editing Services, who reviewed the text in its roughest form and provided essential editing needed to get the book off the ground.

Final special thanks to my mother, Carol Bingham, who helped proof several chapters and also provided encouragement to its completion.

Table of Contents

Johnny

Johnny groaned and pulled the covers over his head. Who had set the volume so loud anyway? He reached repeatedly to the floor for his clock radio, finally managing to hit the snooze button. He shoved the annoying thing back into the war zone under his bed, completing the entire process without waking up. Ten minutes later, the radio came back on—just as loud, but this time less accessible.

Refusing to acknowledge this rude noise, Johnny tried covering his head with the pillow, but as usual, it offered little protection. Not only did it fail to muffle the radio, it also failed to shut out a persistent knocking at his door.

"Johnny Matheson, if you don't get up, you'll miss your flight," called his mother.

He knew that ignoring her was not a good idea, yet facedown with the pillow over his head, his feeble response had no hope of being heard. She called again, this time with a slight edge in her voice.

Johnny sighed and tore off the covers, leaving them in a pile on the floor. He stumbled to his door, opened it a crack, and said, "I'm up, Mom."

She headed back downstairs, instructing him to get ready and come down for something to eat. Instead, he sat down again on the bed. Fearing he might go back to sleep, he arose and threw on yesterday's clothes. He didn't bother looking at himself in the mirror—probably not a good idea—and headed down to the kitchen.

He didn't get far before his mother said, "I am not having Gail and Jim see you in those clothes! Did you sleep in them? Go right back upstairs, and get into the outfit I washed for you yesterday."

11

This was not the best start he could imagine for what should be a great day, but Johnny knew better than to argue and did what he was told. When he returned he avoided his mother's view for fear she might find yet another part of him out of place.

"Hey, the young man is up," Johnny's father said, never looking away from the newspaper.

Johnny hated it when his father called him "the young man," but he knew that complaining not only did no good but also ran the risk of getting him another one of those lectures about the merits of maturity.

"Your plane takes off in four hours—we need to leave soon," his father added, still with his nose to the paper.

"Okay," the boy responded, "I'll grab a bowl of cereal."

Johnny slid into a chair, began to consider his choices, and selected a box.

"Four hours," he grumbled. "I could have slept in at least two more."

Perhaps anticipating this, his father had added, "And we have to leave in thirty minutes."

"Dad, how far away do Ben and Patty live?" said Johnny, thinking it was time for a subject change.

"Well, by car it would take us about three full days—one to the border and two more in Canada. But you should make it in about two and a half hours by plane. Are you looking forward to flying?"

"Oh yeah, Dad, it's great," Johnny lied.

His father loved flying, but Johnny's only flying experience had made him nauseous. Of course, he'd never told anyone about that.

Johnny's mother studied her son thoughtfully. She wasn't at all convinced by his response. After all, this was his first time traveling alone to a place so far from any real city. She recalled the time they had visited her husband's family, just after they were married—beautiful, yes, but just too remote for her liking. She sighed inwardly. It was too late for all that now, and after all, he did love it each time he saw his cousins.

Johnny interrupted her thought, but not his eating.

"Dad, why did Uncle Jim and Aunt Gail move so far away?"

"They didn't move at all. Jim and I grew up there on the lake. It has always been a beautiful place, but I never did like being so far from other people. So I moved from Canada to the States to find a better career. I met your mother, and we settled down here. But Uncle Jim met your aunt Gail in a little town where we used to pick up supplies. They both loved the country, so they took over the store."

"Their place seems so old from the pictures."

"Well, it was built by our grandfather as a combined trading post and homestead. I can still remember him tending the store. Indians used to come down the river from the north and buy fishing and hunting equipment. Their tribe had been selling skins and furs for generations. Old Granddad used to find your uncle and me reading comic books and say, 'You boys shouldn't waste your time with such nonsense. Someday you're going to mind the store. You'd best be learning how to work it.'"

Johnny's dad smiled with a distant look in his eyes, no longer entrenched in his newspaper. Then his expression became more wistful.

"I guess he was right about Jim, but I just lost interest after Granddad left."

"I thought you told me Grandpa still lived there with Uncle Jim and Aunt Gail."

"Your grandpa is still there, but your great-granddad, my grandfather, disappeared one day. It was a shock to all of us. A note was all we found. It said not to search for him, though we did for a month or more. He claimed to have found something that really excited him and said he didn't know if he would ever return. I hate to think of what became of him."

Johnny was surprised at this story. He had never heard this about his great-grandfather before. The story brought visions of a wandering old man being attacked by mountain lions or scalped by Indians, but he knew that was silly. There probably hadn't been dangerous Indians for a hundred years or more. But then, he did wonder. After all, his cousins lived in a very remote part of Canada.

"So what do you think happened to him, Dad? Could he have drowned in the lake? Maybe an Indian scalped him and hid his body somewhere."

"No, there really aren't any dangerous animals in that region, and the few Indians that still lived there at the time were well known and even helped look for him. They missed him a lot. They never did seem to think we would find him though. They kept saying he had found something with an Indian name that no one could understand. It must have been part of some old legend. Someone finally translated it to…oh, I forget…what was it called?"

"I think it was called the 'crystal pool,'" interjected his mother, who hadn't seemed to have been listening.

Johnny's father looked up for a moment and then said, "Yes, that's it…crystal pool. It never made sense to us, and the Indians didn't want to discuss it. Eventually we gave up."

Johnny returned to his breakfast and tried to picture his great-grand-dad. He must have been strong to build a store and cottage all by himself. It was sad that he had left without ever saying good-bye to anyone. But that was long ago, even when his dad was young. He must have walked away and finally died somewhere far from all his friends and family.

Looking down at his bowl, now void of any cereal but having plenty of leftover milk, he glanced up and saw his father had returned to reading the paper. His mother was nowhere in sight, so he quickly lifted the bowl and drained the remaining milk. Wiping his mouth with his sleeve, he put the bowl into the sink and walked out into the cool morning air. He sat down, ignoring the wet grass, and remembered the last time Ben and Patty had visited. It was the best two weeks of his life. A whole summer with them would make his life perfect. Why would his father have wanted to leave the lake? It seemed like paradise from the pictures. Just then he felt something warm and wet on the back of his neck.

"Oh, Checker, cut it out."

The big black lab lay down and thumped his tail on the ground.

"Yeah, I'm going to miss you too. You know I can't bring you on the plane. Besides, you could get lost out there in the woods. There are bears and mountain lions, you know. My great-grandpa used to go bear hunting all the time. Once a bear snuck up on him from behind and tried to squeeze the juices out of him. But old Gramps was too quick. He jumped right out of the old bear's paws like a slick banana. Then he turned around as quick as lightning and sliced him open with his huntin' knife. Cut the gizzard right out of him. Boy, that bear sure never bothered anyone after that. In fact, word got around to all the other bears, and they steered clear of old Gramps. But he's not there anymore. Guess things got too tame for him, and he went off looking for a new adventure."

Johnny looked thoughtfully at the dog. Checker seemed unimpressed with the story but thumped his tail on the ground a few times to prove he was listening. Mom and Dad had given Checker to him on his tenth birthday. This would be the first time in three years they would be separated.

"I sure wish I could bring you with me. Then the summer would be really perfect."

Checker's ears drooped as if to say, "Me too."

They sat there on the grass together, absorbing the morning dew. Johnny surveyed his surroundings and selected a blade of grass. The blade was fat and fit nicely between his thumbs. He carefully pinched it together, first evaluating the likelihood of its musical qualities and then eyeing his dog. Checker looked uncomfortable. Johnny slowly raised the blade to his mouth, keeping one eye on his dog. Checker's discomfort grew to a whining objection that made it clear this was only a signal of the fearful event to come.

The noise proceeding from Johnny's mouth would have caused any adult within earshot to do permanent harm to the boy or at least to the blade of grass. But poor Checker was unable to defend himself, save for competing with frenzied howling and barking. This might seem somewhat beneath Johnny's age, but it had been a tradition of sorts over the past three years, soon to be interrupted by Johnny's departure. After several minutes of this chorus, the blade had used up all the unmusical qualities it once possessed. Johnny discarded it and began to search for a suitable replacement. But the dog's creator intervened mercifully by providing Johnny with distraction enough to lose track of his purpose. Johnny heard a low rumble and looked to the sky to see a commercial jet climbing to cruising altitude. Johnny wondered whether his airplane would look like the one overhead.

"Do you think my plane will look like that?" Johnny asked his dog. "How do they get them to fly anyway?"

Checker wasn't paying attention at all anymore, for the crisis of the moment had apparently passed by. Instead, he was preoccupied with sniffing the base of a nearby tree.

"I wonder if many of them crash," Johnny mused. His father had told him it was safer to fly in an airplane than to walk across the street. Still, he had never flown by himself before, and the thought made his stomach turn. He turned back to his dog.

"You know, I've never flown alone before," he admitted.

Checker ignored him and had even lost interest in the tree. His hair went up on end as he began to growl, looking toward the street.

"Checker! What's the matter?"

Johnny followed Checker's gaze. There was nothing to be seen. The dog suddenly sprang out of the yard onto the sidewalk in front of Johnny's house. He sniffed up and down, searching for an elusive scent. The hair on his back remained standing on end as he continued his low, worried growl.

"Checker, what on earth are you doing?" yelled Johnny, chasing after his dog. "No one's been here—I would have seen it if there had been. What are you looking for?" Checker was too preoccupied to respond and kept running back and forth across the street, sniffing any object that protruded even slightly. Suddenly, Checker looked up the street again, and the hackles on his back went straight up. His worried growl became higher pitched, and he leaped forward in pursuit just as Johnny tackled him.

"Checker, calm down," said Johnny. "What are you looking at?" he added, as he scoured the street with his eyes.

He could feel his dog trembling all over. Johnny stroked his head and back with one hand but held the dog's collar firmly with the other, keeping him close.

"It's okay, boy. There is nothing there," reassured Johnny, not so convinced himself but unable to see a hint of anything other than his normal neighborhood surroundings.

Checker would not take his eyes off the end of the street, nor stop his low growls. He kept quivering and straining forward, but he was unable and perhaps unwilling to free himself from his master's grasp. So both boy and dog stared in the same direction.

Johnny finally saw something. Was there an old man at the end of the street? Johnny blinked, but saw nothing there when he looked for him again.

"Who was that?" Johnny asked his dog.

The question was never answered. Johnny's father stepped out the front door and called to him.

"Johnny, you ready to go? It's time we got your things into the car and headed to the airport."

Johnny slowly turned back to the house, guiding his dog in the same direction.

"Come on, Checker. The plane is waiting!"

Checker reluctantly abandoned his search and headed for the front door. Johnny grabbed his bags and stuffed them into the back of the car.

"Go ahead and let Checker come inside," said his mother. "He may as well see you off too."

Happily, Johnny climbed into the car, pulling his dog in with him. At least they could be together a bit longer. As the car rolled off, Checker looked out the back window at the sidewalk, his head slightly cocked to one side.

The Traveler

The Matheson family turned into the airport parking garage. Johnny's mind was racing. His friends at school were accustomed to flying, and it embarrassed him that he had flown only once before in his entire life, and that experience had definitely not been pleasant. He was far too grown-up to be afraid of flying, but he still felt his stomach churn in anticipation.

Soon he saw the airport looming ahead. He watched three, perhaps four, airplanes stacked up on the horizon, preparing to make their final landing approach, but he lost sight of them as the car entered the parking garage. The entrance spiraled at least seven times before his father finally pulled into a floor. They found an empty slot and parked the car.

"Johnny, would you like to bring Checker into the airport with us?" his mother asked. This was a surprise, and it caught him off guard. Usually his mother could not tolerate the dog, except when Checker was confined to the backyard.

"That would be cool, Mom, but do you think it's okay? The security guards might not like it."

"I think it will be all right. Look, I brought his leash."

The four of them proceeded down the walkway to the elevator, where they headed down to the main floor. When the elevator door opened, they were confronted by a mass of people in the ticketing area. Some were excited, others were bored, and many were tense. Suddenly the reality of the trip began to take hold, increasing Johnny's nausea.

"I'll hold your dog while you go with your mother to check in," said Johnny's father as he handed him his passport. "Keep that in a safe place."

Johnny noticed his father talking to a porter. The porter nodded, disappeared through a door, and returned with a large cage, just as Johnny and his mother were returning with his boarding pass.

"I think this one should do the job, sir," said the porter.

"Come on, Checker," his father urged. "You'll be just fine in here. I know it looks a bit small, but it's really for the best."

Checker didn't look convinced. He crouched down on the floor and whimpered. A look of disbelief mingled with hope came into Johnny's eyes.

"Mom, is he really coming with me?"

"Yes, Johnny. Last night Uncle Jim called and asked us if you could bring the dog. Your cousins were crushed at the thought of not seeing Checker, so they promised that you three would take turns feeding him. They told us they even had an old dog house for him. Your father and I thought we would keep it a surprise."

Johnny jumped down to his dog and gave him a great big hug, not minding the sloppy lick on the face he received in return. Johnny began to coax him into the cage, assuring his dog they would be back together soon and forgetting the nervousness he had felt only moments earlier.

Reluctantly, Checker allowed himself to be guided in. The porter closed the cage, much to the dismay of the dog. Then porter, cage, and dog disappeared around the corner—but it took some time for the howling to fade away.

"Let's get you through check-in. There's quite a line developing in the security area," Johnny's mother urged.

Johnny liked the electronic check-in because all he needed to do was enter a confirmation code provided by his father. He couldn't help thinking that all those questions the machine asked were absurd: who would admit to bringing knives or guns on a plane anyway? Soon they were heading to the inspection area, but there his parents had to stop.

"This is as far as we can go, Johnny," said his father, while his mother quickly began to smooth his hair.

"Oh, Mom, my hair is fine."

He noticed tears in her eyes.

"Gosh, Mom, I'm going to be okay. You don't need to worry. Ben, Patty, and I are going to have a great summer. Having Checker there will make it perfect."

On this final point, his mother agreed. His reassurances didn't stop the tears, however. The three gave each other a warm "family hug," as they often did.

"Oh Johnny, your new clean pants are all grass stained!" his mother exclaimed, but possibly just to stop her tears.

"Be sure to write at least once per week, Son. Don't forget," commanded his father.

"I promise, Dad."

He wished his mother would at least start using e-mail, but it was pointless to bring that up now. Johnny headed for the inspection area, giving them one last wave. He followed the crowd for a while, then tried to get another glimpse of his parents—but it was impossible to see them through the crowd.

Well, I guess this is it, thought Johnny.

Many lines were now forming as people prepared to enter the detection area. Few talked. Some looked nervous, and others just looked suspicious. Could any of them be carrying a gun? An odd-looking man, about to pass through the detector, was stopped by the attendant and told to remove his shoes. Looking uncomfortable, he complied, putting his shoes into a box that was then run through the scanner. As he passed through the detector, it began to squeal.

An attendant took him to another area, where he had to endure a wand search.

Following Johnny's gaze, the man behind him said, "It's no big deal. Look how many others are being re-inspected as well. But if you don't get moving, someone behind you might get annoyed."

Johnny quickly stepped ahead, closing the gap in the line he had created through his distraction. He realized he'd better take off his shoes as well, copying a middle-aged woman in front of him. She passed through with no incident, and next it was Johnny's turn. He wondered if he would set off the alarm.

"I need to see your boarding pass and identification," said a young, uniformed woman.

Johnny rifled through his backpack then handed it to her.

"Okay, you'll need to keep it," she said with a smile, after stamping the pass. "Put your backpack on the conveyor, and then step through the detector."

Johnny, feeling his ears getting red, hurried on. He hoped desperately to get through without any embarrassment. His wish was granted, and he passed through with no further incident. Picking up his backpack, he saw people departing in several directions, and he hesitated.

"Your flight departs from Gate A7. Turn right, go about two hundred yards, and you'll find it on your left."

The voice was that of the same woman who was managing the detector, but this time she called to him across a busy room.

Johnny quickly motioned his thanks and turned in the direction she indicated, trying not to notice the twinkle in her eye. Her instructions were perfect, and he quickly found his gate. He saw the flight was already boarding, so he got in line. After a few minutes, he made it up to the boarding area.

"It's not that precious, and if you don't give me your boarding pass, you'll never get on the plane," said the attendant.

"Oh, sorry," replied Johnny, unaware that he had been clutching it tightly in his fist.

The attendant took the boarding pass, reviewed it quickly, and asked, "Do you like being by the window?"

"I guess so," Johnny replied. "I haven't flown much."

She looked over at a flight attendant standing by, who responded by smiling and then said to Johnny, "Hey, come on with me."

She then turned and headed down the ramp toward the airplane, pretending not to see his nervousness.

"So, what's your name?" the attendant asked, as Johnny trotted to catch up with her.

"Uh, Johnny," he replied. "Johnny Matheson."

"Well, Johnny Matheson," she continued, with a hint of a smile, "I understand this is your first solo flight."

Johnny nodded. "Yes, ma'am...I mean miss."

Johnny felt himself turning red.

"You may call me Michelle," she continued, pretending to see nothing unusual. "I'll be one of your flight attendants today, so if you need anything, just let me know. You are very lucky today, Johnny. It's your first flight, and you are flying on a very new airplane."

"Is this the first time the airplane has ever flown?"

"Not exactly, but it's the newest plane from the best airplane company in the world."

"That's pretty cool," replied Johnny, already feeling more comfortable. "Who made it?"

"Boeing. It's a Boeing 787."

"Oh, yeah—I think my dad was saying something about that."

They walked a bit farther, and she stopped at one of the rows of seats.

"Here you are," she said, pointing out his seat. But then she noticed some grass still sticking to the back of his neck, apparently leftover from the morning's romp with Checker.

"Hold it a minute," she said, as she picked it off his collar. "There, that's better. You want to be sure the girls see how cute you are when you arrive," she added, flashing him a gorgeous smile.

Johnny was stunned and felt himself turn crimson. She must have been expecting that reaction because she laughed, tossing back her hair slightly. Johnny suddenly stopped thinking about the airplane and noticed how pretty her hair was.

"Be sure you put your seatbelt on," she added as she started to leave—but not before giving him another one of her smiles. Johnny watched her until she was out of sight.

He fastened the buckle and waited for the rest of the passengers to settle in. He was glad just to be seated somewhere, but he did hope she would come by again. Looking out his window, he saw many people at work near his airplane. People in jumpsuits with strips of bright reflective tape hauled luggage on odd, train-like vehicles. Before long he felt the airplane move—backwards at first. He wondered how the pilot could see behind himself so he didn't hit anything.

Johnny recalled the times his father had told him that airplane travel was the safest kind of transportation. This didn't stop the butterflies in his stomach as the plane taxied to the end of the runway. Without so much as a pause, it turned and pressed forward. It was moving terribly fast. He watched as runway markers sped by. Which building were Mom and Dad in anyway? He closed his eyes, but that only made things worse as he visualized the plane starting to take off and then falling to the ground, bursting into a giant ball of flame. He opened his eyes and saw the last building disappear behind him. When would the plane take off? What if they ran out of runway?

He was then gently pressed to his seat as he was carried quickly into the sky. Green hills appeared in the distant horizon. Toy houses, cars, buses, and roadways spread out before him. It was as if a living map were rolled out for him to examine. Wonder overcame him, replacing his previous fear. Where were his house and his school? He searched the countryside below but recognized nothing.

Suddenly, everything turned white. Johnny recoiled, certain that his vision of a crash was about to become reality. Everyone around him seemed uninterested. Why, they weren't even glancing out their windows! Johnny looked outside again. All he saw was white.

Of course, you dimwit, he told himself. *A cloud. We flew right into a cloud.*

He wondered whether other passengers could see his fear, but at the moment, he was not up to looking at anyone to find out.

The whiteness was becoming more intense. Johnny knew that the cockpit instruments supplied all the information the pilot would need, but that failed to comfort him. Then, as suddenly as it had appeared, the intense white was replaced with brilliant blue as the airplane pierced the top of the cloud. Johnny's wonder doubled as he saw immense billows of cotton-like vapor just beneath and alongside him as he was surrounded by blue sky. He had never seen anything so beautiful. He could almost touch the clouds—they were like immense pillows calling him to come and rest on them.

"Real pretty, ain't it?"

Startled, Johnny turned and for the first time noticed an old man sitting next to him.

"Yes, sir. It is," Johnny replied, wondering why he had not seen him earlier. "I've never flown by myself in an airplane before."

"Yep, it sure do seem as though one is 'bout to bump into them pearly gates way up here. What do you think? Is heav'n up 'round here somewheres?"

"Well, sir, I guess I never really thought about it much."

"Never thought about it? How could anyone look at those clouds and not've thought about it? What would you do if this plane just bumped up on heaven's doorpost and the Master himself said, 'Boy, what you doin' here on my front porch?'"

If Johnny had had any residual nervousness, it was now replaced by a feeling of awkwardness—and possible annoyance. The old man was clearly eccentric, but he was also loud. Johnny very felt conspicuous but again did not check to see who might be looking at them. He had no idea what he should say to the old man, but the fellow didn't seem to expect an answer and continued in a tone that would have been audible at least three rows in front of and behind them, had the aircraft still been on the ground. Johnny was grateful for the background noise of the engines, wishing they were louder.

"Well, sonny, if you ain't used to flyin,' you must certainly be headin' out on a big adventure, eh? Out to make your fortune in life?"

"Oh, no," replied Johnny. "I'm just heading out to visit my aunt, uncle, and cousins for summer vacation. I don't expect any special adventures on this trip."

"Fiddlesticks! Why, there are always plenty of opportunities for adventure for those that are lookin.' Maybe even for some that ain't lookin.'"

A hint of a smile fell across the old man's face but disappeared nearly as fast as it had appeared, replaced by a look of introspection.

"Not that there ain't nothin' wrong with visitin' your kinfolk," he continued, apparently unconcerned about how to interpret so many negatives in one sentence. "Why, aunts, uncles, and cousins many times removed are real important. Yes, siree! I dare say you probably have lots more relatives to run across than you might imagine. But I sure expect there's a mighty fine adventure comin' your way. Guess I'd better let you discover that on your own. Good thing someone's lookin' out for you." The old man then looked at Johnny with a twinkle and a knowing look, which, this time, didn't change.

Johnny didn't know what to make of all this. He looked back at the old man, who continued to stare at him with the same expression, clearly waiting for a reply. Fortunately, lunch was arriving, and Johnny was able to redirect his attention to the flight attendant. He was glad it was the same one who had assisted him earlier. He realized he was hungry and searched his pockets for his wallet, wondering how much the lunch would cost. He was dismayed to find very little money. Other people were giving her money for their lunches. But the flight attendant flashed him another of her smiles and said, "Don't worry—the lunch is included in the ticket price for you and your friend."

"Oh, thanks," said Johnny, wishing she did not think the old man was his friend.

She handed them both their lunches and started to move along. Johnny looked over the small lunch, wishing it were bigger, but he was hungry and wanted a distraction from his recent discussion. As she moved to the next passenger, Johnny tore into the plastic wrapping and began to devour his food.

With his mouth full of turkey and bread, Johnny came to a full halt. Was the old man sick, or had he just suddenly fallen asleep? He sat with his head bowed and eyes closed. He had not even touched his food. Johnny became worried. What should he do? He started to look for the flight attendant again, but she was busy serving another passenger. Then all of a sudden the old man came back to life with another twinkle in his eye and began to eat.

"Just sayin' thanks to the Master," the old man said and then proceeded to eat his lunch.

Johnny looked at him for a moment longer and then returned to his lunch.

I'll be glad when we land, thought Johnny.

He stared out the window, doing his best to avoid more dialogue with his new acquaintance. Green circles covered the ground for mile upon mile as they slowly passed over the terrain.

Why so many circles? he asked himself.

Drowsiness overcame him unexpectedly, and he slipped into a dream. A very old man entered the dream and tried to talk to him, but Johnny could not hear what he was saying. Then the old man beckoned him to follow and started to walk away. Johnny tried, but his legs would hardly move. The old man disappeared behind some trees in a wood. When Johnny arrived, no one was there, and he saw only a pool of water. He stared at the water, which seemed to churn and boil. His head swam with it, and he began to get dizzy. He felt himself drawn to it, losing his balance. Then he toppled into the pool, which opened into a great waterfall. He fell over its edge, and all went black. He seemed to fall endlessly, wondering when he would hit bottom.

A screech and a bump jolted him awake. Looking out his window, he saw only concrete and runway markers. His heart was racing from the dream, and it took some time to get his bearings. Had they landed already? He wondered how long he had been asleep. He looked to his right and saw the old man sound asleep, despite the bumpy landing. Johnny waited patiently until the plane taxied up to the gate and came to a full stop. The old man awoke.

"Eh, here already?" he asked, half to himself. "Ah, yes—must have nodded off a bit."

The plane found its gate and came to a stop. Getting caught in the anticipation of deplaning, Johnny stood up with almost everyone else and waited for the airplane door to open. Even if he could not move from his seat, it was good to stand up. When the crowd finally began to exit, the old man stepped into the aisle and said, "Here, sonny, step in front of me."

Forgetting to thank him for his courtesy, Johnny grabbed his carry-on bag, stepped into the aisle, and began to proceed toward the door. Then, remembering his manners, he turned around to thank his traveling partner, but the old man was not there. He strained to peer into the line forming behind him, but the old man was nowhere to be found.

"Well, where could he have gone?" Johnny muttered.

"Come on, boy," complained the woman behind him. "The door is in front of you, and I have another plane to catch."

Johnny moved on, wondering whether the old man had been crowded out of line. He walked past the flight attendant, proceeded up the ramp, and passed through the gate into the immigration area. After some confusion getting his passport stamped, officials asking him questions, and recovering his bags only to have them inspected and rechecked again, Johnny paused. He looked around in vain for the old man, who was nowhere to be seen. Finally Johnny and the rest of the crowd passed through a pair of glass doors where security guards prevented anyone from getting back in.

"There's Johnny!" exclaimed a voice.

Looking up, he saw his two cousins bounding toward him, followed closely by his aunt and uncle.

"Where is Checker?" asked Patty. "You didn't forget him, I hope."

"Calm down, Patty," said her father. "The dog is just fine, but they put him in a different part of the plane. It's good to see you, Johnny. I hope your flight was enjoyable."

"Oh, it was terrific. We flew right into a cloud. When we came out on top, it was like we were floating on cotton balls. In fact, the old man next to me—"

Johnny paused mid-sentence and turned to examine the people still coming through the glass doors. The old man was not with the crowd. Johnny felt sorry that he had left so quickly and not even said good-bye. He would probably never see him again. But where could he have gone?

He must have passed by while I wasn't looking, Johnny figured, but this explanation left him a bit unsettled.

Before he could say more, his uncle directed them down the hall, where they picked up Checker and Johnny's luggage. Then they found their car and headed home.

"We still have a three-hour drive," said his uncle, "so why don't you tell us more about your flight when we get on the highway?"

The suggestion fell on deaf ears. Ben and Patty were too absorbed in petting the dog and getting caught up with Johnny on all that had happened since they had been together last.

War Whoops and Peace Pipes

Uncle Jim kept driving. It had been an hour since they had passed through the last town. Johnny could not imagine living anywhere so remote. Finally, they turned onto a country road that slowly descended until it found its way to a small river. It gently went this way and that, occasionally crossing the rushing water with the help of an old wooden bridge. Trees hugged the road on each side, their branches touching overhead as if welcoming the family back.

They turned off this route onto a one-lane dirt road, almost too rough for a car to navigate and barely wide enough for them to fit. They worked their way along the east side of a small lake. Sometimes the water lapped up to the road itself. It followed the lakefront for over a mile until it ended at a rustic log house. A gravel drive jutted out toward the lake, where a small network of docks welcomed travelers needing refuge or merchants seeking to trade goods. On the other side, the cottage was nestled snugly into the forest as if it were carefully wrapped in a soft green blanket. A large, nearly-collapsed barn bordered the edge of their homestead.

"Is that your cottage?" asked Johnny.

"Cottage? Well, I suppose you might call it that," said Uncle Jim. "We just call it home. It seems kind of large for a cottage."

They pulled up and parked the car in a shed. Out jumped Ben and Patty, with Johnny and Checker close behind.

"Mom, can we first play outside for a while?" asked Patty.

"Absolutely not," responded her mother. "You kids help Johnny with his things and show him his room. Then come downstairs for a bite to eat. After that it will be dark and past bedtime. And don't give me those sour looks either. There will be plenty of time tomorrow to show Johnny around to your hearts' content."

"Now, go do what your mother told you," added Uncle Jim.

The three children divided up Johnny's belongings and carried them inside. Ben and Patty led the way heading for the staircase.

"Hey, not so fast," came a voice from the living room. "I may be getting old, but I'm not dead yet."

"Grandpa!" exclaimed Johnny. "I didn't see you!"

"Well then get over here and say hello to your old Grandpa. How's your Mom and Dad doing down there in the States?"

That started a short-lived conversation which Johnny's father's father soon gave up, noticing his other two grandchildren getting fidgety.

"It's not like you don't have all summer to show him the place," Grandpa added with a twinkle in his eye. "Go on, get upstairs and check out your new digs."

They trudged upstairs, went down a long hallway, and turned into the last door on the left.

"Boy, Johnny," said Ben. "You're getting the neatest room in the house. I don't think anyone has ever stayed in this room."

"Fairies come and visit here sometimes," said Patty.

Ben sighed. "Oh, don't be a twit! You know that fairies are only in stories meant for little girls. But I guess you're just a little girl yourself."

"I'm almost as old as you are, so don't be such a creep."

"I suppose you are almost eight, right?" said Ben with a side look to Johnny. Johnny felt like he was getting drawn into something he would just as soon stay out of.

"Ben! You know I already had my tenth birthday. I'm practically eleven!"

"Really!" responded Ben, making an unconvincing expression of surprise.

Patty's face flushed as she prepared to say something futile, but fortunately her next comment was cut short by Aunt Gail's voice calling them downstairs.

"Come on, Johnny," said Ben suddenly, depriving his sister of any more dialogue. Then they scrambled to the kitchen. Johnny waited for Patty, not wanting to take sides and hoping that his first day did not end in a family fight.

"Hey, let's go downstairs, Patty," Johnny suggested, letting her go first.

"He's always such a jerk," she said, as they proceeded downstairs.

After eating a light supper, they were all sent to bed. Johnny surveyed his room and wondered what it had been used for. Someone must have lived in it once. Looking around in the failing light, he noticed that all the furniture was quite old. There was a painting of a young couple sitting by a lake, with Uncle Jim and Aunt Gail's log cabin in the background. The man was fair-skinned but obviously much weathered. The woman was dark skinned with jet-black hair. He wondered who they were.

He heard a knock on the door.

"Johnny, may I come in?"

"Sure, Uncle Jim," responded Johnny.

"Your dog didn't seem too happy in the kennel, so I thought maybe you would like him to sleep in your room."

"Oh, no problem," Johnny answered, trying not to sound too enthusiastic but inwardly very glad to have his dog with him.

Checker trotted into the room and immediately slobbered on Johnny's face. Within minutes, both dog and boy were sound asleep.

All three children woke early the next morning, downed a makeshift breakfast, and headed out to the lake.

"Come on," said Ben, "let's take out the canoe." Without further discussion, he slid the canoe into the water. Patty jumped in and moved to the bow.

"Go ahead and get in the middle, Johnny," said Ben. "I'll shove off."

Ben gave one last heave, stepped in, and sat down with his paddle. Checker ran out onto the dock and started to whine.

"We forgot Checker!" exclaimed Patty. "Poor puppy—we can't leave him here. He might run off into the woods and get lost."

Ben turned the canoe back toward the dock and pulled alongside Checker. The dog continued to whine and ran up and down the dock as if propelled by his wagging tail. Johnny pulled him into the canoe, nearly capsizing it, and off they paddled across the water. Checker lay as low as possible.

"Let's show Johnny the whole lake," suggested Patty. "It won't take too long if we stay in the canoe. It's so pretty, Johnny. Look, let's start with the Stairsteps."

"The Stairsteps?" asked Johnny.

"Oh, it's the most interesting waterfall anywhere," replied Patty. "Two rivers feed into the lake. One comes from the north, and the other from the east. The east one is where you will see the Stairsteps. Come on, Ben. Let's just show him. It's too wonderful to explain; he has to see it himself."

Ben steered the canoe toward a small cove. At the far end loomed a stack of rock shelves, each with a curtain of water flowing over, splashing noisily onto the shelf below. Mist rose from each waterfall, making the scene drift in and out of view.

Ben skillfully guided the canoe to the right side of the lowest waterfall. He was heading directly into a rock wall. But just as Johnny was sure they would crash, Ben turned sharply to the left. There Johnny could see a narrow gap between the falling water and the rock.

"Isn't this just the most gorgeous thing you've ever seen?" asked Patty, as they slid inside the gap.

Johnny stared at the curtain of liquid diamonds. In the morning sun, each drop split the light into dazzling colors that danced on the rock behind. The mist, penetrated by streams of sunlight, created a permanent rainbow they could nearly touch. As he looked to the right, he saw the wall turn sharply away from the waterfall and open into a great cavern. The splintered light from the waterfall danced across the entire cave, providing some illumination.

With a mind of its own, the canoe turned into the cavern and was drawn across the glassy water. A rock ledge appeared before them; it seemed to have been placed there for the single purpose of docking their canoe. But just before they came within reach of it, the canoe began to turn away, trying to proceed deeper into the cavern. Ben reached out and braced his paddle against the rock, drawing the canoe toward the platform and fighting the current. They stepped carefully out and stood on the ledge. Ben pulled the canoe up onto the rock to secure it.

"We call this the Great Council Chamber," announced Ben. "Here is where we have all the secret meetings for our tribe."

"What do you mean by 'tribe'?" asked Johnny.

"Well, Patty and I became blood brothers—"

"And sisters," interrupted Patty.

"Anyway," continued Ben, "we formed a special tribe with an Indian girl who lives nearby."

"You mean there are still Indians? I thought they were gone a long time ago."

"There once was a tribe that lived by this lake. But most of them moved farther up the north river. Dad tells me that when he was a kid, they still used to come and trade at the store. One family really helped old Great-Granddad a lot when he first opened the trading post. Ever since then, we've always hired someone in their family. So they decided to stay, along with a number of other families. Anyway, they have one daughter named Little Flower. We call her Lilly for short. Patty, Lilly, and I decided to create a new tribe. You're looking at our secret council room. Today we were going to ask if you would like to join us."

Johnny thought this sounded like something for kids. After all, he was almost a teenager, and Ben was nearly fourteen. He imagined the ridicule that he might get at school over this, but school was far away, and maybe it would be fun. Besides, he didn't want to offend his cousins. So he pretended he could not have been happier as he looked around the cavern. He realized it went back farther than he had thought at first. How old was this place, he wondered, and how did it get here? It was obvious no one could have made it.

Just then another canoe cleared the waterfall and glided toward them into the cavern. A young, dark-skinned girl was paddling toward them.

"Oh, drat! And everything seemed so nice today too," muttered Patty half under her breath.

"Hey, Lilly!" shouted Ben. "I'm glad you came. This is my cousin Johnny we told you about."

Lilly looked at Johnny dubiously.

"I thought we agreed not to bring anyone here until after they were accepted into the tribe," she said.

"But this is our cousin, and we already talked about him," replied Ben.

"No," Lilly insisted, "this is sacred ground! No one can enter here and live unless he is one of us. He can join only after a secret council and acceptance from the whole tribe."

"Oh, all right," said Ben. "Johnny, can you manage the canoe? We need to have an emergency council. Just take it a little way out into the lake, and we'll come get you in about ten minutes or so."

"Well, okay," said Johnny.

He was disappointed with the new course of events, forgetting that just a moment ago he thought this whole tribe thing seemed silly. But being potentially rejected was something else entirely. Who did this girl think she was? He carefully sat down in the canoe. After a few trials, he managed to navigate reasonably well, and he headed out toward the center of the opening. But he quickly discovered he was making little headway.

"Go next to the edge of the wall and head toward the opening. If you stay away from the middle, it's a lot easier," shouted Ben.

Johnny struggled over to the edge and found his progress improving. He marveled at the strength of the current. It was slightly intimidating, as if the water hid a menace, biding its time. He carefully cleared the mouth of the cave and worked back behind the waterfall, keeping as close to the rock wall as possible.

Well, maybe I'll take a look around, he thought, as he paddled back into the main lake. He looked up at the series of waterfalls his cousins called the Stairsteps. To the left, through an opening in the trees, he saw snow-peaked mountains. The mist continued to rise, hiding the opening from which he had just emerged. His gaze moved back to the lake again, and he noticed another canoe making its way toward him.

"Now who could that be?" he said. The canoe continued to approach. Johnny froze in his seat, staring as it headed directly toward him. Could it be? No, this wasn't possible. Yet as the man paddled closer, there could be no doubt. It was the same old man who had sat next to him on the airplane.

He came right up next to Johnny and stopped. Johnny felt the same discomfort he had experienced while talking with him on the airplane. How did he get here?

"Hey, sonny, welcome to the lake!" said the old man, as if he had been expecting him the whole time. "Why, I realized I plumb forgot to tell you my name on that thar flying machine we was on. Abraham, that's my name. Well, at least that's the one I'm using now. Had it for some time, I have. You can just call me Abe. Fact is, I don't rightly think I never got your name neither."

"Oh, I'm Johnny. Johnny Matheson."

His words were out before he could think, and he realized too late that giving his last name to people he didn't know is unwise.

"Fine name, Johnny—yep, a right fine name. Ever wonder if your name was written down in a book somewheres?"

"Well no, sir. I never really thought about it."

Johnny regretted this statement as soon as he made it. He remembered the conversation about bumping into heaven's doorpost while they were on the airplane, but this time no outburst resulted.

"Well, you never know what books there might be, Johnny, and who might be listed in 'em. Fact is, you never know who might be writin' 'em."

This brought a twinkle to his eye, and he continued.

"Some books are real 'portant, you know. Havin' yer name in one of 'em just could prove mighty useful someday. But anyway, have you found those kinfolk you were tellin' me about?"

"Oh yes, sir—Abe, I mean. My uncle, aunt, and cousins picked me up at the airport. My cousins and some Indian girl are—"

Johnny stopped himself short. He remembered that the Great Council Chamber was a secret—even sacred—place. He certainly couldn't give that away, especially when they were deciding whether he could join the tribe.

"…are letting me use their canoe," Johnny added.

"Well, it's a sure thing that canoe don't belong to no Indian girl, so I take it that it must belong to those cousins of yers. Seems also you brought someone else along."

Checker had been so quiet, huddled in the bottom of the canoe, that Johnny had forgotten all about him. The dog thumped his tail a few times but otherwise didn't move a muscle.

Just then Johnny heard loud cries coming from the direction of the waterfall. He turned and saw the other three children emerging from behind it, with paint on their faces and making what seemed like Indian war cries. They rapidly closed in on Johnny, continuing their cries. Reaching his canoe, Lilly addressed him:

"Big Chief Dancing Bull will make judgment. Come! Judgment will be held in the Great Council Chamber."

Much to Johnny's relief, Ben and Patty were smiling, but Lilly was quite serious. Ben turned the canoe back toward the waterfall and gestured toward Johnny to follow. Johnny looked back toward Abe to say good-bye, but he was not there! No canoe was in sight. Johnny searched up and down the shoreline, even up to the bend in the cove. That was a good 150 yards. How could he have silently paddled away so fast?

Johnny proceeded to follow his cousins and Lilly back toward the Great Council Chamber. The encounter with Abraham left him wondering, but he didn't have time to question the incident as he paddled to keep up. He turned behind the waterfall and then into the cavern. The place was beautiful beyond words. He docked his canoe, and this time he remembered Checker. The canoe nearly tipped again as Johnny dragged the dog out.

Ben had already seated himself on a bench-like rock. Lilly presented him with a long, carved pipe stuffed with what must have been old, dried-up grass. Patty looked thoroughly disgusted. Lilly took out a book of matches and lit the grass in the pipe. Instantly it caught fire.

"This is our peace pipe," announced Lilly. "You have been voted into the tribe. Do you accept?"

"I do," responded Johnny in a solemn tone.

Ben drew in some smoke from the pipe and blew it out.

"As chief of the tribe, I hereby receive you as full member," proclaimed Ben.

He passed the pipe to Johnny. Johnny took in a mouthful of the hot smoke, taking care not to breathe it, and passed the pipe back. Ben then gave it to Lilly, who did the same and handed it to Patty.

"Oh, do I really have to do this?" she complained. "It tastes so awful." But she knew she had to smoke it, so she took in as little as possible and blew it out with a cough.

"Now for the final bond," said Lilly, as she pulled out her knife. "Then blood brothers and sisters we shall truly be."

"Now that is too much," said Patty. "You promised I would have to do that only once, and I simply won't cut my finger again. Last time it got infected, and I got into a lot of trouble with Mom. So did you, Ben!"

"Oh, don't be such a baby," said Ben. "If you had held still, it would have been just a little prick."

"I don't care—I'm not doing it again. You promised, and that's that!"

"Okay, okay," said Ben. "Come over here, Johnny, and hold out your finger. It really doesn't hurt much if you just hold still."

Reluctantly, Johnny surrendered his finger. Lilly made a small cut in Ben's, Johnny's, and her own finger.

Joining them together, Ben announced, "Faithful brothers and sisters we have become, for this life and the next, forever joined and never parting."

The Secret Library

Johnny was hesitant to say anything about Abraham as they returned home. Lilly had separated from them shortly after leaving the falls, heading back to her village. Johnny paddled in front, allowing him to keep his thoughts to himself.

Patty leaned forward and whispered to Johnny, "It's okay, Johnny. I'm not so sure I like being part of that silly tribe either."

Johnny turned to her momentarily and smiled.

"Oh, it's not the tribe; I'm just thinking."

Before long they came to their dock. Johnny and Ben put the canoe away as Patty ran to the house. The two boys then followed at a leisurely pace.

"So what did you think?" asked Ben, also perceiving his cousin's changed mood.

Johnny looked at Ben and then cautiously said, "Ben, a weird thing happened on the lake when I was out by myself, and I don't know what to make of it. If you promise you won't think I'm crazy, I'll tell you and Patty, but maybe we could leave Lilly out of it for now."

"Sure," said Ben. "Hey, don't worry about the tribe thing—that's just something we do to pass the time. I know Lilly takes it pretty seriously, but it really is just for kicks."

Johnny nodded as they entered the house. Patty was already helping her mother make cocoa—which, due to a mother's intuition, was almost ready when they arrived. Patty brought in a cup for each of them, and the three sat down in the living room.

"Hey, thanks, Patty," said Johnny, focusing on the cocoa rather than his cousins. He then glanced at Ben and Patty. Both looked at him expectantly.

"Okay, look," began Johnny. "I think the tribe is great, especially as something fun to do, but I need you two to take something seriously for a minute. It is really strange, and it's starting to creep me out. Anyway, here goes…You know, when I got off the plane, I was looking for an old man who had sat next to me. He was kind of weird. Well, he let me walk in front of him as we left the airplane, but when I turned to say thanks, he wasn't there. I watched for him when I met you guys, but he never came out. "

"Maybe he went out the back door," suggested Patty.

Ben was about to say something but thought better of it.

"No, they only let you out the front," responded Johnny. "Anyway, I decided to just forget it. It was great seeing you guys and getting Checker, and besides, I knew I would never see him again—but I did feel a little rude not saying good-bye and thanking him."

"Well, it wasn't your fault," said Ben. "I wouldn't worry about it, I think."

"Oh, I know that. In fact, I had almost forgotten about him until today. But remember when I took the canoe out of the cave while you guys talked? Well, I went out, I don't know, maybe a couple of hundred feet from the falls. Then I saw another canoe clearing the point on the north side of the bay. It headed toward me. Now—don't laugh at this, I'm dead serious—when the canoe got close enough, I recognized who was paddling it. It was the same old man!"

"It must have been someone else," said Ben. "There is an old guy on this lake, but no, it couldn't have been him."

"And he is always in a wheelchair and just talks to other old people on his front porch," added Patty in an unusual display of support for her brother.

"Yeah, that's right," continued Ben. "There is no way he could even get into a canoe."

"Ben, the canoe came right up next to mine. I could not have mistaken who was in it. Besides, he talked to me, just like he had in the airplane. He always says weird stuff about heaven and family and things that don't make any sense. No, it was the same guy. He was really friendly and polite. He introduced himself as Abraham, but it sounded like he went by other names too. He didn't say anything scary, but he did scare me. He kept talking about some adventure we would go on—I think he meant you guys too."

Johnny proceeded to fill Ben and Patty in on each detail of his conversation with Abraham, both on the airplane and in the canoe. When he was finished, all three of them were very quiet.

Patty broke the silence.

"I think Abraham sounds very nice," she said. "After all, he helped you on the plane, and he even welcomed you to the lake."

"But how did he get here?" said Ben. "He couldn't live near the lake or we would know who he was. What really bothers me is that we didn't see him ourselves. When we came out of the cavern, we headed right toward Johnny. I remember seeing Johnny as soon as we cleared the waterfall. But there wasn't any other canoe. It just doesn't make sense. Johnny, are you sure you weren't watching for us for a while and he just kinda snuck off?"

"No, because I was talking to him when I heard you whooping and hollering. When I looked back toward the cavern, you were just coming out from behind the waterfall."

"I bet Lilly would say he is an evil spirit from an old tribe that used to fight with her people," added Ben, with a sidelong look at Patty.

"I told you to stop talking about old spirits," complained Patty. "I don't like them, and even Mom says not to talk about them. You know it gives me bad dreams."

Ben leaned over to Johnny and whispered, "She really can be a little baby sometimes."

Johnny smiled in return, but secretly he was glad that Patty had put a stop to that subject. The old man seemed nice enough; he didn't seem creepy like you would expect from a ghost. But he said such unusual things. And his way of coming and going had left the realm of the curious and entered into the impossible.

"What do you think of him, Checker?" Johnny asked his dog.

But Checker was too busy enjoying the freedom of being out of the boat and was already curled up next to the fireplace. He simply offered a few thumps of his tail and closed his eyes.

The children finished the day by making plans for the next. It would be very busy, since they still needed to tour the rest of the lake. After dinner they decided to head to bed. It had been a big day. Everyone was too excited to sleep—except Checker, who should have been dismayed at their plans for the next day but instead was blissfully captivated by whatever dreams dogs may have.

———

The next morning they all awoke to a steady, drenching rain that gave no hope of letting up. Their plans were at best delayed, if not totally ruined. Grandpa looked up from his morning paper.

"Why don't you kids go up to Johnny's room and play a game? Rain always takes longer to go away if you watch it, you know."

This seemed reasonable—especially to their mother, who was more than ready for both the kids and the dog to leave the kitchen. So they all scrambled upstairs before one of the adults thought of a job that needed doing.

"Hey, your room is cooler than I thought," said Ben. "Grandpa told me this morning that this was Great-Granddad's room. That's why there's so much old stuff in here. Nobody ever uses the room anymore. In fact, Johnny, I think you are the first person who has ever stayed in it, at least since I can remember."

"Look how old and faded everything is," said Patty. "It seems a bit musty, even though I know that Mom cleaned it up a lot before you came. Look here. What a big book this is."

She pulled a large black book off a shelf, opened it, and began carefully to turn the first few pages.

"It's a Bible," she exclaimed. "Look how tattered the pages are. It must be very, very old. Look at this page."

"Hey, let me see," said Ben, taking the Bible from her. "It has family records inside. And look at this!"

All three looked at the opened page, which read:

> *This Bible is hereby presented to*
> *John William Matheson*
> *on the twenty-fifth day of December*
> *in the year of our Lord*
> *nineteen hundred sixteen*
> *by his godfather, Robert Isaacson,*
> *to celebrate his first Christmas.*

"Johnny!" Patty exclaimed. "Why is your name in this Bible?"

"Don't be silly," said Ben. "Look at the date. This Bible was given to John Matheson way back in 1916. That's even before Grandpa was born. Look—it was given to Great-Granddad when he was a baby. Boy, no wonder the pages look so old. I wonder how long it's been sitting here."

"Probably a very long time," said Patty. "Look how dusty it is. Poor thing! It must have been very lonely all this time, with no one reading it."

Ben shook his head in disgust but decided to change the subject. "Johnny, you must have been named after Great-Granddad. Did your mom and dad ever tell you that?"

Johnny had not been listening to the conversation. Instead, he was staring at a wooden lever on the wall behind the bookcase where the Bible had been. He reached up to touch it. It was very smooth, yet unpolished. It seemed to be attached only on the lower side. So he tried pulling it toward himself.

"Johnny, what are you doing?" asked Patty. "I think we shouldn't touch that. Mom might not like it. Now, be careful and don't break it."

But it was too late.

"Oh, no! Now look at what you've done," cried Patty.

The wall itself had silently separated in the middle, and one side began to swing open toward them. Looking inside, they saw a small room filled with ancient books. It took them some time to recover from the shock. The room could not have been more than ten feet wide and five feet deep. It was lined from floor to ceiling with books laden with the dust of years upon years. Ben was the first to break the silence. "I'll bet no one even knows this place is here. These must have been all of Great-Granddad's old books. I wonder why he kept them hidden."

"Well, I'm not sure I like this place," said Patty. "It just doesn't seem right, with walls opening up into doors. I think we better go tell Mom."

"No, no—at least not yet. We should tell Lilly about this before we tell anyone else. After all, she is part of the tribe. This is much too important to tell grown-ups, at least not yet anyway."

Patty stomped her foot.

"Ben Matheson, you are really going to get us in trouble yet. I'm getting tired of that tribe of yours anyway. I have to smoke that awful pipe every time you think of something new. You and Lilly make me cut my finger, and it gets infected, and now old Great-Granddad's room comes apart in the middle of a wall, and you want to keep it a secret! Well, you can just forget it. I'm going downstairs to tell Mom right now." She darted out the door.

Johnny looked concerned, not wanting to offend his aunt.

"Don't worry about it, Johnny. Mom is tired of all the complaining Patty has been doing lately. Patty will be back up here sooner than we'd like."

The boys stepped inside the tiny library. The books were of all sizes and shapes, and each seemed very old. Johnny tipped his head to one side and started reading the titles, most of which seemed quite boring. At first they looked like the kind of books you might get in school. Then he saw one titled *Old Indian Legends in the United States and Canada*. Then he saw a small notebook in the far corner.

"I wonder what this is," said Johnny.

He carefully removed it from the shelf and started leafing through the pages. They were old and fragile. Johnny looked at them in some awe, turning and examining each page carefully. Just then, Patty sheepishly appeared at the opening.

"I thought you were going to get Mom," said Ben.

"Well, I did, but she was kind of mad when I came down. Anyway, we're supposed to be quieter."

"Hey, look at this!" said Johnny. On the front of the notebook, written in a neat flowing hand, he read, "'The Journal of John William Matheson.' Hey, it's Great-Granddad's own personal journal!"

Johnny continued to turn the pages. Some were hard to read. There were a lot of dates and people's names he had never heard of. He continued to carefully turn the pages until one section caught his attention.

"Hey, look here," said Johnny. "He writes a lot about when he first got here and started to build the place. It must have been tough. I guess there were two tribes of Indians. One tribe was okay, but the other was really nasty. He says he even got shot at a few times. They almost hit him more than once."

"That must have been that rotten tribe Lilly was talking about," said Ben. "Just think of it: the same Indians that shot at Great-Granddad are now ghosts wandering around somewhere in the woods."

"Ben, I told you to stop it!"

"In fact, sometimes I think I hear them outside at night, yelling and screaming their old war cries."

Patty said nothing more. Johnny noticed the tears beginning to well up in her eyes.

"Oh, come on, Ben—lay off. Besides, this is really interesting. It seems as though old Great-Granddad ran into some pretty bad luck his first winter. In fact, he says here he wouldn't have made it at all if it hadn't been for this one Indian family that helped him out."

"Hey, that must have been Lilly's great-grandfather. That's the same story that Grandpa told us," added Ben.

"Well," Johnny continued, "he goes on to say how they became really good friends. His name was Great Bear. Now listen to this. I guess this Great Bear told old Great-Granddad some legend about pool of water they called 'Crystal Mirror.' Wow! Dad already told me about that. He said Great-Granddad went off searching for something, and no one could find him. The Indians said he'd found a crystal mirror, but nobody knew what they meant. So, the crystal mirror must be a pool or pond somewhere. In fact, it must still be there!"

"Keep reading, Johnny," urged Patty, who had become very interested all of a sudden.

"Hmm. He goes on now about their first spring at the lake. Here's some stuff about the store and some other stuff about trappers from the north. Boy, looks like one year they darn near had trouble with that other tribe, but Great Bear and his people scared them off."

"Look further in, Johnny," complained Patty. "This part is boring."

Johnny ignored her and kept reading.

"Seems as though he got to know the trappers pretty well. He did a fair amount of trading with them. Hey, here he talks about starting to take some trips in the woods and around the lake with Great Bear. He says they were looking for the Crystal Mirror. I guess the Indians didn't even know where it was."

"Why were they so interested in it anyway?" asked Ben.

"He really doesn't say. But they sure seemed interested. Maybe there was gold there. I'll bet an old pirate treasure had been buried there for years and only the Indians knew about it."

"No way, not this far from the sea. No pirates ever came close to this part of the country," said Ben.

"I'll bet fairy princesses lived there and could give magic gifts," suggested Patty.

"Just like a girl—never thinking about anything practical," said her brother. "Besides, why would anyone want to go see a bunch of silly fairies anyhow?"

Patty started to turn red in the face and was about to make a sharp reply when she noticed that Johnny had turned white as a sheet.

"Johnny! What's the matter?" she cried.

But Johnny didn't reply—he just stared at Great-Granddad's journal.

"Hey, Johnny, what's the problem?" asked Ben, looking over Johnny's shoulder.

But Johnny just kept reading silently, looking almost as though he were about to faint. He slowly handed the notebook to Ben and sat down on the floor without saying a word. Ben looked at the page Johnny had been reading and gave a low whistle.

"Well, read it out loud!" said Patty.

"Oh my gosh," said Ben. "This is enough to make your hair stand on end. Let me back up a couple of pages." Ben turned back the leaves and began to read.

APRIL 16, 1936

Great Bear and I continued our search again this spring. We spent most of the morning near the layered falls. I still am amazed at their beauty. But, as usual, we found nothing. The time is never wasted seeing the beauty of God's creation. Somehow it would be more encouraging if we could find a hint of the old legend. The silver curtain—what could possibly be meant by that? I often wonder if the legend is just a pack of old stories, but Great Bear is so sure.

APRIL 30, 1936

We were able to get some time off from our duties, and so we continued our search. Bear's sister went with us again. She is truly a beautiful girl. I just can't see why it is supposed to be wrong for a white man to marry an Indian. All my old friends would be shocked that I even could consider it. But Bear says I am Indian myself since we became blood brothers.

We searched all day but found nothing of this silver curtain.

JUNE 1, 1936

The strangest thing happened today. I'm not sure what to make of it. Great Bear is sure that it is our first clue. We wandered with our usual luck. I was at the point where I was ready to give up for good. I think Bear felt the same. But just as we were making our way home past the layered falls, we met an old man sitting on a large rock next to the lake. He spoke with a strange accent. He seemed to know all about us and of our search. Since I am still confused about the whole affair, I will write it all down as best I can recall, including his strange mannerisms.

"Hey, boys," he said. "Now why are you spendin' all your time lookin' for what's right thar in front of you?"

"What do you mean, sir?" I asked.

"Now don't ask me what I mean when you rightly know just what I'm talkin' about. That thar silver curtain."

He pointed to the lowest of the falls and said, "Here it's been in front of you the whole time, and you just haven't never even seen it. But now that you've found the key, I 'magine you'll be headin' over thar to unlock it, eh? But now don't you go forgettin' those great-grandchildren of yours, neither, 'cause they need to find it too.

Great Bear and I turned and stared at the falls, trying to figure out what on earth he could mean about its being the silver curtain. Certainly the falling water was beautiful enough to be called silver, but why a curtain? Did it perhaps hide something? We turned back to ask the old man if he knew why the waterfall had been so named. But as we turned around, we discovered he had disappeared. We could not imagine how he could leave so quickly without our knowing. (Bear says he is a spirit of some ancient tribe, but he hasn't the look of someone with Indian blood to me.) So we turned toward the waterfall to study it, but we saw nothing unusual. Tomorrow we will take the canoe to study it more closely. I simply cannot bring myself to go to sleep, as I am consumed with anticipation. And what could he possibly have meant by my great-grand-children? I'm not even married!

Ben stopped reading. All three children were staring at Great-Granddad's journal. Johnny remained sitting on the floor with a stunned look on his face. He was the first to break the silence.

"It was him. I know it."

"But it just couldn't have been," said Ben. "Great-Granddad must have died a long time ago. And he was pretty young when he wrote that journal—only twenty, according to the dates. But he said the man in the woods was old, even way back then!"

"No, it was him!" insisted Johnny. "He talked like him, and he seemed to know all about the lake, just like it belonged to him."

"And he disappeared too," said Patty, "just like he did with Johnny on the plane and in the canoe."

"Well, then, he must be a ghost," said Ben. "Otherwise, he couldn't still be alive."

"Oh, Ben! I keep telling you to stop talking about ghosts and spirits. You know it gives me nightmares. I think it's really mean. Besides, the old man couldn't possibly be a ghost. He always seems so nice. After all, he did tell Great-Granddad about the silver curtain. I think the old man is really a nice fairy."

Ben rolled his eyes and said, "Girls!"

"Wait a minute," said Johnny. "I don't know who the old man is, but we're forgetting something really important. This silver curtain they were looking for was just the key, not the main adventure. They were trying to find something called the Crystal Mirror."

"Yeah, you're right," said Ben, "and he was pointing to what they were calling the 'Layered Falls.' Do you think—"

"Yes, of course! What else could it be?" interrupted Johnny. "That's what we call the Stairsteps. Where else around here is there a place that could be called 'Layered Falls'?"

"Nowhere," admitted Ben. "And this is a matter that must go before the council. We will have a meeting this very afternoon. I will summon Lilly to come to the council chamber at two o'clock."

"Oh bother!" complained Patty. "We'll probably have to smoke that wretched pipe again."

Delays and Frustrations

The three children were hardly hungry, but that didn't prevent lunch from being ready when they arrived downstairs. They were all excited about heading back to the Stairsteps. But Aunt Gail insisted that they sit down and eat. Now, you must not think badly of the boys, even though they devoured their food more like animals than people. Aunt Gail looked at the boys and then at Patty, shaking her head.

"See, Mom, what I have to put up with?" Patty said.

Uncle Jim entered through the kitchen door and studied each of them individually.

"Now there's just what I'm looking for," he announced. "Three healthy volunteers. Gail, could I borrow this crew after lunch, or do you have some other purpose for them?"

"They're all yours, but you may find they have more energy than you counted on. They nearly escaped without lunch, but now they're eating as if there were no tomorrow."

"Excellent! Their energy is just what I need. I have a job that'll take at least the rest of the day."

Ben and Johnny looked horrified. This was simply unfair. But they knew they'd better not complain. Uncle Jim was obviously in no mood for arguing. Patty was also unexcited at the prospect of a job that would take at least the rest of the day, but the thought of avoiding another meeting with Lilly and that horrible pipe was a relief.

Uncle Jim's afternoon job turned out to be much worse than expected. He had finally followed through with his threat to tear down the old barn. The tearing down wasn't bad, since it had been on the verge of falling down on its own. Aunt Gail had complained for years about its being an eyesore, but lately she had insisted that something be done because it had become a death trap. Grandpa was the only one who really hated to see it go. He said it reminded him of "the old days."

At first the boys didn't mind the project as much as they thought. Tearing something apart that wanted to fall down anyway was somewhat interesting, even spectacular, if not a bit dangerous. Uncle Jim took a lot of precautions with the sequence of the demolition, noting carefully who was where and when. By early afternoon the barn was down, but then it was time to clean up the mess. A heap of broken wood marked where the old barn had stood. Ben and Johnny stared at the pile. Patty had managed to talk her mother into letting her help in the kitchen.

"You boys start taking these hammers and pulling the nails out of the wood," said Uncle Jim.

"The good nails go in this bucket, and the bent or broken ones go in that one over there. Then I want the wood stacked up next to the firewood. Don't worry about saving any of it. It's only good for fuel now. I'm heading off to town for the rest of the day. I want to see good progress when I get back."

They realized now that tearing down the barn was the fun part of the job. Cleaning up the mess was going to take a lot of work, but Ben and Johnny got right to it as Uncle Jim headed for his pickup. Checker trotted up beside the boys and flopped over on his back, his tail wagging between his legs.

"Oh, not now," said Johnny. "We've got work to do. I just wish you knew how to work this hammer."

"What timing!" complained Ben. "We were on to something big, and we get stuck doing this."

"Maybe we should have told them about Great-Granddad's journal. They might have been interested enough to go check it out."

"Nah, Dad would have just read part of it and said, 'Hmm, I'll show this to your grandpa. He'd probably like it.' Then he'd've brought it to his room, and that would've been the end of it. Dad just can't concentrate on anything that doesn't help him work the store."

They both turned back to their work. The pile of wood was depressing.

"Oh, I hate it when Dad gets his mind on these projects," added Ben. "There's no end to it until it's all finished."

By dinnertime, they were not even halfway done. Uncle Jim had returned from town and seemed pleased with the boys' progress, but he had no intention of letting up until the project was complete.

"Tomorrow we'll see if we can't finish it up. I'll stay and help this time," said Uncle Jim.

Johnny and Checker headed upstairs shortly after dinner where Johnny collapsed facedown on the bed.

"I thought this was supposed to be a vacation," he said to Checker.

Looking up, he noticed that they had never closed up the ancient library. With some effort, he got back up and stepped into the small room. There was the book. They'd never put it back where it belonged. Johnny reached for it and took it back to his bed. Opening the journal to the page at which they had left off, he tried to read.

"Checker, I wonder what Great-Granddad was really like. He sure seemed to like adventures. I suppose if I read more of his journal here I'll find out."

Checker let loose a huge yawn and curled up next to Johnny's bed.

"What are you tired for anyway? Ben and I did all the work. You just kept trying to chase the ducks."

Checker ignored all this and closed his eyes. Johnny turned back to the journal but had trouble focusing.

"Oh, this is useless. I'll read it tomorrow."

Johnny forced himself out of bed and put the old journal back in the little library. He then pulled the door shut. He felt better with the library wall looking like a solid wall again. As exciting as the secret library was, it seemed strange all the same, and he did not like the idea of going to sleep with the place all opened up like that.

He picked up the old Bible and returned it to its place on the shelf, where it concealed the lever controlling the hidden door. He paused for a moment as he considered the old book.

"I wonder what old Great-Granddad used it for. It's too big to read the whole thing."

He removed it once more from its place and began to carefully thumb through its ancient pages. He tried to read part of a page, but after going through a few sentences, he found he couldn't remember what he had read. Besides, the words were hard, and there weren't even any pictures.

Johnny gently returned it to its place on the shelf. He slid back into bed. Never had anything felt so good. It was only a few moments before he and his dog were both sound asleep.

A Stranger in the Dark

Johnny awoke suddenly with a most uneasy feeling. It was still quite dark, except where a sliver of moonlight leaked through his window. Checker was sitting up erect, staring at the wall that hid the library. He let out a low growl.

"What is it, Checker? What's the problem?" Johnny whispered.

Checker thumped his tail a few times in response but did not take his eyes off the wall. He let out a few more growls, but there seemed to be nothing to warrant them.

Johnny slipped out of bed, crept up to the wall, and listened. Checker was next to him, sniffing the floor.

"Shh," whispered Johnny, as he stroked his dog's head in an attempt to keep him quiet. Both boy and dog searched the entire wall. Johnny stopped. He remembered closing the door to the library before he went to bed. But here it was, slightly ajar. Johnny felt butterflies starting up in his stomach. Slowly he reached for the edge of the door and tried to pull it open, but it would not budge.

Oh, yes, the lever, he thought.

He went back to take the old Bible off the shelf, but it was already lying on its side, exposing the lever to plain view. Johnny looked at the Bible for several moments. He remembered trying to read it, but he was sure he had put it back—or had he?

Johnny pulled on the lever. The wall silently opened, just as it had before. His heart was racing as he peered into the little room. Barely visible in the weak moonlight stood an old man, reading Great-Granddad's journal. He had a strange yet not unkind smile on his face. Johnny let out a gasp.

The old man looked up and simply said, "Oops! I knew I was takin' too long!" Instantly he and the book vanished.

Johnny stared at the empty space where the old man had been only seconds before. There was absolutely no question this time. It was definitely Abraham. Fear suddenly welled up inside him, and he bolted from the room with Checker at his heels. Down the hall he raced, flying into Ben's room.

"Ben! Ben!" said Johnny in an excited whisper.

Ben sprang up to a sitting position.

"What on earth are you doing, Johnny? You scared the wits out of me. What time is it?"

"Ben, listen! Old Abraham was just in my room. I saw him, and so did Checker."

"But how did he get into your room?"

"Beats me, but that's not even half of it. Checker woke me up with his growling. But he was growling at the library wall. Now, I know I closed the door, but when I looked, it was a bit open. What's more, someone had moved the old Bible. So I pulled the lever and looked in. There was Abraham, standing in the library. He looked surprised that I saw him. Then he said something and just plain disappeared. I mean, right in front of me!"

"Come on, let's go back and see," said Ben.

Ben started down the hall, with Johnny following a bit reluctantly. They crept back to Johnny's room. Ben peered in first. There was Johnny's bed, obviously slept in. His pants, shoes, and shirt lay in a heap on the floor. His suitcase, still half unpacked, lay on the easy chair where he had left it. So everything seemed quite normal.

"So what's there to see?" asked Ben. Johnny looked in after him and saw the library closed up as if it did not even exist. The Bible was back in its proper place. All was as it should have been.

"Are you sure you didn't just have a bad dream?"

"No! I tell you, he was here—just as plain as you and me!"

"Was your light on, or was it all dark like this?"

"Oh, cut it out. I tell you, I saw him. Come on, let's go back and look in the library."

The two boys walked over to the Bible and started to pull it from the shelf.

"And just what do you boys think you're up to?" said a deep voice behind them.

Both boys spun around. There, in the doorway, stood Uncle Jim, looking not at all pleased.

"Do you realize it's two o'clock in the morning? You're making enough racket to wake up Grandpa. How long have you been up?"

Ben looked back to the wall and said, "Dad, I think you had better see this."

He pulled the lever and the wall opened back up, exposing the library.

"I see you've discovered the old library. I guess that might excite boys your age. I probably should have told you about it. It belonged to Grandpa's dad. But I'll tell you all you want to know about it tomorrow, when we get back to work cleaning up that wood pile. If you boys don't get some sleep, you won't be any use at all—and the job will take an extra day. Now get back to bed, both of you!"

The boys said no more and hurried back to their beds. Uncle Jim closed up the library, said goodnight to Johnny, and shut the door.

"Boy, oh boy, Checker, what do you think of that! We'd better stay awake in case old Abraham shows up again. Besides, there's no way I could sleep now anyway."

Johnny threw his pillow down by the foot of the bed and turned himself around, facing the wall that hid the library. He stared at the wall and prepared to keep a vigilant watch throughout the night. Ben found him in the morning, sound asleep with his fists pressed into his eyes.

"Hey, wake up, sleepyhead. It's already nine thirty. Dad wants to know when you're going to get up and help us finish with the old barn."

Johnny groaned and rolled over. Then he shot out of bed as he realized he had fallen asleep. His head swam, and darkness started to close in, forcing him to sit back down.

"Did he come back?" asked Johnny.

"Who?"

"You know, the old man, Abraham. Don't you remember? He came to my room last night and got into the library. He even took Great-Granddad's old journal."

"Oh, yeah. You better not bring that up around Dad. He wasn't real happy with us for being out of bed in the middle of the night. First thing he told me today was that he expected us to stay in our beds at night until breakfast time."

"Oh. I guess we did make too much noise. But let's at least go check the library."

"Well, okay—but we'd better make it quick, 'cause Dad's expecting us downstairs."

Johnny went back to the bookshelf, removed the Bible, and pulled down the lever. The library wall opened up, and the boys walked in slowly—half expecting the old man to be waiting for them. The little room was just as they had left it, except that the journal was nowhere to be seen.

"Well, I guess we'll never see Great-Granddad's journal again," said Johnny sadly.

"That's kinda weird," replied Ben. "I remember we left it right here."

He looked thoughtful for a moment and then shrugged it off.

"Come on. Let's get the job finished so we can get back to the lake again."

The cleanup operation took not only all that day but most of the next. Aunt Gail and Uncle Jim decided to go to bed early, telling the three of them they could stay up late if they were very quiet.

"Thank you, boys, for your work. You've been a big help. Tomorrow is all yours," said Uncle Jim.

"You were a big help too, Patty," added her mother as she headed upstairs. "Don't stay up too late."

The children kept their thoughts to themselves for some time. Checker was making the most of the fire left by Uncle Jim. Grandpa was leaning back in his easy chair, still smoking his pipe. He then blew the biggest smoke ring Johnny had ever seen.

"Well, Johnny, you haven't told me what you think of our house and lake since you've been here," said Grandpa. "It must be a lot different from what you're used to."

"Oh yes, Grandpa. It's even better than I ever dreamed."

"I imagine you youngsters will go exploring that lake tomorrow. It's a good lake. There is just something peaceful about it, yet it is mysterious too. I suppose your dad told you about the mystery of the lake."

"No, I never heard about any mystery." However, Johnny immediately thought about Abraham and his strange appearances.

"Well, I can't believe Ben never told you about it either. Why, there's no lake like this one. Ben, didn't you tell him about the rivers that feed the lake?"

"Oh yes, Grandpa, but I guess I forgot to mention that other part."

This turn in the conversation was making Ben nervous. Sure, the lake was beautiful, but the only real mystery was hidden away in Great-Granddad's journal. Ben knew that no one else had discovered the cave behind the Stairsteps. He stared at Johnny as if to warn him not to blurt out anything that might give it away.

"Well, Johnny," continued Grandpa, "the lake has two rivers that feed it. The closest one goes over what we used to call the 'layered falls' back in the old days. The other river is clean on the other side of the lake. Neither river is all that big, but both of them run into the lake and not out of it. Try as you might, you can explore every inch of lakefront for the rest of the summer, and you won't find any river, stream, or creek that leads out. Now here's the real mystery:

since I've been a kid, the lake has never gotten any bigger. So where does all the water go?"

"I know, Grandpa!" cried Patty, who just loved it when Grandpa stayed up late with them. "The water just flows out of the bottom of the lake like it does out of the bottom of a bathtub."

"Then where do you think it goes after it drains out of the bottom of the lake?" asked Ben.

"Well, that's easy. It goes into the Great Underground Ocean. That's what I think happened to all the water from Noah's flood."

Grandpa smiled, but Ben rolled his eyes.

"Well, you youngsters think about that for a while. But now it's time for old fellers like me to get some sleep."

Grandpa stood up, rubbed Checker behind his ear, and started upstairs. "Good night, kids."

"Good night, Grandpa," they responded.

Ben waited until he heard Grandpa close his door.

"Tomorrow will tell us if old Great-Granddad really found anything," Ben said. "Let's first pick up Lilly and tell her what happened and then go straight to the Stairsteps."

"But I don't get it," said Johnny. "The silver curtain has got to be the waterfall. We've been behind it into the cave, so what's left?"

"I don't know," Ben retorted. "It's really too bad we lost Great-Granddad's journal. Maybe he found something and wrote it down later on. But it's gone now. I guess we'll never find out."

"Yeah, that was wild when Abraham disappeared right in front of my eyes."

Ben looked at him doubtfully. "Are you sure there was anyone in your room? I mean, it really was late, you know. Maybe it was just a shadow."

"Look, Ben. I saw what I saw. If I imagined him, how come Checker was growling at him?"

"I don't know, but I do know that no one has seen him but you."

Patty stood up with her hands on her hips.

"Now, you boys think you're so smart, and you can't even figure this out! It's simple. The old man in Great-Granddad's journal is the same old man that Johnny saw on the plane, on the lake, and in the little library. He's obviously magical. For one thing, he would have died a long time ago if he weren't magical. And besides, he disappeared right in front of Johnny. Well, he took the journal away because it would make things too easy. He told Great-Granddad to go behind the waterfall, so whatever we're looking for has to be there. And don't forget: he told Great-Granddad about us. So we are meant to follow him there and find the magic in the cave."

"All right, then why haven't we already found the magic? We've been there over and over again since we discovered it two years ago," retorted Ben.

"Because we were never really looking. We never have looked any farther than the landing."

"Oh, why try to reason with girls? There is nothing back there. We can see the back of the cave from the landing."

"Ben, you are really stuck-up. You think you know everything just because you're older."

"No, it's because I'm not a girl."

Patty's face started to turn red, and things would certainly have gone further downhill had Johnny not interrupted.

"Wait a minute. Just wait a minute. Something is starting to make some sense. Yes, of course! Why, it all fits. Can't you see it?"

"Well, no I can't, unless you tell us," said Ben a bit irritably.

"I think there is something to what Patty is saying."

Ben glowered, and Patty smirked at the same time, but Johnny ignored them both and went on with his thought.

"You see, the lake does need to have a drain somewhere, and it must be in the cave behind the waterfall. The day you took me in there in the canoe, there was definitely a current. The canoe turned itself into the cave. You had to hold the ledge where we landed, and I had a tough time getting out."

"Yeah, that's right," said Ben. "I told you to go by the edge, where it was easier. I've known that for a long time. But I never really thought much about it. I figured it was just caused by the water being all stirred up by the waterfall."

"But it can't be that. Water has to get out of the cave somewhere, or it would just fill up."

Ben looked thoughtful and said nothing for a few moments. He then broke the silence.

"You know, you're right. Grandpa is right too. Both rivers flow into the lake, and no one can figure out how the water gets out. It has to be in the back of the cave."

"But why hasn't anybody found the cave before?" asked Johnny.

"Because you can't see it," responded Patty. "We only accidentally got close enough to see it. About two years ago, we lost control of the canoe and almost went right under the waterfall!"

"That's right," interrupted Ben. "There is so much spray that we almost missed it. You saw how close you have to get before you can see the space between the waterfall and the rock wall."

"So then," concluded Johnny, "nobody ever gets close enough to notice the passage to the cave. There's so much action in front of the waterfall that you wouldn't feel the current at all."

"And don't forget the nice old man that keeps showing up at the strangest times," said Patty. "I think he wants us to go and find out where the water goes."

"And I'll bet you anything that's the way old Great-Granddad went when he took off and left his note," added Ben. "Boy, I wish we could go right now and find out for sure. I'm going to bed. The sooner we get to sleep, the sooner morning will come and we can find out for sure."

Any adult would have been amazed to see what happened next. All three scampered off to bed as if their lives depended on it. But sleep did not come easily for any of them.

The Journey Begins

The next morning held promise for a beautiful day. Uncle Jim was in a particularly good mood, as was usually the case when large tasks were behind him. He looked at the children thoughtfully from across their large oak table as they gulped down their breakfast.

"You kids were really a big help these past few days," he said. "The weather looks like it should hold out for some time. I think you could probably get a lot of exploring done if you went on an overnight."

"Oh, could we really?" said Ben. "That would be just terrific!"

Aunt Gail looked disapprovingly at her husband.

"What do you propose Patty will be doing on this outing?"

"Oh, Gail—she'll do just fine. The boys will take good care of her. There is absolutely nothing that will hurt any of them on the lake. You have to admit, she's proven herself to be a pretty strong swimmer this summer."

Now this started what adults call "a discussion." But if you'd heard it, you might have called it something else. The long and short of it was that Aunt Gail agreed to let them go only if they took Checker and promised never to get out of sight of the lake. So she packed up enough food to last them through the next day's lunch, with strict instructions to be home for dinner the following day.

Soon the canoe was filled with kids, dog, paddles, backpacks, sleeping bags, and canteens. Waving good-bye, they began to glide across the lake.

"Where are we going first?" asked Patty. "To get Lilly, of course," said Ben.

Patty groaned.

"Why do we always have to do things with her anyway? I thought this was going to be an overnight just for us."

Ben looked shocked.

"We can't possibly leave out Lilly! Not on something as important as this. We've got to explore the depths of the cave. Why, it would be breaking the secret oaths if we left her out."

Patty threw down her paddle into the canoe.

"Well, you've just ruined the whole trip, and I refuse to go any farther. You always get your way just because you're bigger than I am."

Ben ignored her and kept on paddling.

"She's just being a baby, as usual," he said to Johnny.

Johnny looked up at Patty, who had folded her arms and was looking away from both of them. She couldn't hide the tears that were beginning to well up. He slid up toward the bow, next to her.

"Patty, I don't really like Lilly either," he whispered. "How about if you and I make sure we have a good time and just don't worry about anyone else?"

Patty didn't say anything but nodded her head in reply. Looking up, Johnny could see a rustic-looking log cabin. A young, dark-haired girl was standing on the shore, looking across the lake but not at them.

"Lilly!" Ben called out.

But Lilly ignored his cry. She continued to stare until the canoe reached the shore. Ben jumped out while Johnny dragged it up onto the beach.

Without acknowledging their arrival, Lilly spoke.

"There are great wonders in the sky. I have watched them since before dawn."

Patty rolled her eyes and said something under her breath.

"We have much to discuss," said Ben. "It's all secret tribal business and must be done in the council chamber."

Lilly nodded. Noticing the food and gear the others had brought, she went back into her cabin. A few minutes later, she emerged with a sack and threw it into her own canoe. She appeared ready for an indefinite journey. Johnny wondered where her parents were. She couldn't be living there all alone.

"Johnny, take Patty in our canoe. I'll go with Lilly. Just follow us. We'll head to the Stairsteps."

Both canoes headed back across the lake. Johnny looked up at Patty, who appeared dejected. She was paddling half-heartedly, so Johnny matched her pace to keep the canoe going straight. They lagged behind the other canoe, and after they were separated by some distance, Patty broke the silence, speaking in a low voice.

"I don't know why we always have to have *her* do everything with us. Just when things start to get fun, either she shows up or Ben has to go and get her. It isn't fair!"

"Yeah, she is kind of strange," answered Johnny.

"No, she's just plain creepy, and she makes me sick to my stomach. Sometimes I wish she'd fall out of her canoe and drown."

"Patty, isn't that kind of harsh?"

"No, it isn't! She always spoils everything, and she does it on purpose too. What makes it worse is Ben likes her. Last year he wouldn't have anything to do with her, but now it's always the tribe this and the tribe that. I wish we had never started it at all."

"Well, why don't you just quit the tribe altogether?"

"Then what else am I supposed to do? No one our age lives anywhere close."

"Is it really that bad being part of the tribe?"

"How would you like to smoke that horrible pipe practically every time Ben or Lilly thinks something up? It's always stupid too—usually about some secret information that no one cares about. I think Lilly would just die if anything ever happened to her old rotten pipe. She always has it with her."

"Where did she find it?"

"Find it? Oh, no—she didn't find it. It's been in her family for a long, long time. She says for over five hundred years, but I'd like to know how she found that out. They used to tell me that if I didn't smoke it, old spirits would come and get me in the middle of the night. One day I had an awful dream about it, and Mom had to wake me up. That's when I told her what Ben and Lilly had been telling me. Ben really caught it that time. Served him right too."

Patty looked as if she was about to boil over, but she had finally run out of words. The discussion seemed to help her paddling, however. Even with this new energy, Johnny and Patty were only just entering the bay when Ben and Lilly were disappearing behind the waterfall.

Five minutes later, Johnny and Patty slipped behind that dazzling sheet of liquid crystals. Johnny felt the cool spray on his face as they carefully worked their way to the cave's mouth. He asked Patty to stop paddling as he steered toward the center of the opening. This time, there was no mistake. The canoe suddenly turned and was pulled into the cave by the current. Ahead, a canoe was docked at the familiar rock platform.

Ben reached out to stop their canoe as it moved up to the ledge. He helped Patty out, but she offered no thanks and proceeded to sit down on the far side of the landing. Stepping out of the canoe, Johnny called Checker, who looked unhappy with the whole arrangement. After some effort, and a few threats, Johnny succeeded in pulling the dog onto the ledge without upsetting the canoe. Lilly was studying the far side of the cave with no expression whatsoever. Ben leaned over to Johnny.

"I told her on the way over what we thought about the other end of the cave."

"Did you tell her about old Abraham and Great-Granddad's journal?"

"Nah—well, actually I was going to, but she said it should wait until the whole tribe gathered at the council chamber. And since we're all here, we might as well get started. Lilly, it's time for the council to begin. Bring out the pipe. Patty, come on over here."

Patty glowered at her brother but came a few feet closer. Ben surveyed the other three with a very solemn look. After a moment of silence, he opened the meeting.

"Today we must explore for the secret of secrets. The lost pool may yet be revealed. Each of us must share all that we know about the strange things that have occurred recently and long ago. Lilly should begin by telling the old legends."

Now, Ben didn't really think of himself as sounding quite so mystical as his performance indicated, and consequently it didn't come off nearly as well as if Lilly had said it. Patty rolled her eyes but said nothing. Her brother talked like that only when Lilly was around.

"Legends, the white men may call them," said Lilly, "but they are ancient truths held by my people. They tell of this lake before the white man ever came. It was a time when all my people knew of secret ways of travel that led to lands of wealth beyond the imaginings of foolish men who wanted nothing but gold."

Johnny was becoming increasingly interested in all this, but Patty was beginning to regret she had come at all. She walked over to Checker and began to stroke his head, pretending not to listen any more. Lilly stared off into space as if she were trying to recall an old memory. After a moment's pause, she continued.

"Many, many years ago, my tribe wandered away from the southern plains. It is said that a wicked tribe drove them from their homeland. Long they wandered, seeking a new home. Many died on the journey. Scouts were sent out in all directions to search for a place with many buffalo. The scouts came back, saying that the land was either barren or filled with white men. Some good Indian lands remained, but no tribe would have us. A few scouts never came back."

"When our people were near to despair, one lone scout returned from the north. He said a wonderful land, empty of people, awaited us. There were no buffalo, but much water, deer, and other game. Our people rejoiced, except for one old man who said he had heard of the country. He told my people that it had a secret place with a deadly peril. When the chief asked him what the deadly peril was, the old man did not respond—for he died as soon as the words left his mouth."

"Fear swept through our people, but suddenly a warning cry came from a brave. The wicked tribe that had chased us from our homeland had pursued us and was bursting into our camp. Thinking we were trapped, the wicked tribe retreated just out of arrow shot and waited for an opportunity to attack. Our chief was very wise. At night he discovered a way out. Our people can move in perfect silence, and they escaped without notice.

"After many moons, we arrived at this lake, tired and hungry. We found the report of fish and game true, and soon there was plenty for all. Finally, the white man did come but never in great numbers. Your great-grandfather and mine became blood brothers and gave us peace. But my tribe dwindled and dispersed, and now we know of only a few others in northern regions."

"But what about the deadly peril that the old Indian warned you of just before he died? Did you ever find it?" asked Johnny.

"Only rumor and guesses. Once, a wandering Indian from another tribe was found at the point of death in the snow. We revived him. He said he was searching for a pool that he called 'Crystal Mirror.' He said he had heard of it once as a child and knew only that it was near the lake. Before leaving, he warned us that the pool was wonderful but dangerous."

"Well, if this pool is so dangerous, why on earth are we trying to find it?" asked Patty, who had also found the story much more interesting than she would let on.

Ignoring her comment, Ben interrupted. "Okay, now we know the ancient history of this lake. Now I will tell you everything that has happened since we saw you last, Lilly."

"Johnny should tell that, Ben!" objected Patty, who no longer pretended not to be listening. "You didn't even believe half of it anyway."

So Johnny recounted all that had happened relating to the discovery of the library and Great-Granddad's journal. He described waking up in the middle of the night to find old Abraham in the library reading the journal and then disappearing with it in his hand. Finally, Ben wrapped it up with Grandpa's comment about the water flowing into the lake but never out.

"I still think there is a hole somewhere in the bottom of the lake, and it all drains away like a bathtub," added Patty.

"Yes, in a way I suppose you're right," said Ben, "but the drain has to be in this cave."

"Did you notice how hard that current is when we come through the opening?" asked Johnny. "I steered the canoe away from the edge when Patty and I came in. It was strong. I think if we were to shove off this rock and head back into the main current, we would find that drain in a hurry."

Johnny's words echoed on the cavern's walls with no response. The impact of what Johnny had just suggested suddenly dawned on everyone. They all knew that the moving water must lead to an opening, but to what else did it lead? What was this great peril that died on the lips of that old Indian so long ago?

Unexpected Adventure

Lilly stared for a moment into the dark regions of the cave.

"Let us seek the adventure that has been prepared for us and find the secret ways of the flowing waters," she said, a bit dramatically.

Ben nodded, and together they began pushing Lilly's canoe off the ledge. Patty grabbed Johnny's arm and pulled him away from the others.

"We aren't really going to go back there in the dark, are we?" she whispered.

"Well, I think those two want to."

"What do you want to do, Johnny?"

"I don't think it would hurt just to find out what's back there. The water flows really smoothly. Besides, the current isn't too strong if we stay away from the center."

"But we promised Mom that we wouldn't leave the lake. You wouldn't want us to be liars, would you? And especially to Mom!"

Johnny paused a moment. No, he certainly did not want to lie to his aunt and uncle. He knew lying was wrong, but he couldn't miss out on finding out the answer to this mystery either. Besides, he couldn't have Ben thinking he was a coward.

"But, Patty, we won't leave the lake at all," Johnny said. "You see, the lake flows right here within the cave. As long as we stay in our canoes, we'll never leave the lake at all."

Patty looked doubtful as she thought this over.

"Johnny, I'm really scared," she whispered. "I don't trust Lilly at all. Ben is never the same when he's around her. If something goes wrong, she would probably just let us all drown."

Even in the dim light, Johnny thought he saw a tear running down his cousin's cheek. "Look, Patty, Checker and I will be right by you in this canoe. Ben wants to go with Lilly anyway. Checker and I have been through lots tougher adventures than this. We'll let those two go on first, and if anything goes wrong, you'll be safe with us."

"I don't want Ben to drown either," she objected.

"No one is going to drown. I'm sure they can take care of themselves, but if they have any problems, Checker and I will rescue them too."

"Just Ben—I don't care what happens to *her*."

"Come on, you two," yelled Ben. "What are you waiting for? Let's go!"

Johnny called to Checker, who wagged his tail several times but made no attempt to move off the rock. In the end, Johnny had to pull him into the canoe, nearly upsetting it again. Patty took her place in the bow. Johnny stepped into the stern and looked disgustedly at his dog.

"Some hero you're turning out to be. What's so bad about a little boat ride?"

Checker looked back at his master sheepishly, but he didn't seem concerned about being a hero at all. He curled up on the floor of the canoe with his tail between his legs and watched the cavern walls glide silently by.

For some reason, the light did not totally fail. This was fortunate for them all. Patty would not have tolerated total darkness, even for a moment. It was dark enough, however, to lose track of how far and how fast they were actually traveling. Patty's tension continued to grow, but before she lost her patience altogether, Lilly's canoe came to an abrupt stop. Johnny and Patty both dug in their paddles to avoid collision, but it was not really necessary. The current, which had been so effectively carrying them along, suddenly boiled and swirled, heading in no direction at all.

"Which way do we go from here?" shouted Johnny. He had not realized that the noise level of the water had been continuously growing.

"I think I see the back wall over to the left," responded Ben. "Let's go look."

Immediately, Ben and Lilly starting paddling across the turbulent waters toward the far wall of the cave, but Johnny and Patty tried to stay where they were.

"I don't like this, Johnny," said Patty. "Something doesn't feel right. Why is the water getting so noisy? Besides, I've been splashed in the face twice now!" Suddenly she gasped. "What are those two doing? Have they gone crazy?"

Johnny and Patty watched Ben and Lilly, now in the middle of the cavern. But instead of continuing toward the far wall as was their intent, they were moving in a broad circle and much too fast. Ben and Lilly were gripping the sides of their canoe. In little time they had turned completely around and were rapidly heading right back toward Johnny and Patty. They did not collide, however. Their canoe continued in an ever-tightening circle, moving faster and faster with every moment. Johnny and Patty watched helplessly, failing to realize that their own canoe was moving toward the same area as Ben and Lilly's.

All at once, Johnny and Patty felt their canoe lurch forward. Patty fell backwards, on top of Checker, while Johnny was pressed back into the stern. The water had taken on a will of its own. It was no longer flat but rather sloped toward the center of the circle in which they were now traveling. He looked to the side and saw Ben and Lilly's canoe spinning madly, almost on top of itself. There was no mistake: Ben and Lilly were clearly inside this whirling vortex and underneath them. He heard screams of terror that were suddenly cut off. Ben, Lilly, and their canoe had simply vanished.

Horror struck Johnny's very core. The canoe was riding at such an angle that they would have fallen overboard if they hadn't been pressed so tightly into the bottom. Patty was sobbing out of control. Even in his terror, Johnny's thoughts turned toward his parents, his home, and his friends at school. No one would ever know what had become of him. He remembered going along with some of the school bullies when they'd been so cruel to the new kid with the red hair. He knew it was wrong, but he didn't dare cross them.

What happens to people who die with too many bad deeds? he wondered. Had he done enough good to make up the balance?

They were now spinning so tightly that everything was a blur. He felt like he was going to be sick. Water was all around him. The canoe's bow was pointing straight down. Below him, he heard Patty scream horribly and realized he was screaming himself. Then all noise was absorbed by the crashing of water as he was smothered by it from all sides. He felt himself being sucked downward as if by a giant, relentless hand of twisting water. Suddenly, his fear left him altogether. He was aware only of the water's intense grip and the sensation of plunging downward. Instinct caused him to hold his breath. Then without warning, the water loosened its awful hold, though it still surrounded him. He could feel himself falling, falling, falling. Then suddenly he hit hard and felt himself plunging into a pool of water.

Blackness crowded into Johnny's mind. Fighting for consciousness, he instinctively swam upward. Just when he was sure his lungs would burst, he shot through the surface. Water was crashing all around him from above, but he was blinded by dazzling light from every direction. Yet somehow he managed to swim away from the falling water. Squinting through the glare, he saw a dog vainly tugging at the limp form of a young girl's body. Someone else swam up to help, and together they dragged her to dry ground. With a last desperate effort, Johnny swam to the same place and collapsed on an overhanging ledge with his legs still dangling in the water as he lost consciousness.

Johnny was forced awake by a persistent whining and the nudging of a wet, furry face. Checker began biting at his clothing, tugging until Johnny dragged his legs out of the water. After a few moments, he could see through the dazzling light. There was Lilly, bent over Patty and blowing air into her mouth. At first there was no response, but then Patty gasped and began to cough. Finally, she broke into a good, hard cry. When she looked up and saw that it was Lilly who had saved her life, she reached up and hugged her like a long-lost friend.

"Where is Ben?" asked Lilly.

Johnny felt a wave of nausea come over him when he heard Lilly's words. He desperately but vainly scanned the water and the shoreline. Lilly did the same, but Patty had fallen asleep in her arms, making it difficult for her to move. Lilly carefully laid her down and walked up to Johnny. Both continued searching without success. Ben was nowhere in sight.

Lilly collapsed to the ground, dissolving into tears. Johnny looked helplessly at her. He was torn by his own grief and confused by this part of Lilly that he had never seen. He stared at her for a moment and then turned his gaze back to the water.

For the first time, he observed his surroundings. He was overwhelmed by the violence and the unbelievable beauty of the pool of water before him. It formed a perfect circle at least a hundred feet across. The water drained into a river at one end and disappeared into a long tunnel, which then bent out of view to the right. A column of water fell from the roof—at least thirty feet above them— and thundered into the center of the pool. In one area of the cavern's roof, several narrow fissures formed slits in the rock, allowing sunlight to penetrate. Throughout the cave, jagged crystals caught and scattered the sunlight, casting a dazzling light everywhere. This turned the column of water into millions of falling diamonds. The shore was smooth where they had collapsed, though hard and any-thing but comfortable. As his eyes drifted away from the falling wa-ter, he marveled how well it reflected the image of the cave they were in, at least until it reached the cavern from which it exited and then became dark.

Johnny's gaze moved back to the water. He noticed an object being forced to the surface by the turbulence. It came quite close to the ledge. Johnny reached for it, but it slowly sank and drifted back toward the center of the pool.

"It's Ben's jacket," said Lilly.

They both stared at the water, saying nothing in hopes that it would reappear. But they never saw it again.

A soft whimpering caught their attention. Lilly returned to Patty, who was beginning to cry again.

"Where are we?" asked Patty.

"We're safe on the ledge," responded Lilly, as she sat down next to her.

"I'm cold. I want to go home."

"Put your head on my lap," said Lilly, as she took off her own jacket and wrapped Patty with it. Patty obeyed without a word and quickly fell asleep again.

"We've got to figure out how to get out of here," said Johnny. "We must have fallen right down that column of water."

"We did," agreed Lilly. "We were caught by the whirlpool and sucked right down through it. I was thrown out of the canoe. I didn't see what happened to Ben or my canoe. He must have—"

A lump in Lilly's throat stopped her short. Tears welled up in her eyes.

"Oh, I wish I had never talked him into starting that stupid tribe. Nothing good ever comes from what I do. He was the only true friend I ever had, and now he's gone."

"It's not your fault," said Johnny. "Ben, Patty, and I all wanted to go. We had been planning it for days. Patty at least had some sense.

She wanted to go back when we were in the cavern, and I should have listened to her. We've got to find a way out soon, especially for her sake. If only we hadn't lost everything. We have no canoe, no sleeping bags, and—worst of all—no food."

Lilly said nothing.

"Well, let's think it through," Johnny continued. "You fell through the opening and got separated from the canoe. What happened next?"

"All I remember is falling and plunging into water. I went in feet first…at least I think so because I went down really deep. I wasn't sure I was going to make it back up."

Johnny recalled the horrible smash when he hit the pool.

I wish I had gone in feet first, he thought.

"When I came up, I was blinded by the light. As soon as I could, I looked up at the falling water. Your canoe was just coming through. I never saw you at all. You must have been in the middle of the column, but Patty and Checker were thrown free. Patty landed on her back and went under. I swam over to where she hit, but Checker got there first and dragged her closer to the ledge."

"That's when I saw you pull her up," said Johnny. "You were really great."

They both studied their surroundings for several minutes. There was no hope of returning the way they had come. Johnny studied the fissures in the ceiling and the walls leading up to them. They were much higher than the opening of the water jet, and the walls leading up to them gave no hope for a foothold.

"I wonder where the cracks in the ceiling lead to," continued Johnny. "They must be just beyond the back of the cave where we fell through. I wonder why no one has ever discovered them. They must be hidden somehow. If we could just get to them, we might be able to yell for help. There is no way we could fit through any of them. Besides, I can't see any way of getting up there."

Johnny's eyes again followed the moving water, which drained out on the far side as an underground river. It flowed for a few hundred feet before the water wandered to the right and out of sight.

"That has to be the only way out," he muttered. "But we can't possibly make it without our canoes. Who knows how long we'd go before we could find a place to rest?"

"Or where it finally ends up!" added Lilly.

Patty suddenly sat up and studied her surroundings.

"Are you okay?" asked Johnny.

"Yes, but I want to go home now," said Patty.

Johnny and Lilly said nothing more but again considered their options. Things looked bleak. They walked back to the water's edge and carefully studied the two exits again, but neither seemed possible. There was nothing but crashing water coming through where they fell, and there was no way to navigate down the exit tunnel. Then Lilly pointed across the pool. With their eyes more adjusted to the light, they could now make out the opposite shore. There was an opening of some kind, but was it just another cave or a path out?

Patty started to do some exploring of her own. She had no desire to go anywhere near the water, so she began to look over the cavern walls, somewhat away from Johnny and Lilly. The cave was pure crystal, with an occasional sandy area made of pulverized quartz. She tried uncovering the sand in places, but it was always shallow and revealed nothing. Then something unusual near her feet caught her eye. She uncovered it and saw a blood-red stone, very smooth to the touch. It must have been buried for a very long time, since the sand around it had nearly turned to rock. After much effort she finally freed it. Looking her prize over, she saw that it was nearly circular, about three inches across and half an inch thick at the center. One could almost see through it, though it was murky. While one side was completely smooth to the touch except where it had one deep crack, the other side had worn markings.

Patty studied her new treasure. It was hard to tell, but she could almost make out the markings to be a sun above a moon.

Who could have made this? she wondered.

She sat down pondering why this stone, so different from all the crystal around it, was there at all.

There must have been a great people living here once, she mused, her mind now drifting into an imaginary world of kings, queens, and princesses who had wars and adventures of their own.

A low growl broke her dream. Checker was staring across the pool. His ears were well forward, the hair on his back bristling. Patty heard the growl and, without thinking why, slid the stone into her pocket.

As she wondered why he was growling, she thought, *Perhaps he heard Ben. I am going to check and see if it's him.* So she moved in the direction of where she thought Checker was looking but saw nothing herself, so she sat down again to see if she could find another gem like the one she had just unearthed.

"Hey, take it easy, boy," reassured Johnny. "Believe me—there's nobody here but us, and if there were, we'd be yelling for help."

Checker wagged his tail for a moment in response but did not take his eyes off the opposite wall of the cave. He let out another low growl. Lilly looked at Checker, then studied the wall herself. She knelt down next to the dog and began to stroke his ear.

"Good boy," she whispered.

"What's the matter?" asked Johnny.

"Shh," whispered Lilly. "I think we'd better hide."

Johnny and Lilly hid themselves as best they could, taking Checker with them. The crystal rocks that formed the cave provided less-than-satisfactory cover, but it was all they had. Lilly continued to calm the dog as Johnny peered back around to the other end of the cave. He studied the opening in the wall just above the water. It was, at most, six feet high and three feet wide. He ducked back under cover.

"That's an opening at the other end, I'm sure. If we could get to it, we might find a way out of here!"

"Shh," commanded Lilly. "Checker heard something again."

Lilly, Checker, and Johnny crouched down out of sight of the back wall and waited. After a few minutes, Lilly and Johnny could hear strange and eerie voices. As they listened, the voices became louder and more ominous.

"I've got to see what's going on," whispered Johnny.

"Just don't let them see you!" responded Lilly.

Johnny peered around the rock a second time. This time he saw men with torches, wading into the water, and others proceeding from the opening. The men were dressed in rough brownish material like leather. Their faces were painted with gruesome designs. Each was armed with a bow and a quiver of arrows.

The men formed two lines and waited for something as they looked back toward the mouth of the cave. Without a sound, they all dropped to their knees and bowed their heads so that their faces were just above the water.

Suddenly a man dressed in a spectacular, brightly colored cape jumped through the opening and surveyed the pool. Johnny ducked back under cover.

"You've got to see this!" he whispered to Lilly. "I'll hold Checker."

Lilly changed places with Johnny and carefully peered over the ledge. She saw the brightly clad man being helped into a small canoe that was pushed into the pool. The others went back into the cave and reappeared with several smaller canoes. They followed their leader into the water.

Lilly jumped back.

"They're coming this way! Don't move!"

Johnny and Lilly pressed themselves back into the crystal rocks, which only partially shielded them from view. Johnny glanced at Lilly. An expression of horror came over her face. When he looked out again, he saw why: Patty was in plain view. There was absolutely nothing they could do without attracting attention, so they watched and waited. Patty clearly had not seen the men and was sitting on the sand, studying the various rocks she had collected.

Johnny and Lilly watched as the canoes paddled behind the falling water. Fortunately, the strangely dressed men were preoccupied and did not look in Patty's direction. They began their chanting again, moving their torches in a rhythmic pattern. The leader stopped paddling and stood up in his canoe with arms outstretched. Without losing his balance, he wailed in a loud voice and waved two torches in opposite circles. Then, as if with one will, all the men raised their voices to a single climax and abruptly stopped.

Johnny watched helplessly as he saw Patty, whose attention was captured by the noise. A look of terror came over her face, and she screamed and ran back to Johnny and Lilly. Disturbed from their ritual, the men turned toward the noise and saw that their sacred pool had been invaded by outsiders.

Valley of the Shadow of Death

Ben lay in a half dream with his eyes still closed. He felt very uncomfortable, wondering what was wrong with his bed. As he attempted to turn over, he found himself stuck in what appeared to be a hard crevice. Having no desire to struggle, he lay where he was. A dull throbbing came into his head, driving him into more complete consciousness. He thought back to his dream: the awful spinning and falling, then the horrible crash. He shuddered as he put the memory behind him and reached vainly for his pillow.

Forcing his eyes open, Ben attempted to survey his situation. It was difficult to see in the weak, grayish light and what he did see was confusing. Above him, he felt wood; it was the underside of a small bench.

Sliding out from under it shouldn't be difficult, he thought, but when he attempted it, pain shot through his back and arms.

"I feel like I've been through a wringer. It must have been that old barn Dad had us take apart," he said out loud.

His voice sounded strange, as if someone had snatched away his words before they could be heard. Despite the pain, he slid out from under the ledge and sat up. Dull, gray walls drifted slowly by. The occasional sound of moving water was all that greeted his ears. He looked again at his surroundings and saw he was alone in Lilly's canoe, being carried along by a small river and completely surrounded by solid rock.

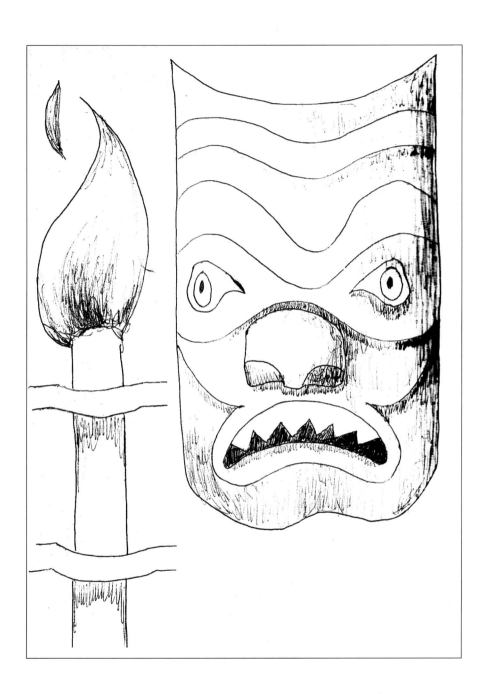

The light slowly diminished as the canoe glided toward a deepening gloom. He pinched himself hard, hoping to force himself out of his dream, but this only added to his pain. Ben felt a knot tightening in the pit of his stomach as he remembered the horrors of the cave behind the waterfall. Turning, he searched upstream for the other canoe but saw no trace of the others. Fear rose rapidly within him.

"Johnny! Lilly! Patty!" he shouted. The rock walls swallowed his cries.

"Johnny, can you hear me?" he screamed. No response came— only the deepening darkness of this glowering rock prison. The canoe continued to drift, as if being pulled by some dark sinister force.

Minutes ticked by; what light there was turned gray. Then, even the gray ebbed away as blackness crept over him. He looked back upstream, straining his eyes to use what was left of the departing light. Finally, all traces of vision left him save what his mind provided.

He crouched back onto the floor of the canoe, tightly shutting his eyes as if to ward off the blackness.

How on earth did I get here? he thought.

He traced each step from the time they left their platform in the cave behind the waterfall. Johnny and Patty had been behind them as they explored the rear wall. The water had seemed strangely turbulent. Then it had suddenly gone mad as they spun in ever-tightening circles. He remembered Lilly screaming and being gripped by water all around him. Then there was the awful twisting and falling, followed by sudden blackness.

"So why am I back in the canoe?" he asked. "What happened to the others? Did they escape the fall somehow?"

The thought of them lying underwater somewhere in this horrible cave sickened him. It struck him harder than the blast that had knocked him out. Shivering to the bone, he realized that he was soaking wet.

"I must have fallen out of the canoe—in fact, I remember being thrown from it. So why am I lying in it now, floating down this wretched river?"

On and on he drifted: how fast was he going, and how far had he traveled? The lapping of the water grew louder, though he could detect no change in the rate of his progress. Occasionally, the canoe bumped against the rock wall, making him fearful of capsizing, but even fear became wearisome as he drifted on and on.

He began to envy the others. Why couldn't he have died with them? This living death was more than he could endure. Would the river never end? If only it would suddenly cascade over a ledge carrying him to some crashing ruin! What awaits us after death? Anything at all? Lilly had spoken of a great spirit who gathered every soul into the everlasting tribe—but that was just a game. Then he thought back to his grandmother before she had died; she had said that heaven was for those who had put their faith in God's only Son. That had never seemed very important before, and now it was too late. Did Patty go to heaven? Lilly? Johnny? Had he been denied eternal life and condemned to this blackness?

Ben began to see ghostlike images frolicking before him. He wanted to run and hide, but there was nowhere to go. The images continued to dance in front of the canoe, approaching close and then receding away. Throwing his hands in front of his face brought no relief. Only then did he realize that his eyes were still tightly shut; he opened them in hopes the ghosts would flee, but it made no difference.

Ben began to despair. How long would this last? He had lost everything he'd known and treasured, with no hope of reunion. Was this what happened when you missed out on going to heaven—just traveling on aimlessly in the blackness, separated from anything good and accompanied only by frightful images darting through your mind, whether your eyes are open or closed?

The thought of Mom, Dad, and Grandpa brought a lump to his throat. They would never know what had happened to him. Searching the lake for days would produce no clues; the lump swelled as he thought of the beauty surrounding his home. He could almost feel the heat on his back from the memory of the sun beating down upon him as he fished at the end of the dock, his feet dangling in the cool water.

Tears welled up in his eyes. There was no one to turn to for help, and he had never felt so alone. His tears turned to sobs, but only the invisible cavern walls were listening, and they had no sympathy. They merely slid by silently, making their presence known by occasionally reaching out to scrape the side of the canoe.

Ben's thoughts suddenly grasped a childhood memory of his grandmother kneeling by his bed. What would she say each night? It had always comforted him, yet it had been so many years since she'd died. Those words had even been carved into her tombstone— yes, now he could remember.

Yea, though I walk through the valley of the shadow of death, I will fear no evil; for Thou art with me.

If ever there were a valley of the shadow of death, this black, endless cave must certainly be it. Grandma had always said that God was everywhere and we could always trust Him. But He certainly wasn't in this horrible cave. There was no one here except himself. He was utterly alone and abandoned. Or was he? Could God hear him even in this place? Would He listen?

"Help me, please help me," he said weakly. "God, if you can hear me, please get me out of here."

Ben stopped his prayer. He didn't dare open his eyes for several minutes. When he finally did, his despair reached bottom: nothing had changed. God either didn't hear or didn't care. Grandma had trusted Him for nothing.

Actually, something did change—quite drastically. But Ben was too overwhelmed by his fear to see subtle but significant changes.

He did not notice that the ghosts that had been plaguing his mind had fled. Only a single, tiny light remained, flickering yet staying in one place. In time he recognized it as distinctly different from the hallucinations that had been torturing him only moments earlier. He tried to reach for it but succeeded only in blocking it from view. Experimenting, he slowly passed his hand in front of it then moved his hand to the side. Each time, it came in and out of view.

Pondering it for a while, he saw the light slowly grow larger, flickering only slightly. His hope started to rise. The darkness was fleeting and he could make out more details on the cave walls. It seemed as though there were deliberate markings, perhaps even drawings on the walls that had been worn with time. He tried to make out what they were in the improving light as he got closer to its source. He watched the light morph into a definite flame. It loomed closer, until he realized that his canoe was passing it by. There could be no mistake: it was a torch, attached to the side of the cave. Ben lunged for it, nearly upsetting the canoe—but to no avail, for the torch slid cruelly by.

He stared at the torch as it grew smaller and smaller, slowly disappearing from view. He'd had his chance at light and muffed it. Why hadn't he steered the canoe closer? He could have snatched the torch and at least had some comfort on this hideous journey. Melancholy overcame him again as the light diminished to a flickering speck, finally disappearing altogether.

Again Ben sat alone in pitch-darkness with nothing but despair for company. Certainly this must be that place Grandma had told him about—where there's no hope, only eternal separation from God. But before he could dwell on that thought for long, another pinpoint of flickering light came into view in the distance. Was he going to be given a second chance?

Awaiting his next opportunity, he studied the growing light source, judging that this time the light was on the opposite wall of the cave. Another scrape of the canoe against the wall told him he was on the proper side. His hopes stirred as he watched the light steadily approach. Distance was so hard to judge. As the light came closer, he realized he'd have to stand up to reach it. This would be tricky, and he feared upsetting the canoe. Finally, when the torch was next to him, he carefully rose to his feet. Ben grabbed at the torch, bringing the canoe to a halt. The bow jammed into the wall as Ben held the torch handle. Water began to pour into the canoe, threatening to capsize it. Ben wrestled with the torch as he tried to free it from its holder. With a last desperate pull, he succeeded and fell backwards into the canoe, burning himself in the process.

Forgivingly, the canoe somehow righted itself and continued its journey down the subterranean river. Reaching over the side Ben thrust his wounded hand into the water. The pain subsided immediately. The water was far colder than he had expected. He had won the torch but at much greater risk than he'd anticipated. The consequences of upsetting the canoe had never entered his mind, but death would have come quickly in water that cold.

Turning his attention to the hard-earned prize, he studied its beautifully carved handle. He wondered who had fashioned it and then placed it into the cave. His mind froze: not only *who* but *when?* Since the torch was still burning, it obviously had not been there long. Looking up, he saw another torch approaching and another one far beyond it.

The torches continued to appear closer together until they were spaced no more than fifty feet apart, always alternating from side to side. The entire cavern was now visible, but the canoe's shifting shadow seemed eerie as he drifted from torch to torch. Ben peered ahead into the distance in hopes of spotting a landing area—or, at the very least, some explanation for the torches. Before long, he saw an area where many torches were tightly clustered in a circle. He wished he had a paddle to hurry his progress. From the circle's center, a grotesque face carved into the wall stared menacingly at him. Its features were distorted: the eyes bulged as if they were about to pop out, and its huge, sadistic grin revealed fangs falling down to its chin.

As the canoe dragged slowly by, the face with its horrific eyes followed him silently. Ben sank down, trying to escape its terrible gaze. What kind of people would carve such a face? Were they the ones who had lit the torches? What would he do if he met one of them in this awful place?

The face proved to be a false threat as he drifted out of reach of its surveillance. No living thing challenged him, but the torches continued tirelessly to generate flickering shadows of a boy and a canoe—one shadow fading and then another growing, until it was in turn replaced by the next. And with only shadows for company, he continued his relentless trip downstream.

After perhaps a dozen more torches, he saw a change in the pattern. The torches now lined both sides of the cavern wall and were only twenty feet apart. Suddenly, they ceased as a vast openness greeted him. The dismal cavern came abruptly to an end. As if with a last purpose, the current carried him out into what appeared to be a great underground sea. Oddly enough, it was not devoid of light, nor was it brightly lit. A subdued violet glow illuminated the scene. Ben looked back and saw that the sea was bordered by a beach of pure white sand. He reached into the water to paddle with his hands. It was still as cold as ice.

Managing the canoe without a paddle was a challenge, but he slowly worked his way to shore. This vast lake glowed with pale phosphorescence. Yet despite the unnatural ambience, Ben was relieved at the change. He was still underground but no longer suffered from the stuffy claustrophobia of the darkness. Ben pulled the canoe up onto the beach and collapsed onto the sand. There he fell fast asleep.

The Underworld People

Johnny and Lilly had ceased wondering what had become of Ben. Their situation was rapidly becoming dangerous. They had no way of knowing that Ben was lying unconscious in the bottom of Lilly's canoe, drifting down the river that drained this dazzling but treacherous crystal pool. If they had, they might have envied him for avoiding what was about to befall them.

They watched in horror as the strange men in the small canoes trained their arrows upon Patty. Lilly cautiously moved into view, holding up one hand as a gesture of peace. The leader turned his attention toward her. He spoke a few words in a strange tongue. Instantly, three of his men aimed their arrows directly at her. Fear struggled against honor within Johnny as he watched the scene from his hiding place. Lilly's eyes did not waver. Looking straight into the leader's face, she carefully spoke a few words that Johnny couldn't understand. No response was offered. Finally, honor conquered as Johnny stepped up beside her, Checker at his side. He could sense the tips of the arrows piercing his chest, even though they remained motionless in the fully drawn bows.

The chief now moved his gaze over all three children and Checker. No one said a word. Checker growled, but Johnny held him by the collar. The chief broke the silence by asking Lilly a question in that same unknown tongue. Lilly looked uncertain but attempted a short response. The chief, unmoved, paused as he considered her words. Then, quite suddenly, he gestured toward his canoe.

"Come on, Johnny," said Lilly in a low voice. "Don't do anything suddenly. He wants us to get into his canoe."

"But what about Patty?" Johnny objected. "You keep talking to them—it seems to help—and I'll go over and get Patty."

"Be careful and move slowly. They are very dangerous."

Johnny eased across the rock ledge to get next to Patty. She was obviously terrified but had brought herself under control.

"Johnny, are they going to kill us?" whispered Patty.

"No, no. They're just trying to scare us," Johnny responded. But the tone in his voice betrayed his words. "Now, don't worry—we'll be just fine. We've got to get into their canoes, so come with me and don't make any sudden moves."

"But where are they going to take us?"

"I imagine the same place they came from. Now, come on. I think we'd better not stand around talking any more. They don't seem to be the patient type."

Johnny took Patty's hand and led her back toward Lilly. Unexpectedly, the chief began to shout angrily at one of his men. Unlike the others, this man had tattoos covering his face, arms, and chest. A great eye painted on his stomach stared at you, no matter where you were standing. He looked displeased, fixing his gaze at the children, and then shrugged his shoulders, uttering a final and unintelligible protest to the chief.

"What was that all about?" Johnny asked.

"I'm not sure, but I think we just had a close call," said Lilly. "While you were over with Patty, that man with the tattoos made some complaint. I think he meant us no good. At first the chief ignored him, but then he got more insistent. Finally, the chief got mad. He told him to be quiet, and you saw the rest."

"Can you understand them?" asked Patty.

"Only some of the words. Some of them sound a lot like the ancient language of my people, but others I can't recognize at all. I wonder if—"

Lilly never finished her thought. A strong hand gripped her arm and led her into the canoe. But Checker, baring his teeth and snarling, sprang between the men and Johnny. The chief himself fitted an arrow to his bow and drew back the string, preparing to fire at the dog's throat.

"No!" yelled Johnny, throwing his arms around his dog. "We'll come, all right."

Lilly spoke some words to the chief as Johnny coaxed Checker into a second canoe. Patty followed, sitting as close to Johnny as she could. Checker wagged his tail as she sat down, even managing to lick her cheek. She didn't mind, and she gave the dog a big hug. One of the men got into the canoe with them. The chief had gone with Lilly and had already shoved off.

Patty put her hand back into her pocket and felt the unusual stone she had found.

Perhaps it will bring me good luck, she thought.

She cast another look around the pool and took in its great beauty. Everything was crystal except the water itself. Into the center of the pool fell millions of liquid diamonds, which produced continuous crashing and a glistening spray. Never had she seen a fountain so beautiful—Mother would love a picture of it! Ben probably wouldn't appreciate it at all. Ben! Where was Ben?

"Johnny!" Patty looked panic-stricken. "Where is Ben?"

Johnny felt sick. How could he tell her that her brother was probably under many feet of water? Only his coat had appeared after their horrible fall.

He looked at her thoughtfully, then lied, "He got away."

"Oh, hurray!" said Patty. "I know him—he'll follow us at a distance so he won't be seen. Then, when he gets his chance, he'll rescue us! Those men don't have a chance. Do they know he got away? Did they see where he went?"

"No, they didn't see him; they don't even know he was ever here."

"Oh, good. That means we have a good chance of getting away if we're patient. That's really important now. We don't want to mess up Ben's plans."

Johnny thought about this as the canoe skirted the column of crashing water. He figured he hadn't really lied. After all, Ben *had* gotten away. But it just wouldn't do to tell Patty about what really had happened, at least not now.

He was not given much time to think about this as they approached the little cave. The chief, who had arrived first, gestured for them to get out of the canoe. Stepping over the side, Johnny found the water only knee-deep. The canoe was pushed up to a sloping flat rock that emerged from the pool in front of the cave's opening.

Johnny peered into the cave. It was a long, straight tunnel that rapidly disappeared into blackness. He shuddered at the thought of entering it, yet he was sure that was just what they were about to do. Patty would not tolerate it. She was deathly afraid of the dark. However, much to his relief, the chief had secured several torches. He watched him head into the passage, with Lilly walking behind.

A heavy shove sent Johnny stumbling forward into the gloomy tunnel. He nearly lost his footing but managed to catch himself and avoid a cruel fall. Looking back, he saw the same man who had been arguing with the chief, now grinning with a wicked sneer. The eye on his stomach stared with a mind of its own. Checker again bared his teeth, ready to spring, but Johnny called him off. The dog reluctantly walked back to his master. The tattooed man shouted a command in his strange language, and Johnny had no trouble understanding his intent.

"Come on, Checker—just leave him alone. Let's catch up with Lilly before we lose sight of the torch."

The chief negotiated the path easily, despite the many forks in the tunnel. Johnny looked back once to see how Patty was doing but regretted it when his eyes met those of the wicked man. Murder was written there. Johnny could see that none of them would survive long, if it were not for the presence of the chief.

They had walked no more than a half hour when torches began to appear on the sides of the cave. At first they were separated by some distance and alternated from side to side. But soon they lined both sides of the tunnel, illuminating grotesque faces; their eyes always stared at you until you were well beyond them. The faces were horribly unnerving, each having its own hideous grin and unique sadistic features. Patty clutched Johnny's hand.

"Johnny, I'm really scared. Those faces are just awful. How can they keep looking at me when we walk by? Can they really see us?"

"No, they can't see us at all. They're just faces carved in the rock. They were designed to seem like they are looking at you, no matter where you are."

"Why are they so mean looking? Who would have made them like that?"

"I don't know, Patty, but I'm sure they were made a long time ago, and the people who made them are no longer around."

Patty's voice dropped to a whisper, "It doesn't matter, even if they are, 'cause Ben will help us when he gets a chance. I think I heard him behind us."

"Patty, listen," began Johnny. "I know this won't be easy, but—"

Another blow from behind sent him sprawling headlong. Stunned, he lay facedown on the rock floor. Something warm began to flow down his cheek. He wiped his face with the side of his hand and found it covered with blood. Patty screamed and rushed to his aid.

"Johnny! Johnny! Are you all right? Oh, your poor face. It's bleeding!"

A threatening voice from behind issued an unintelligible command. Patty turned and saw the assailant, his painted eye looking even more evil in the weak light. He was gesturing with his spear to move on. She stood up with her fists clenched and her eyes flashing.

"You wicked, wicked bully! Do you always go around pushing people half your size? If my dad were here, he would teach you a lesson you'd never forget!"

The man advanced toward her, threatening them both with his spear. Rage seethed in her now as she held her ground. The man began to smile sadistically. Even in her fury, she noticed just how similar he looked to those faces on the tunnel wall. But she was beyond thinking of herself and would not budge. He raised the spear and prepared to strike, but it never found a target. Checker, finding his master wounded and seeing Patty threatened, lunged at the aggressor—knocking him onto his back. Instantly, the dog was on top of him, almost unrecognizable in his fury. But before he could do serious harm, Lilly pulled Checker off.

Recovering his spear, the evil man pulled himself back to his feet and returned his gaze to Patty. He was no longer smiling as he lifted his spear to strike her. Again his intentions were frustrated. He dropped his weapon with a scream of pain. An arrow had struck him in the arm!

The chief approached and picked up the spear. He then thrust it into the cavern wall, shattering it. Several others rushed to the aid of the wounded man, who stared at the chief for some time in disbelief. Then the disbelief transformed itself into hatred. Finally, he muttered a few words in a low voice, shrugged off his helpers, and walked ahead of the company down the tunnel. The chief watched him until he disappeared from view, then sighed and shook his head.

Despite his pain, Johnny tried to get up.

"Just lie down, and I'll take care of you," said Lilly soothingly.

Johnny obeyed, and Lilly produced a small jar of ointment and a clean, white cloth. Johnny couldn't help wondering where she had kept them hidden all this time, but it was no time to ask questions. Lilly dipped the cloth into the ointment then cleansed his wounds with it. It stung horribly, but Johnny was determined to be brave.

"You'll be all right," she said. "Probably was bad blood anyway."

Johnny picked himself up and regarded the scene. The chief was studying Patty with what appeared to be admiration. He spoke a few words with her and then motioned to his remaining followers. A new guard was assigned to the children, and he proved to be less threatening and not violent. Much to everyone's relief, the chief ordered a rest. Johnny sat down next to his dog.

"Boy, we'd better be careful from now on," whispered Johnny to Checker. "These guys can be really unpredictable."

Before long, the rest was over, and they all proceeded further down the tunnel. This time the children stayed close together.

"That was a mighty brave thing you did, Patty," Lilly said. "He would have killed you without a second thought. It's a good thing the chief doesn't like him. But I'm worried that we haven't heard the end of it yet. He seems to have some power over the chief that the others don't have. Almost as if he were a medicine man—but he just isn't old enough. Still, I don't think the chief would normally have shot him. I don't know why he's helping us this much."

"Well, for that matter, the chief doesn't look very old either," responded Johnny. "Probably not even twenty. Are you sure he's their chief?"

"No, but for right now, he is. Everyone seems to do what he says without question."

"Hey, do you hear a noise ahead?" asked Johnny. All three children listened intently. A low, distant roar seemed to echo up the walls from ahead. As they walked, it became more and more noticeable.

"It's water falling, just like at the Stairsteps," said Lilly.

"Oh, if only it were," said Patty. Despite her bravery, tears began to well up in her eyes. "I wish Ben would come."

Some distance ahead, they could see the end of the tunnel. It opened into an enormous cavern, and mist flowed around the opening. Several minutes later, they emerged from the tunnel; but as they stepped out, the source of the mist was revealed. Water flowing from one of the cavern walls splattered into a small pool. The pool drained into a creek that meandered into the center of the cavern.

They could not take in the cavern's wonder all at once. First, it was huge, giving them the impression that they had found their way outside again. It was also illuminated throughout with a bluish glow. As the children's eyes followed the wandering creek, they saw a village made entirely from crystal and other beautiful gemstones. Some were blue and others green, but all emitted the same strange light in this sunless world.

Many people walked to and fro in the village, occupied with various tasks. But no sounds of laughter were heard, no youthful or frolicsome playfulness was to be seen anywhere. An expression of deep-seated fear marked everyone's face as they went about the village's business.

The chief himself stared at the village, and Johnny saw the sadness in his eyes. His expression was not one of fear, like those of the people in the village. Yet the chief appeared wistful, as if he were trying to recall an old memory. But then he shook it off and ordered the march to continue. They paused for a quick drink in the pool and then proceeded down to the village.

An Old Friend

The first thing Ben noticed when he awoke was a terrible thirst. He had no idea how long he had been asleep on the strange shore. He tried to roll over, but his right arm would not respond. It seemed to belong to someone else who had recently died.

"Oh, I hate it when my arm falls asleep," Ben said out loud.

His voice echoed. This seemed strange in such a wide-open place. As far as he could see, white sand formed a shoreline bordering a massive, underground ocean. Huge, cylindrical rocks jutted from the water in various places; the ones closest to the beach rose up twenty to thirty feet.

The shore had almost no depth. Only ten feet behind him stood a jet-black stone wall. It was incredibly smooth and stood perfectly straight up, towering far above his head.

His gaze worked its way up the wall until it locked onto a rock ceiling laden with huge stalactites. Thousands upon thousands of them hung menacingly, their razor points daring the earth to loosen them with even a mild tremor. He wondered how long it would take for one of the stalactites to fall to the shore.

It will make an awful impact when it hits, he thought.

Then his mind froze. He considered the massive cylindrical rocks in front of him. Of course! They were just the upper portion of fallen stalactites. But how often did they fall? He shuddered at the thought of being in the wrong place at the wrong time.

Ben forced his eyes back down and contemplated the great ocean before him. Something about it was wrong, even unnerving. The violet glow it made was unnatural enough, but it was too peaceful. All was dead quiet unless he spoke. But words seemed alien in a place that probably had never hosted any living being. Quiet—so quiet. In fact, that was the very thing that made it so odd. The sea was completely calm, like glass, but it was devoid of waves and made no noise whatsoever.

His parched throat reminded him how thirsty he had become. He stared at the water: was it fit to drink, or would it be salty? He struggled to his feet and walked to the shore. Both arms functioned now, so he knelt down and gingerly scooped some water to his mouth. It was as fresh as a mountain stream. He immediately thrust his head into the water, creating the only ripples within sight.

The fresh water tasted so wonderful that he was able to ignore, at least for the moment, how deathly cold it was. After drinking his fill, he sat back down. The same strange light was present everywhere—not very bright, but it illuminated well enough to see for nearly a mile.

A gnawing in his stomach reminded him that water alone would not be enough to sustain him. Ben looked intently at the sand. His mind drifted back to when his parents had taken him to the ocean so many years ago. The beach there was dark gray, bubbling with activity. Clams had squirted up small bursts of water, exposing their whereabouts, but here, the sand was not even wet, let alone capable of supporting life. No surf pounded the shore. No silt, no mud, not even water had left its mark on the shore. The water's surface remained motionless, as if time had wound down to a complete halt.

Suddenly, an ominous cracking sound from directly above him intruded upon the serenity of the motionless sea. Looking up, he saw—to his horror—one of the giant stalactites breaking away from the rock ceiling. Running back to the wall, he turned just in time to see the massive spear pierce the water not far from the shore. Great waves rose up in raucous protest of this disturbance, forming the only observable movement throughout the vast ocean.

"I've got to get out of here!" said Ben. Even the noise of his own voice made him uneasy. He wondered how many more of the huge stalactites were ready to fall. He shuddered to think of what it would have been like to be hit by the giant projectile. His eyes searched up and down the shoreline, looking for some escape from the perilous beach. There was, of course, the opening of the river that had led him here, but nothing could compel him to reenter that horrible place. Besides, he would never be able to fight the current.

It is just too ironic, he thought. *Patty hit the nail on the head in saying it was "just like a bathtub." And here I am, like a spider that went down the drain, only to find—what was it?—oh yes, the water from Noah's flood.*

Ben surveyed the ocean again.

Boy, I suppose if this were Noah's flood waters, it could have done a lot of damage. In fact, it probably would have flooded just about everything, he thought.

But why is the water fresh if it once had been part of the ocean? Could the ocean have become much saltier since the great flood?

Another cracking sound and a splash farther out in the sea reminded him that he had best find a safer place to ponder the possibilities of a global flood.

Well, since I'm not about to get near that wretched river, I might as well start heading in the opposite direction.

But what about the canoe? I guess it won't do me any good to carry it, and I don't have a paddle anyhow.

But a sense of self-preservation prompted him to pull the craft as far away from the water as possible.

Ben set out on his trek, hugging the rock wall as best he could. The prospect of being hit by one of the stalactites was unnerving. He found himself hurrying along, even though there was no obvious destination in sight.

After several hours of travel, he lost some of his fear of the falling projectiles. They seemed to fall less frequently now. His fear was replaced by an aggravating hunger. Frequently he drank by the shore, but even an abundance of water failed to satisfy the gnawing need for something to sink his teeth into.

Suddenly, he came to a dead stop. He stared into the distance ahead of him, where he saw an ordinary, cylindrical rock protruding from the sand—obviously a former stalactite. But what was that on top of it? Ben moved along, scrutinizing it more slowly as he drew closer. Again he came to a stop. Could it be? It was almost certainly a man sitting on the rock, looking out over the underworld ocean. Ben felt exposed on the beach but cautiously drew closer. There was no question: it was indeed a man. Ben looked around, but there was nowhere to hide. Was this person friendly? He remembered the grotesque faces on the cavern wall. Could this be one of the people who had made it?

Ben continued to work his way along the wall, more slowly than before. What would he do if the man saw him? But the man never looked toward him and continued to study the motionless sea. As Ben approached, he realized that the man was quite old, yet far from frail. His path led behind the man—between the rock platform and the sheer wall along which he was traveling. Ever so quietly, he proceeded, in hopes of passing by undetected. Worried that any noise might betray him, he held his breath as he passed within fifteen feet of the stationary figure. The old man never stirred but simply continued to contemplate the sea.

Just when Ben was sure he would make it undetected, the old man let out a long sigh. Ben froze in his tracks. The old man slowly shook his head without taking his eyes off the water in front of him.

"And I was sure he'd at least say thanks for the help," the old man said to the ocean.

Ben made no response. The old man ceased shaking his head but continued to stare, unblinking, at the sea. He sat there motionless, as if he belonged to ocean and rock. Ben began to wonder whether he would speak again, or if he had really even spoken at all. But he dared not move. Then the old man stirred again, still without taking his eyes from the sea.

"What d'you think of that, anyhow?" continued the old man, with such an expectation of a response that Ben found himself looking at the ocean to see whether it would somehow reply.

"Well, sure, I know he's had a rough time, but is that any excuse to be ungrateful?" continued the old man.

The ocean maintained its silent but ominous response.

"Humph—well, that'll take a lot of convincin' as fer as I'm concerned. I think he's just plain ungrateful, and that's that. Just like his old great-grandpappy. Yep, that's just who he's like, all right. I told you before, you shoulda picked the other one."

Ben wondered at this unusual one-sided dialogue. Who was this old man talking about? More importantly, how could he sneak by without disturbing him?

"Oh, all right! You've always been right about these things. But I can't figger out why they can't just learn to trust a bit. I mean, they cook up these desperate prayers and can't even see when they've been answered—and far better than they ever dreamed. But do they thank anybody? No, siree! And with all this special attention by the Master himself too! I just don't see how he can be so patient with them!

"No, no, no," he continued after a short pause, "you just can't convince me of that. I mean, he ought to've at least asked himself why he's even alive. Floatin' down the icy river when he knew full well he would have been thrown clean out of that silly little boat if we hadn't helped. But did he ever think that someone was watchin' out for him. No, of course not! Probably just wrote it off to good luck or somethin' else equally foolish. Okay, okay—I'll stop this here bellyachin' and get on with the program. But I must admit, I'm a bit disappointed in the whole affair. Such an opportunity for these youngsters, and they have no trust. But then, as you say, how'd they ever've learned it? The Master gave us the job, and we'll get there yet."

The old man ceased speaking and continued to stare at the silent ocean. No stalactites had dropped for some time. All was deathly quiet. Ben felt sure that even his own heartbeat would give him away. He waited until he could bear it no more. The old man seemed to have joined the stone that supported him. Had he fallen asleep?

Judging that this was his opportunity for escape, Ben began inching away from the old man ever so slowly. The man did not stir. But before Ben had moved even five feet away, the old man spoke again.

"Oh, just stop that-there sneakin' around, as if I didn't know where you was, anyhow. Why don't you just climb on up on this here rock, and we'll talk this thing out. Besides, yer about to take the wrong turn, and we don't have enough time to let you wander 'round here forever. We got ourselves a job to do, and it's about time we got down to the real business. Oh, yes—I dern-near forgot about this here sammich ol' Mike thought you'd want, so if yer a bit hungry, you'd better git on up here."

The promise of a sandwich was more than Ben could resist. He was too hungry to wonder where the old man could have acquired it. Slowly, he walked from behind the cylindrical rock into plain view. The old man never so much as glanced at him but continued his long stare, penetrating the depths of the ocean itself. A distant splash reminded Ben of his previous fears, helping him to find a quick pathway up to the old man's perch.

"Mighty peaceful here, ain't it?" said the old man, as Ben found a place to sit.

Ben did not want to disagree, so he just sat quietly. His eyes searched for the promised sandwich, but it was not forthcoming. He sat patiently and waited for the old man to make a move.

"Yes, sir, I'd say it was real peaceful-like, all right. No noise, no hustle-bustle at all. You know, there's lots of partyin' wheres I come from. Yep, parties all the time. Now, don't misunderstand me. These ain't bad parties at all. Fact is, they's great parties. We only hold 'em when someone new wants to join up with the Master himself. Ol' Mike, now he's one that just loves them thar parties. Says it makes the kingdom all that much better every time someone new joins us."

The old man's eyes suddenly twinkled, and he looked at Ben for the first time.

"Oh, yes—that thar sandwich. I don't want ol' Mike to think I've got a mean streak in me. No, no—that wouldn't do at all."

He reached under his cloak, producing one of the finest turkey sandwiches Ben had ever seen. Ben eagerly received what now seemed to be a long-awaited lunch and began immediately to devour it.

"Now, just hold on there," said the old man with a stern look.

Ben stopped in mid-chew.

"Ain't there even an ounce of gratitude somewhere in those young bones of yers?"

"Oh, I'm sorry," said Ben. "I'm just so hungry! But thank you very much."

Ben proceeded to the second bite.

"Hey, I didn't make that there turkey yer enjoyin' so much. Nor the lettuce nor the t'maters neither. Fact is I don't have a clue on how they're made at all. So what're you thankin' me fer?

Ben stopped eating altogether. He was feeling most uncomfortable. Somehow he felt a bit uncivilized. What did this old man expect? What should he say?

The old man looked hard and long at him. Ben was too nervous to see it, but the twinkle never had left the old man's eyes.

"You really don't know what I'm talkin' about, do you? Well I guess it ain't really yer fault. Besides, that's partly why yer here anyway. Look, all that there food is provided by the Master himself. Sure, he uses some of us to gather it up sometimes and put it together, but he's the one that invented it in the first place. So we need to thank him! But never mind, he really understands. I'll do it fer you."

The old man bowed his head and offered a prayer for the food. Ben bowed his head too, until he was finished. The old man then looked up.

"Well, go ahead and dig in!" he said.

Ben was happy to comply. The sandwich knocked the edge off his hunger but left him wishing for another. No second sandwich was forthcoming, however, and it did not seem to be an opportune time to inquire about it. The old man appeared friendly enough, but he certainly was strange. Ben wondered where he'd come from and how he had ended up down here by this vast underground ocean.

"Sir, I wonder if you would tell me your name," Ben said awkwardly.

The twinkle in the old man's eyes became a full smile.

"Why, I suppose it's only fair for you to know my name, especially since I know yours, Ben."

Ben stared at him.

"How did you find out my name? I never told it to you."

"Oh my goodness! It's not hard for me to know your name. How could I possibly take on this assignment without knowin' all your names anyhow? But to answer your question, I guess you could call me Abe. Short for Abraham, you know."

The Narrow Way

Ben stared at him in disbelief. Was this the same Abraham that Johnny kept talking about? So Johnny wasn't making it up after all—but the thought of Johnny brought back a flood of memories. He felt his throat choke up as he remembered their fate and the loss of his friend, sister, and cousin.

"Abraham, did—did you—ever meet a boy named Johnny on a plane?"

Abraham looked at Ben thoughtfully.

"You look upset, young'un. Now, I guess I can give you a bit of good news. I suppose yer thinkin' that the others met a bad end back there in the pool. But you can stop worryin' about that. They all got outta that pool safely enough, even Checker. Not that they don't have a sizeable adventure of their own to deal with—oh, yes siree, that they do. Fact is they probably could use your help soon enough. But at least for now, they's okay. I think we'd best focus on ourselves a bit. We've got a lot of travelin' to do, so if yer finished with that thar sammich, we'd best get on with it. I think we've spent more time here jawin' than we ought."

With amazing agility, Abraham scampered down off the rock platform and landed lightly on the sand. Ben followed, but not nearly as easily. The old man was staring hard at the sheer rock wall behind them. Ben wondered whether it was pure jet. It was hard to tell in the odd light. Flawless in its finish, it spread both left and right as far as the eye could see and rose up at least two hundred feet to the ceiling of stalactites above them.

"Ah, yes," said Abraham, "thar 'tis. Been so long, I almost had trouble recognizing it. Can you see it thar, Ben?"

Ben looked hard but didn't quite know what he was supposed to see. Abraham spoke again before Ben had a chance to respond.

"It's that door there in the wall. Can you see it? Now look real close. It's very narrow, and you could miss it."

Ben could see nothing but smooth blackness in front of him. There simply was no door anywhere—just a vast, jet-black wall spread out before him, bordering this subterranean ocean.

"Abraham, how about if we keep moving along this wall? The path here is broad. The sand is firm, and it's easy to walk here."

Abraham looked at Ben disapprovingly.

"You'll find many broad paths in life, my son, that lead only to destruction. No, you don't want to go that way at all. The sand may seem firm, but it really just fools you. If you walked 'bout another mile that way—why, you'd find the sand creepin' into yer shoes. You'd then take off them shoes to empty 'em out, but you'd sink down to yer ankles as soon as you tried. Next you'd pull out one foot, but the other leg would slip down up to yer knee. Then you'd drop to yer hands and knees to try to pull yerself out, but yer hands and knees would start to sink too. The last thing you'd do is try to pull yerself back the way you came, but it would be too late. Down, down, down you'd go into that sand. Yep, it sucks you in for sure. People say that the earth has no foundation over there. No, Ben, that broad path *looks* good, but it's really nothin' more than sinkin' sand. We need to go this narrow way through the wall."

Ben stared at it again, trying to find this narrow way, but he could see nothing at all. A sheer and impenetrable black wall stood before him, reaching all the way to the ceiling. He couldn't return the way he'd come, since that led only to that horrible river. And continuing the way he had been heading led to sure death.

"Come, come," said Abraham. "Let's just walk right up to it. The door ain't like what you expect. It's a very narrow opening to a passage through the wall. Yer a mighty privileged boy to get to see this here door. Selected by the Master himself, according to ol' Mike."

Abraham started toward the rock wall, followed by Ben. Then he stopped in front of it. Clearly, it consisted of solid jet. Ben wondered whether this old man was really just a little bit crazy or trying to make a fool out of him. Somehow he knew that Abraham was neither crazy nor deceptive. But where would all this lead?

"Now, you must just step on through," said Abraham.

"Right into the wall?" protested Ben.

"Now's the time to take a step of faith," responded Abraham. He looked somewhat proud of himself, having uttered this comment, but the hint of a smile left as quickly as it had come.

"Oh, I'm sorry," Abraham said suddenly—as if he had returned to talking to the ocean.

"But I thought it was kinda cute; a step of faith and all. But I know, this is really important and not a joking matter. Abraham's countenance suddenly changed, not dark or angry but introspective and deliberate.

"All right, Ben, now's the time. Just trust me. Look hard, and you should be able to see a part of the wall that's darker than the rest. You're standing right in front of it. It is narrow, very narrow. Believe me, it's not only the right way—it's the only way through this wall."

Ben looked hard at the wall one more time. There *was* something there, now that he thought about it. It was just as Abraham had described it: one portion of the wall was actually blacker than the rest. Of course—it was obvious now. How could he ever have missed it? It must be pitch-black on the inside. He wondered whether he could tolerate it, after his experience in the cavern's river. But somehow he felt reassured knowing that Abraham would be with him.

"Abraham, could you go first and I'll follow you? I think it would be a lot easier that way."

"I'm sorry, son. I can't take you through this one. This is what you might call—hmm, well—let's say it's a solo flight."

Ben was horrified. Abraham not with him? No, this was impossible. The terrible journey down the icy black river was still too close to home.

"Oh, Abraham, I don't want go in there by myself. I know I'm not that brave. I just can't do this one on my own."

"Oh, I know that, Ben. So does the Master. In fact, I'm glad you found that out yerself. That trip you took down that river wasn't the same as this. That was like hell itself. Separated from all of God's goodness. But this trip is different. For one thing, you'll find hope right away and know yer on the right track. For another, this trip leads you in the right direction rather than the wrong direction. This is between you and the Master. He don't tolerate nobody gettin' in the way of Him and His chosen ones. I'd just mess up the whole picture if I went with you. In fact, Ol' Mike thinks I've already said way too much. Now's the time, Ben. You've got to step on through."

Ben stared at the opening. He began to take a step but then hesitated.

"Abraham?"

There was no answer. Ben turned around; Abraham was gone. He looked up and down the beach, but there was no sign of him anywhere. He could still see their footprints in the sand, leading up from the rock platform to the passage entrance. But there were none leading away.

Ben remembered Johnny's accounts of Abraham and how he would suddenly disappear. Turning back to the entrance, he sighed.

"Well, here goes," he said out loud. He closed his eyes and stepped forward—then a second step and a third. He opened his eyes and stared ahead, with nothing but blackness to greet him. But it did not feel the same as it had felt in the black cave housing the icy river. This somehow was warmer, more reassuring.

Ben continued his walk. The floor was smooth and level. He occasionally bumped against one wall or another. At one point, the path became so narrow that both walls brushed against him at once. But just at that point, he thought he detected a weak light in the distance.

Ben watched its reflection dancing across the shiny, smooth floor, its source being out of view. The path was certainly as narrow as Abraham had promised. It meandered through the shadows, widening and narrowing only slightly as he moved along. Eventually he was able to see a small campfire in the distance, with something or someone near it.

Ben cautiously made his way toward the fire. As he came near, the narrow tunnel ended, emptying into large cave. He stopped short of committing himself to open view. Sounds of crackling logs echoed in the cavern before him. Ben strained to hear any voices or see any clues of human presence, but there were none. Gathering his courage, he peered around the corner. There, in the middle of the cavern, sat a frail, old man, his head heavy with slumber. He rested in a rickety chair before the fire. His hair was as white as cotton, and his beard flowed halfway down his chest. Deep lines ran from his eyes and mouth. No one else was present.

Ben silently stepped into the cave, proceeding slowly up to the sleeping man where he studied his face. He had never seen anyone quite this old before, except maybe Abraham. But Abraham was different—you just couldn't be sure how old he was. Abraham *seemed* ancient, yet his full share of strength belied that. This man was different: as if he had lived beyond his apportioned years, but some inner peace or purpose would not allow him to pass on.

Ben's gaze moved to the old man's lap. What was he holding? It was not a normal book, but more like a notebook. The old man's hand covered the title, concealing it from view. Curiosity overcame his fear of being discovered, and he gently pulled the notebook from his lap. The old man did not stir. Ben looked at the front cover. There, just as he had remembered it from the secret library, were printed the words: *The Journal of John William Matheson.*

Ben stared in disbelief at the sleeping man.

How could he have found Great-Granddad's old journal? he wondered.

Whether he sensed Ben's presence or the absence of his journal—or both—the sleeping man began to stir. Captivated, Ben waited for him to fully awaken. The old man opened his eyes, which immediately locked with Ben's. After a brief pause, he spoke.

"Well, I'll be!" he exclaimed in a rough, cracking voice. "I guess he knew what he was talking about after all! How might you have managed to come all the way to me, young sir?"

"It's a long story," Ben said. Judging wisely that he should be brief, he added, "Abraham sent me."

Surprisingly, this answer satisfied him. He smiled and closed his eyes. Although Ben was sure he would fall asleep again, the man forced his eyes back open and straightened up in his chair.

"Come, come, sir! We have much to discuss. Why not pull up that other chair and catch me up on what's been going on topside?"

Ben pulled up the extra chair and sat down next to him.

"Now, before we get into all that, I have one question for you," stated the old man. "Is it true that your name is Ben?"

"Why, yes, that is true, sir," responded Ben.

Maybe Ben should have been taken aback by this question, but he was becoming accustomed to the display of unexplained personal knowledge by complete strangers.

"Well, I think that's just terrific. Old Abraham is seldom wrong about these things."

"Sir," Ben interjected, "I was wondering—please don't misunderstand me—but I was just trying to figure out how you came across that journal you're reading."

"Well, funny you should ask, since I'd forgotten where I'd put it and then it showed up here just a few days ago. I was really upset I'd misplaced it. But now that you mention it, I recall Abraham did say something about having to borrow it for a few days. Maybe he just brought it back."

"You mean Abraham may have borrowed it from you?"

"Yes, I imagine he must have. I really wish he wouldn't though. I've spent a lot of years writing this journal. Losing it would be more than I could bear."

"But then—this is your own journal?" asked Ben, feeling butterflies beginning to stir in his stomach.

"Why, of course it's mine. It's my whole life's story!" he replied. Quickly settling back down, however, he looked somewhat thoughtful and added, "But I'm not sure it's of much importance—after all, who's going to read it down here? Certainly not those village people. I tried reaching out to them many years ago, but it didn't do any good."

Ben studied the old man with a new sense of understanding and awe. He must have been very tall and strong in his younger years. His skin still showed signs of being weatherworn, although he probably hadn't been exposed to the sun for many years.

"Did Abraham tell you I was coming?" asked Ben.

"Why, he sure did! He told me just this morning that I needed to wait here for a youngster like yourself to come by. He said you were called Ben, though he didn't tell me your last name—least I can't seem to remember it. Seeing now that you know my name, what is yours?"

"Matheson. Ben Matheson is my name."

The old man's eyes narrowed.

"Why, that is really strange. That's my last name too. I suppose Matheson isn't that unusual, but it does seem odd."

"Sir, I think it's really supposed to be that way. What I mean is, I think you are my great-grandfather who left the lake a long time before I was born. We found your journal in our house—your house, I mean. It was in a hidden library we found upstairs in an old room. Anyway, we got a chance to read only a little bit before Abraham came back and took it."

Great-Granddad looked at Ben hard before he spoke again.

"You mean to tell me that you're my grandson's boy? No, that can't be. Both my grandsons were about your age when I started off on this here journey. Of course that was many, many years ago. So whose boy are you?"

"My dad is Jim Matheson."

The old man pushed his eyebrows down so far Ben was sure they would touch his nose.

"Well, now—can you believe it?" He sighed after a considerable pause. "Jimmy always did like the cabin the best. And now he's up and grown, and his boy comes way down here just to visit his old papa."

Ben looked confused.

"Papa?" Ben inquired.

"Well, that is what your dad and your uncle would call me when they were young. I got kinda partial to it. In fact everyone started calling me that after a while."

"Well, I would like to call you 'Papa' too, especially if Dad did."

Raising his eyebrows as well as his voice, he exclaimed, "Now that I think of it, you do look the spittin' image of him. Yes, call me Papa! But now I would like to know…how did you come to get yourself down here?"

"Well, that's kind of a long story," responded Ben.

"I don't see anybody rushing us. Why don't you just take it from the beginning and tell me everything that happened up to right now. Don't miss a single point!"

So Ben started his story with picking Johnny up at the airport, recounting each step of the adventure. At times he had to stop and back up when his great-grandfather would nod off. But he eventually made it through the entire tale, including the horrible trip down the river. When he finished, the old man sat staring into the dying embers of the fire, deep in thought. As Ben looked upon his great-grandfather, a feeling of awe overcame him. How could he have survived down here for so many years? And how old was he anyway?

After all, Grandpa was in his early seventies, so Papa must be well into his nineties.

Papa looked back at Ben.

"Tell me again about that trip through the river that led from the pool," he said. "What did you do when you realized you were drifting all alone?"

"There really wasn't much I could do. I didn't have a paddle, and even if I had, I don't think I could have fought the current. Besides, I was cold and soaking wet."

"But you must have been thinking something through all that. You had been drifting for hours."

Ben hesitated. He thought back to drifting endlessly through utter blackness, vividly recalling the gripping fear and despair that had overtaken him. He remembered his grandmother's words about the valley of the shadow of death and his first, apparently unsuccessful, attempt at prayer. Ben looked back at his great-grandfather, who waited patiently for his response.

"I'll bet it was tough, wasn't it, Ben?" Papa interjected, seeing that his great grandson was struggling for words. "Tell me, what went through your mind? What did you think and do?"

"I guess I wasn't very brave," Ben admitted. "I gave up on the inside. I didn't think there was any way out. I didn't know if the river would just go on forever or if it would end up at a waterfall somewhere and I would die suddenly. I almost was wishing that would happen, just to end it all. But it didn't, and I kept drifting on and on. I really don't know how long. It seemed like days."

"So how did you deal with it?"

"I, um—well, I remembered some stuff that Grandma used to say. Something about a valley of the shadow of death. Grandma used to tell me that God was everywhere and wanted to help us. So I tried to pray like I had seen her do sometimes. But it didn't help. I just kept drifting."

"But I thought you said some torches started appearing?"

"Yeah, they did. I missed the first one though. It was on the wrong side of the cave. I was pretty upset when it went by. Then another one showed up, and I grabbed it. It was tough getting it out of its holder. I darned near flipped the canoe over, wrestling with it."

Papa looked very grave.

"It was a mighty good thing you prayed, son," he said. "You probably wouldn't ever have gotten here at all if you hadn't."

"Yeah, maybe so; that water was cold. I probably would have frozen right there on the spot."

"I don't mean that," added Papa. "That first torch you missed. Did you look at the cave carefully there?"

"Well, no, not really. It wasn't that bright, for one thing. But once I figured out what it was, I tried to get the canoe close to it, but I couldn't grab it."

"That first torch marked the most perilous part of your whole journey. There is an ancient Indian tribe living down here. They keep those torches lit. That first one is important because it marks a fork in the river. The fork you took that led you here is actually the tributary. It takes you to the big sea where you ended up. The main part of the river goes the other way. No one knows where it ends up. The Indians have gone some distance down it until the current gets too strong. Some have ventured too far. They never came back. No, Ben, I'd say your prayers were answered, all right."

Ben felt a knot growing in his stomach. If he had taken the wrong turn, he might still be drifting in utter blackness. Both Ben and his great-grandfather fell into silent thought for a time. Papa was the first to break the silence.

"Ben, I think I see what I've missed all these years. It's all in God's own book. It's His journal in a way. You see, he says we're supposed to take the narrow way. Just like you did in the black river and just as you did to find me through that rock wall. He keeps talking about a narrow way in His journal, and He says it's the only way to heaven. I think He's telling us to keep looking for it and we'll find His kingdom."

The old man stopped speaking and looked at his great-grandson. Ben frowned.

"That sounds just like what Grandma used to say, but I never could understand it," responded Ben.

"I'm not sure I ever understood it either, but I *am* sure we have a mission in front of us. While were gabbing, we forgot about your little sister and your cousin Johnny. Johnny—now, there's a marvel. I always thought that uncle of yours was heading for trouble when he grew up. Never was interested in the lake. But now he's gone off and named his son after me. Well, isn't that just grand? And you probably don't know this, Ben, but you were named after my Pappy. And there's this Indian girl too. I think I know more about her than any of you even suspect. Come on—let's go. They are sure to need our help soon if they've tangled themselves up with those who I think they have."

New Light on an
Old Problem

Papa started to rise from his chair, but quickly sat back down.

"Humph! This old chair is harder to get out of each time I use it. I'll be glad to leave it here. Help me up, son, and we can get on our way."

Ben grasped one of his great-granddad's hands. He felt a faded grip that must have once been very strong but now trembled with age. Ben wondered how he would find his way back to the others with the added burden of his great-grandfather, but there was no point in worrying about that. Even if they never made it, at least they would be together.

This is really unbelievable, Ben thought. *I never imagined that Papa was still alive, but then to find him here, of all places. In fact, finding him anywhere—even if I had known he was alive—should have been impossible! But never mind all that. Here we are, and we need to find Patty, Johnny, and Lilly.*

His heart leapt with the thought of his sister, cousin, and friend being alive, giving him a greater sense of urgency to move on.

"Okay, son, I think I can manage it," said the elder John Matheson, releasing Ben's hand. "I may not be quite as fast as you, but I can get around reasonably well—at least if we don't get in a big, fired-up rush. Besides, I know the way out of this place, and I think I know exactly where you dropped in—so to speak. I imagine you wouldn't mind going back by a different route than the one you came on, eh?"

Shuddering, Ben nodded.

"Now, let's head off toward that opening up ahead. The sooner we get going, the sooner we'll be there. Our hike will take the better part of the day."

The better part of the day? Ben mused.

Startled, he realized he had lost track of time. What was a day down here anyway? There was no sun, no moon, nor any other measure of the passing of time. Instinctively, he glanced at his watch and was a little surprised to see that it still worked, dully showing three thirty. He hadn't thought to check it since leaving home.

"Three thirty," he mumbled. But was it morning or night? Ben's preoccupation with time abruptly stopped, however, when something went whizzing past his head.

"Quick, duck in here," said his great-grandfather. "They won't dare come up this tunnel, but they will shoot into it."

Fortunately, they were already at the opening and could scuttle in. Several more arrows whistled past, narrowly missing the two of them and glancing off the rock walls.

"Who are they, Papa, and why are they shooting at us?"

"Don't ask questions now; just keep moving along the wall as fast as you can. They'll be at the opening soon, and we've got to be out of range before they get there."

Ben didn't argue but stayed close behind his great-grandfather. He was amazed at how fast they could move when pressed. He couldn't help but look back. There, he saw human shapes at the tunnel opening. One of them fitted an arrow into his bow, drew it, and released the arrow.

"Duck, Granddad!" shouted Ben.

Both fell to their stomachs, just in time to hear another arrow whizzing over their heads. It fell harmlessly to the tunnel floor about thirty feet in front of them.

"Stay down, Ben, and keep moving," said the old man. Both half-crawled and half-scooted along the tunnel floor, while several more arrows fell around them. One last shower of arrows proved they had finally moved out of range.

Papa stopped and looked back. He sat with his back against the wall while he caught his breath. He said nothing—just shook his head and watched them go into a frenzy of unthinking rage, yelling incomprehensible threats and curses.

Ben spoke after a couple of minutes, interrupting his great-grandfather's morose silence.

"Who are they, and why did they try to kill us?"

The old man said nothing in reply for some time, as he continued to regain his breath. Finally, fumbling in his pocket, he produced an old handkerchief and wiped the sweat off his brow. He then turned to Ben.

"I bet you didn't think I had that much energy left in me, eh? Well, to be honest, I haven't had to pour on the coal like that for some time. I really didn't think that group was anywhere near us, or I would have left long ago. They are a vicious lot, Ben, and lucky for us, very superstitious. Their tribe makes those gruesome masks that stare at you with a wicked sneer—remember? You saw them as you floated down the river. They keep the torches lit as well, but they will never come up this tunnel. Their religion forbids them trespassing in this area. It probably makes them even madder that we came this way.

"But why did they attack us?" asked Ben. "We didn't do anything to them."

"Ben, that group is nothing but evil. There isn't one shred of human good anywhere in them. Not only would they kill us for sport, but their culture requires it. They will kill each other for the smallest reasons. At times, they even kill their own children."

As if his condemning words held some strange power, their attackers stopped their cursing and chanting and just peered into the cave, none daring to enter. Finally, as if their mission had been accomplished, they left for regions and reasons unknown. Surprised to hear about the depravity of this people, Ben could not help wonder whether Papa was exaggerating. Then he thought of his sister, Johnny, and Lilly.

"Are all the people down here like that?" Ben asked.

"No, not all," he admitted, "but some are." We narrowly escaped disaster, and it's time we moved on. We won't have any more trouble with that bunch, although we could stumble into some of their friends, if you can call them that, when we leave this tunnel. But we'll get there long before they can alert anyone."

The two continued on carefully, listening to every imagined noise behind them. Papa's last few comments had left Ben feeling very uncomfortable—not just because of the imminent danger but also because he had never imagined such evil.

The two of them walked in silence for some time. It seemed odd, now that he thought about it, that the light never completely faded as they walked on. Could the tunnel walls actually be glowing by themselves? Yes, there was a pale light all around them that never dimmed. Then Ben became distracted by a faint trickling sound growing more and more noticeable.

"What's that noise, Papa?"

Ben momentarily forgot the trauma they had left behind.

"That's where we will take a break shortly," he responded. "It is called the Oasis. Some of the natives call it Second Wonder. The noise you hear comes from a small stream that feeds the Oasis. The stream actually begins from the same pool of water you fell into— that's the source of all the water down here. The pool itself the natives call First Wonder. Before I came down here, we knew it only as a legend. We called it the Crystal Mirror."

"Crystal Mirror!" Ben exclaimed. "That's what you wrote in your journal. That must be the place we call the Crystal Pool!"

"Crystal Pool?" mused the old man. "Well, I suppose that's okay, but it really leaves an important part out. Didn't you take a close look at the water while you were there?"

"I only remember getting sucked down into that whirlpool and feeling like I got hit by a freight train," Ben responded. "Next thing I knew, I was floating down that horrible river in Lilly's canoe. And then everything became pitch-black."

"Hmm, looks like we'll have to make a trip by the Crystal Mirror too, but not right away. We've got to get to the Oasis first and take care of some business there. Anyway, I think you might be a bit surprised at what you'll see. It'll sure make your stomach happy anyway."

The sound of that last comment reminded Ben that he hadn't eaten since that sandwich given to him by Abraham.

Abraham, Abraham—now where could he have gone? Ben thought.

He remembered Johnny warning him how he would come and go unexpectedly. But it seemed like if he would just stay around a bit longer, he could solve a lot of problems.

The two trudged on, Papa slowing his pace. Ben could see he was getting tired, and he thought it best not to talk anymore, letting his great-grandfather use his strength in just making it to their destination. The old man didn't initiate any more discussion either, and the two walked on, sometimes stopping for a short break. Before long, the sound of water started to become more noticeable, reassuring Ben that a resting point would soon come.

After more trudging, the strange light intensified. Then the source came into view: "Second Wonder" was an appropriate name, indeed. Water sprayed from a thousand sources in a wall to their left and coalesced into a pool at its base. The pool itself was not large, maybe only fifty feet wide and a hundred in length. It drained on the side opposite its source, forming a creek that wandered through a small, rock-strewn meadow filled with lush vegetation. The plants were nothing Ben had ever seen before. They all had huge leaves, like oversized rhubarb, but they were mostly pink and violet. The light itself was a mystery, being present everywhere but coming from no apparent source.

Ben noticed that they had stopped walking and were just taking in the natural wonder. Cool mist from the spray curled around them. Great-Granddad walked to the pool's edge, removed his sandals, sat down, and dangled his feet into the water. Ben followed his example, ignoring the wetness of the rock surface they sat upon. The water was refreshingly cool, yet not uncomfortably cold as was the horrible lightless river that he unwittingly had traveled after falling into the Crystal Pool. The two sat in silence for some time; Papa was clearly exhausted from the events of the day.

"You can eat these plants, Ben," said the old man. He picked some huge leaves off a nearby plant and tore them into pieces. He then broke off the stem of what appeared to be a mushroom, although it was much too big. The stem fell apart into large slices in his hands with little effort on his part.

"Ben, go get one of those purple plants behind you," he requested.

Ben pulled it up easily and brought it to his great-grandfather. Looking under one of its leaves, Papa found a brown fruit or nut of some kind. Plucking it off, he sliced it, in a manner much like the stem. He placed pieces of the broken brown fruit between slices of the stem, along with some of the green shredded leaves. It resembled an oversized sandwich. Finally, on another plant he found a small red fruit and tore off the top end. A thick paste oozed out, like ketchup. He spread it on the sandwich, closed everything up, and handed it to Ben and then began the same process for himself.

"Go ahead and eat it, Ben," he urged. "It tastes a lot like a turkey sandwich. The red stuff looks like ketchup but tastes more like cranberry sauce—maybe not quite as strong.

Ben took a bite. Papa was right: it was much like Thanksgiving leftovers, perhaps a little blander, but it wasn't bad. In fact, considering how hungry he was, it was downright delicious.

The two of them sat together and ate their fill. Afterward, they made several more of these sandwiches and wrapped them in the large leaves.

"Unlike turkey sandwiches, these will last for several days without being refrigerated," said Great-Granddad. "Maybe even a week. There are several places like this down here. I discovered one that the Indians never found—at least they never go there. I used that as a hideout for a long time. Making these sandwiches, and traveling near water sources, you can get along down here quite well. You do have to be careful not to get lost, however. The caverns and tunnels get complicated."

"Granddad, how long have you been here?" asked Ben.

A look of reflection came into Great-Granddad's eyes, as if recalling years and years of memories. But whatever memories were present, he tucked them back into the depths of his mind and became more preoccupied with something that seemed to be happening deeper in the Oasis. His eyes squinted, probing the weak light.

"What is it, Papa?" asked Ben, noticing the change in his expression.

"Hmm," he responded in a hushed tone, "it seems we are going to have visitors."

The Vision

Ben followed his great-grandfather's gaze and saw, to his horror, a dozen or more Indians coming directly toward them from the opposite end of the Oasis. Papa watched them closely but didn't move a muscle. Then, speaking so low that Ben could hardly hear him, he said, "Say nothing, do nothing. Absolutely nothing. No matter what happens, don't move, don't ask me any questions, and don't take your eye off them for even a moment."

The old man became completely still, watching them intently. It didn't appear as though the Indians had seen them yet. In this weak light, perhaps they could crawl out of view and hide among the giant rhubarb-like plants.

The intruders continued toward them, becoming more and more visible as they approached. They carried an assortment of clubs, spears, and knives. Some were armed with bows and arrows. Ben could see that they all had masks with the same gruesome expressions as those he had seen on the cavern walls. They walked on silently, single file, directly toward them. Ben felt he could not just stand there any longer. A sudden urge to run came over him, but he knew that running would only give them away. Even his pounding heart threatened to betray him. The large plants were no longer accessible, and discovery could not be more than a few moments away.

Fortunately, the hostile men were focused on the water, simply not expecting anyone else in this secluded place. Ben and his great-grandfather glanced at each other with the same thought: detection would be inevitable if they did not move, yet movement might attract attention to them. Without a word, the two inched their way backward to the edge of the cavern. There was nothing but the poor light to hide them, yet somehow they went unseen as they slipped into the darker shadows of the cavern wall.

Upon reaching this wall, Ben found that it was perfectly smooth, forming an impassable barrier, except for one location. Forgetting his fears he explored this irregularity and discovered an opening about one foot wide, invisible in the weak light. He was able to slip into it sideways and realized that there was room enough for two. Stepping back out, he reached for his great-grandfather's hand.

"A hiding place," he whispered, gently pulling him in.

The old man had more difficulty with the passage than the boy, but being trim himself, he managed it. Fear of the natives superseded the sense of claustrophobia as they squeezed themselves between millions of tons of rock. Ben continued to work his way down the crack in the wall, trying get as far from the opening as possible. He probed for the end of it, feeling elated that the pathway went as far as it did. Perhaps they could avoid discovery after all.

Step by step, they continued down this unexpected path. They imagined the fissure to narrow and render the route impassable, but the end did not come. With each small step, the threat behind them was replaced by a growing apprehension of what lay ahead. Ben's curiosity won out over his wariness as he continued on. The old man followed without a word, interested only in getting as far from the Indians as possible. The two groped their way onward for an incalculable amount of time. Fear of discovery had long since passed, so Ben finally stopped and risked some words.

"Papa, you didn't tell me about this passage."

"Well, that's because I never knew it existed. I'm amazed you found it in that weak light. It's almost like it just sprang up here out of nowhere, just for us. Darned good timing too."

"But where do you think it goes?"

"It could go anywhere, but most likely it's just a small fissure in the earth caused by some earthquake a long time ago."

This thought made Ben shudder.

Suppose another earthquake comes again, with us in it, he thought. Sensing his discomfort, the old man continued.

"I doubt there are many earthquakes around here. In all the time I've been down here, I've never experienced one."

This was comforting, to an extent, but the topic motivated Ben to start moving again.

"Which way should we go, Papa? Should we keep going on ahead or go back to the cavern to see if those guys have left yet?"

"No, I really don't think we'd better go back. They were getting ready to perform a ritual ceremony. It's not pretty, and we really don't want to be there when they're doing it. They take a lot of time at it—sometimes several days."

"Well, we can't stay in here for several days, that's for sure. Let's keep going until we find where this ends and have to turn around—or at least find a place where we can sit down."

They continued their slow progress, sidestepping down the passage with rock walls brushing against backs, arms, and at times, their faces. With time, they found their journey had become gradually easier as the fissure opened slightly. Soon they were able to face forward as they walked, though still needing to travel single file. This encouraged them to pick up speed.

"Ben, I've got to stop for a bit. My wind just isn't what it used to be."

Ben paused, but at the same time looked intently forward.

"Papa, I think it's a little lighter up ahead. Can you make it just a little farther?"

The old man looked ahead but saw nothing.

"Perhaps my eyes aren't as good as yours, Ben. What do you see?"

"Well, really nothing yet, but the way ahead just seems to be a little brighter. What do you think that means?"

The old man's voice betrayed a glimmer of hope as he mustered his resolve once again.

"Okay, Ben, I think I can manage it. We'd better go check it out."

They continued on. The farther they went, the more apparent the light became. Even Papa could see it. Ben did not notice that he was hurrying at a pace beyond what his great-grandfather could manage. The two quickly became separated.

"Papa!" Ben called out, no longer mindful of the previous threat behind them. "It's an opening! I can see it! This path leads out!"

Ben broke into a dead run, unable or unwilling to hear his great-grandfather crying out for him to stop.

"I'll be right back, Papa! I want to see the opening!" he yelled, dashing full speed to what he thought was their salvation, failing to heed his great-grandfather's desperate and fading cries to stop.

Ben raced directly for the opening. It was close now, and very bright, as if illuminated by natural sunlight. In fact, those were precisely Ben's last thoughts as he plunged through the opening, convinced they had not only found their way out of this mountain but also found their way back to the earth's surface.

Ben saw too late the edge of the precipice toward which he was rushing. The path took an abrupt turn and before him loomed a sheer drop to a vast depth below. With nothing to check his fall, he plummeted over the edge. Ben reached out vainly to grasp at the protruding rocks that bordered the pathway. Nothing could stop the momentum induced by his rash sprint. Panic gripped him. Down he fell, to unknown depths below. Not wanting to see his doom, Ben shut his eyes. But he could not shut out the sensation of the falling, falling, falling in this nightmare come true, until his consciousness was suddenly snatched away.

A narrow pathway meandered up a rocky slope void of anything hospitable, green, or even remotely resembling life. It simply struggled through its difficult way, threading itself ever upward around loose boulders and threatening precipices. There was a kind of unexplainable peace to it, despite the hazardous and uncertain terrain. Far below, there was a hint of movement. Something was working its way up this narrow, difficult trail, little by little. It took some time before a small party of people could be discerned in the depths below. Along their route lay many dangers, unperceivable until they were reached. As the path precariously negotiated the huge boulders and sheer cliffs, it somehow managed to allow passage, even if only for one person at a time.

He wondered at these pilgrims. The perch from which he observed this procession seemed to have been placed there solely for him to witness this unusual event. It did not occur to him to question how or why he stood on this precipice, nor did he make any attempt to move. He felt ordained and purposeful as he waited and observed the scene below him.

His eyes moved farther up the path where the pilgrims were heading, visually exploring the journey the pilgrims had yet to see. The trail traversed the mountainside, folding itself back and forth along its perilous journey. Each twist brought it nearer rather than farther, until at last—much to his surprise—the trail eventually led to him! It no longer made steep ascents or crossed chasms; but rather the pathway prepared itself for its ultimate destination. Ben's eyes continued to follow this route above him as it wandered toward an enormous golden gate, itself dwarfed by an immense city towering behind it. The city seemed to go on forever, rising higher and higher—as if built upon a great hill. A song emanated softly from all parts of the city, beginning first in very low tones and then building into an awe-inspiring crescendo that conveyed a sense of worship to anyone who could hear it.

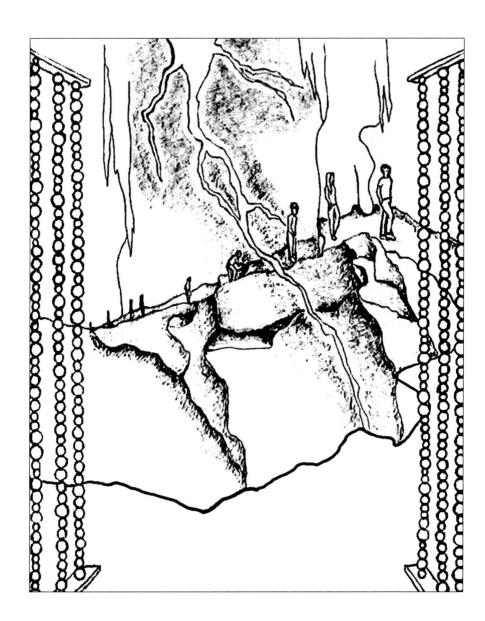

Coming from nowhere, a woman appeared, possessing many years of life yet not appearing old. He stopped short, looking into her kind face, and realized that he knew her. Though it had been many years since she had passed away, he could not fail to recognize his own grandmother. He knew he should be stunned to see her, and perhaps frightened as if by a ghost, yet somehow her presence in this place seemed right. If anything, he felt himself to be the intruder.

Then she spoke.

"Ben, look back down the path. Look way down the mountain at the people making their way along that treacherous path."

Turning back toward them, Ben was surprised at the progress they had made since he had first seen them. The party was moving single file across a fallen rock that formed a narrow bridge across a canyon of which the bottom could not be seen. A strange wind buffeted them, threatening to push them into the abyss below. He imagined himself with them, wondering how anyone could get enough nerve to cross such a foreboding bridge. But instead of clinging to the rock, inching their way across on their bellies, they simply walked slowly yet deliberately, stopping occasionally when confronted by a wicked gust of wind—one at a time, they all crossed, none of them perishing.

Ben continued to watch as they proceeded. They made steady but slow progress toward him through many dangers and toils, yet always surmounting them. As they passed around the last bend, their demeanor transformed from patient determination to total joy. They beheld the city and its gate, continuing the last few steps of their journey, passing Ben and his grandmother as if they did not exist. They approached the gate and it opened by its own accord to receive these pilgrims.

Drawn to this magnificent city, Ben got up without a second thought and attempted to gain access to the path and follow them. His grandmother, however, gently laid her hand on his shoulder, and with her touch he became paralyzed.

"You cannot go this way, Ben, at least not yet," she said. "Everyone who journeys on this path must start at the beginning. The city is accessible only to its citizens, but you have not yet become one."

This gentle rebuke struck a sense of great loss and grief within him as he looked upon the forbidden city, so close to being within his grasp. He watched as the last few wayfarers passed through the gate and as it slowly, noiselessly, and firmly closed behind them. It was clear that no one could force it open. Studying the wall that protected this golden fortress, he heard his grandmother speaking, responding to his unspoken thoughts:

"You can enter only by the gate, Ben. If anyone tries to go in any other way, he will immediately be thrown out. It would be useless to try. The Master can see everything, and he keeps watch over the gate. You might even say that He *is* the gate"

"I don't understand, Grandma," Ben blurted. "I thought—I thought—well—"

"I know you are confused," she responded with a genuine and warm smile. "It is to be expected, of course. After all, you're being treated with special attention, and you should feel very special. But The Master will not wait forever for you to respond. He is calling you, you know."

"Grandma, I'm not trying to be disrespectful, but I really don't understand what you're saying."

"Ben, it's not your time now. It's a good thing too, for you're not ready. Remember that you've been called by the Master. You must respond: it's a great gift He offers you. Do not turn Him down, Ben."

"Grandma, I won't turn Him down. I would love to go into the city now and do whatever He asks me, but how do I get in?"

"This gate is the only entrance. But you must first take the narrow path, like those people you just saw. It's a rare privilege that you have seen it, but there are others you must also lead."

"Grandma, what do you mean? The path is right here." But even as he spoke, Ben became less sure about what he was seeing. The city shimmered, just slightly, but the shimmering made it look surreal. Ben rubbed his eyes, but when he opened them again, the city was less in focus than before. The path, as well as his grandmother, began to shimmer—even dissolving in front of him.

"Grandma, I'm having trouble seeing you. What's happening?"

Ben's grandmother seemed unconcerned about the situation, though her voice became more deliberate. She looked toward the vapor that had once been the magnificent city and spoke slowly, her voice lowered.

"Ben, this is the most important message of all. You may not understand now, but you will later. Remember this: Take the narrow way, Ben, and put your trust in the Lamb. Don't forget that. Say it over and over—Take the narrow way, and put your trust in the Lamb."

"The lamb? What lamb?" Ben responded as the entire scene began fading from his sight. Although the city had now disappeared into a mist, along with most of the path, his grandmother's form lingered;.

"Ben," she repeated, "say it after me: Take the narrow way, and put your trust in the Lamb."

Ben obeyed, repeating her words but beginning to panic; she herself had become mist, shimmering as if made only of light.

"Grandma, don't leave me! I don't understand what you mean."

"Trust in the Lamb, Ben; no matter what, trust in the Lamb! He will help you find the narrow path, and then you must take it yourself, leading as many others who will follow. That is all, Ben. I must go, for my task is now complete. You must remember: find the narrow path. Reach out to the Lamb, and He will accept you. "

Her image, now shimmering and wispy—almost as if it were blowing in the wind—stubbornly refused to disappear altogether.

"Grandma, please stay," Ben pleaded. "I still don't understand what you're telling me. I don't know about any lamb, and I can't get onto the path. Please don't go!"

Her image swayed, remaining as a thin, wispy form, yet her voice persisted.

"The Lamb, Ben, Reach out for the Lamb," the voice commanded over and over.

"What lamb?" repeated Ben.

"The *limb*, Ben; reach out for the *limb*," the voice now commanded, this time more insistently.

The ethereal form that had once been his grandmother lingered as a long, slender object wavering in front of him. The voice returned again, in a more commanding tone:

"Ben! You must reach out and take hold of the *limb*. You're on a very narrow ledge. If you move the wrong way, you will fall. Take hold of the limb now!"

It was not his grandmother's voice at all; it was his great-grandfather. Ben peered up the rock face and saw he had fallen perhaps ten feet, and it had knocked him out cold. The limb was more like a vine and dangled before his face, his only hope of rescue. He sat up and made the mistake of looking down, nearly becoming sick with dizziness. He clutched the limb offered to him. The narrow ledge onto which he had fallen was barely two feet wide. How he had avoided falling off in his earlier rash chase toward this precipice was way beyond luck.

Grasping the limb, Ben pulled himself up.

I hope Papa secured this thing, he thought.

A rock came loose under his feet and plummeted down the abyss. Ben waited in vain to hear it hit bottom. He shuddered to think how high he must be, but he didn't dare risk another look. Instead, he gripped the branch with both hands and braced his feet against the rock wall before him. Hand over hand, he drew himself up, finally reaching his great-grandfather at the cliff's edge. Ben pulled himself over the edge with some effort and with as much help as the old man could offer. With one last struggle, he cleared the edge and rolled over on his back, now safe on the path from which he had fallen only a few minutes earlier. He lay there regaining both his breath and his wits.

Rebirth of the Journey

"Are you okay?" came the reassuring voice of his great-grandfather. "Any broken bones? That was one nasty fall you just had. You must have more lives than a cat. Look how short that ledge is, and this is the only place on the cliff where there's any ledge at all. I can't believe your luck in hitting just in the right spot."

"Yeah, I guess you're right," Ben replied. "I must be the luckiest guy in the world."

This response left him suddenly empty. He thought of his grandmother, the narrow pathway, and the city. Was it a dream, or was it real? It was all so fuzzy now. What was this lamb she was talking about so insistently? Was it just his great-grandfather desperately trying to get him to take hold of the limb?

The limb, the limb, he mused. Where on earth could he have found a branch in this place anyway? But he was not given much time to ponder it, for he clearly saw his great-grandfather's anxious face.

"I was sure you had killed yourself," said the old man. "You should never run in a place where can't see what's ahead. But now look!"

They looked cautiously over the great precipice. Ben shuddered to think of his reckless race down the stone corridor and of the disaster that he had so narrowly escaped. He could not have known that had been rushing toward a precipice defined the boundary of an unimaginably huge underground cave. The word *cave* did not do this place justice. "Country enclosed by granite walls" might be a better description. Its roof was supported by gigantic rock pillars formed by some natural process of an age gone by and not understood by man.

"Ben, are you able to walk? The path traverses along the face of the cliff. It doesn't look too steep, but I've never been here before. The sooner we can get away from this ledge, the better I'll like it."

Ben didn't argue. He tried to get up onto his feet. Other than a rapidly developing bruise on his leg, everything appeared to be in working order. He stepped ahead of his great-grandfather, glad to be alive and glad to be getting away from the edge. His mind replayed the vision of his grandmother, reassuring himself that the experience had really happened—or was this merely the plaything of his unconscious self? Regardless of his desire to get down to the cavern floor, the pain from his bruise slowed him down.

"Sorry I'm so slow, Papa. I'm okay, but my right leg hurts with each step."

"Oh, don't worry about me," came the response. "I prefer this easy pace at my age. I'll be down right behind you. Just keep on going, but watch yourself this time."

With this they both stopped talking and concentrated on their footing. Before long they could hear a faint sound of rushing or perhaps falling water. They looked at each other momentarily, saying nothing but proceeding onward side by side in the widening path. The thought of a waterfall brought fear to Ben—certainly with reason, considering that his last experience with one had been anything but positive. The noise of water, gaining volume with each step, could hardly be ignored. Ben chanced a look to his right, beyond the edge of the path they were traversing.

"Not a good idea, Ben," said his great-grandfather. "I imagine you've already had enough looks at that cliff to last a lifetime."

Ben failed to heed the advice, however, taking one more good look down the cliff—and then immediately regretted it. The path was a narrow overhang precariously attached to a vertical rock wall by some strange act of nature. It was scarcely two feet wide. Perhaps this was not so bad, however, because it served to slow Ben down even more.

The sound of water kept increasing, yet it still was not within their view. The path continued to bend to the left, following the shape of the cliff. The gentle downward descent was reassuring and made traveling easier. So strong was the desire to get off the cliff, the thought that they were moving ever deeper into the bowels of the earth did not enter into Ben's mind.

Spray could now be seen ahead of them. As the mist thickened, Ben kept his left hand on the cliff's rocky face to avoid drifting to the deadly drop on his right. The spray's volume did not match the torrent they could hear nearby. Curiosity drew them on, but the swirling gray mist made it impossible to see very far.

"Ben, don't drag your hand on the wall," said his great-grandfather. "There are still a lot of jagged crystals that are sharp." The old man was shouting, reminding them both of how loud the sound of the water had become.

Ben reluctantly obeyed and focused only on their path which was visible for only a few feet ahead of them. Relinquishing the assurance of touching the wall may have avoided injury, but it also left them presuming that the wall would be there as they moved along. Years of rushing water had polished the path on which they were traveling. It was fortunate that their route had become very straight and level in this region, and as long as they took each step with care, they were not under too great a risk of slipping to what would certainly be a grisly end. They could now hardly see anything, but both of them felt secure in their belief that if they stayed away from the path's right edge, they did not risk falling. Some distance ahead— perhaps tied to the form of the rocks—the mist brightened a little, encouraging the two of them to press on and get to a place where they get a better view. Oddly enough, the sound of water crashing now came from their left and not their right, though it was hard to pinpoint its source.

As they approached the clearing, they got some relief from the spray, and consequently, their steps became more sure. Their ability to see also improved, but there are times when blindness is a blessing. The view to the right was much the same as it had always been since they started—a sheer drop-off to unknown depths below—but the view to the left was paralyzing. A one hundred-yard gap had developed, separating them from their once reassuring rock wall. A thousand jets of water issued from it, spraying directly toward them, and then collecting together into a massive waterfall falling beneath them a thousand feet to the valley floor.

Ben and his great-grandfather were so transfixed by this wonder that it took them a while to grasp that this footpath was a strange phenomenon in itself. It had become a natural rock bridge, delicately spanning an irregularity in the cliff formed by the many jets of water forming a huge, narrow, wet bridge with no protection on either side.

"Let's keep moving, Ben. We only have another hundred feet." They started to walk, but with much greater trepidation knowing the peril was now on both sides.

"I think I feel sick," said Ben, after they finally reached the other side of the rock bridge.

It was some time before the racing in Ben's heart subsided. The path, again firm rock on the left, was no longer a sheer cliff, nor even an overhang on the right. Although it had begun descending steeply, the absence of a sheer drop set their nerves more at ease. They both sat down to rest.

"Dangerous, yet mighty beautiful," said Ben's great-grandfather. "I've never seen this place in all the years I've been down here."

Ben didn't comment, but the two of them stared back at the waterfall in wonder and watched the water shoot out of the wall toward the path they had so boldly crossed. From this distance it seemed safe, almost planned by design, as the water fell just short of the bridge, cascading underneath it to the valley below.

"Give it a name, Ben," said his great-grandfather. "What do you want to call it?"

Ben thought for a moment, not realizing that it is always the privilege of great explorers to name new things.

"Crystal Falls, Papa. I want to call it the Crystal Falls."

"Nice name, Ben, but why did you choose that?" he responded.

"Because the water has to come from the Crystal Pool. And it was the legend of that pool that brought you down here, you know, the legends you wrote about in your journal. They made us curious about this place too. I think I understand what's happening. The lake by our cabin, the one that never gets bigger but has two rivers that feed into it, empties behind the layered falls. Remember, you wrote about that. Then it drops down that whirlpool, which is how we got here in the first place."

"Yes, go on," said his great-grandfather.

"Well, that has to be the main source of water for this whole underground world. And the water empties into that dark river that I went down. But remember the river split into two directions. One went to that great underground sea, but the other went somewhere unknown. Well, I think it gets trapped on the other side of that cliff, and over the years it has forced itself out in all those jets of water. So all this water must come from the Crystal Pool, and if you think I should name this place, then I would like it to be called the Crystal Falls."

"Then Crystal Falls it is," said his great-grandfather, soberly wondering if this truly explained the fate of some Indians that had explored too far down the wrong fork in that dark underground river.

They paused to study this ancient phenomenon that had just been christened. They watched the water fall, fall, and fall more, hitting the cliff wall as it went and creating a violent yet beautiful fountain. Down and down it went, until it crashed into the valley floor with a profusion of mist and turbulence. Eventually it re-formed itself into a river completely out of character with its origin—it lazily threaded its way into what appeared to be farmland, just as one might find on the surface of the earth.

"And then shall we call the river down in the valley 'Crystal River'?" asked the old man.

"Yes!" said Ben with much enthusiasm, feeling very much the explorer and adventurer that he had indeed become.

They watched the river meander back and forth across the valley. The valley was green near the river, then almost whitish beyond with some areas of blue and yellow. The river's journey was occasionally punctuated with what appeared to be a village or two along its path. The areas surrounding the villages were groomed and clearly cultivated. In the far distance, the river headed into a more desolate region, where it was accompanied by a narrow line, possibly a road.

The road crossed over the river. Soon afterward, the river bent to the right, remaining parallel to the road until the two were separated by a tall, narrow, wedge-like cavern wall connecting the valley floor with the rock roof above them. The river then flowed out of sight behind the wall, but the road continued onward in front of, but on the opposite side. In this way the road and the river followed the same general direction, yet each out of sight from the other.

Ben looked back to where the river crossed the road, because something had caught his eye in the far distance. Perhaps his imagination was playing tricks or perhaps he had a sudden longing for his companions, but he thought he saw dust rising or some other kind of movement there. He stared long and hard, hoping to see more evidence of life, but with no success. Eventually, he shrugged his shoulders and looked back at the path they needed to follow and then stood up.

"Ready to go, Papa?" he asked, helping his companion to his feet.

"Yes, I suppose we must go on," was his reply. Ben noticed a look of weariness and pensiveness in his eyes. It soon passed, and the two of them resumed their long trek down into the valley.

A New Hope

Lilly watched the sister of her lost friend with silent concern. Patty was staring intently at the cavern wall from which they had emerged, scanning the road they had traveled. The young chief had ordered a rest, supposedly for his own men, yet they seemed fidgety, wanting to press on and apparently uncomfortable in this open place. For Patty, it was an opportunity to watch for something—or someone— she so obviously expected to appear at any time.

Lilly joined her, looking in the same direction. "Where do you think he is?" asked Patty. "I know he's there somewhere. He's waiting for his chance to rescue us. There are just too many of them, and we are too much in the open. But when he gets a good opportunity, he'll come to set us free and show us the way home. He just needs the right chance."

Lilly was silent for a moment, continuing to look over the same terrain that Patty had just examined.

Finally she responded, "When you see him, tell Johnny or me quietly. You must be careful, because they will sense any change that comes over you."

"Yes, of course," Patty responded. "We can't let them know he's here."

Lilly then walked away from her and sat down next to Johnny, saying nothing. He was absentmindedly drawing in the soil with a sharp rock he had found. Without raising his head, he said, "Yeah, I know—I'm worried about her too."

Lilly said nothing but surveyed their surroundings. She sensed the men's tension, but the chief seemed oblivious to it. He was having all the water sacks filled at the river. Throwing two empty ones toward two of his men, he nodded toward the river. His men rose in obedience and went to the water's edge to fill them, taking the opportunity to bathe their hands, feet, and face as well.

Lilly studied the area. It was an unusual place. Her eyes followed the river upstream and across the valley until it met the vast cavern wall. She thought she could see water falling from a great height, but she was not sure. As she brought her gaze back to where they were seated, she looked ahead to where a small bridge spanned the river. The water then proceeded onward, bending to the right and disappearing from sight behind another massive rock wall. She knew that escape by water would be impossible.

Suddenly one of the men shouted. Johnny and Lilly sprang to their feet, but the yell had come from behind the bridge. Now there were many shouts, followed by a scream from Patty. The two raced up from the river bank to the bridge. About a hundred feet down the road, they saw Patty running away and being quickly overtaken by several men.

"Stop!" shouted Johnny as he joined the chase. "Don't hurt her!"

Johnny's voice was lost in the confusion, and—perhaps because he himself was trying to join the chase—he did not see what Lilly saw. Just before Patty was overtaken, she appeared to stumble, but Lilly saw her unfasten something yellow from her hair. It flittered to the ground alongside the road as one of the men swept her up and began to carry her back. Johnny had been restrained by another of the chief's men, and both he and Patty were escorted by force back to the chief. Lilly had anticipated this and had positioned herself closer to the chief, yet not so close as to seem disrespectful.

Lilly then turned to Patty and spoke to her, sternly but not without compassion. Patty made no further protest. The chief then gathered his nervous men and began to speak to them in their language.

Lilly moved closer to Johnny and said, "I think the chief is protecting us. His men are very nervous and think we are a curse to their tribe, but I can tell that the chief doesn't believe it."

"You really can understand them, can't you, Lilly?" Johnny was rather impressed.

"I cannot understand them perfectly, but their language is similar to the ancient language of my forefathers. I have studied it and listened to the elders of our tribe speak it. I think I can pick out enough words to get their meaning."

"What are they saying now?"

"Some of the men are saying they should have let the shaman kill us at the pool. They're worried about what his father will say and do when they return to their city. But the chief made some angry comments to that, which I couldn't understand. Wait—they want to talk to us directly. This means you, Johnny—they're going to ask you some questions."

"But I can't understand them at all. How am I supposed to answer anything," Johnny responded, a bit fearfully.

"Don't worry. I'll translate the best I can, but you must address them directly. Never look at me at all. Listen to the chief both when he's talking and when I'm translating. Look at him alone when you're responding and while I translate for you. Never look at me. If their culture is like that of my ancestors, it would be a great insult. Now, don't talk to me again, because they are coming."

The chief, followed by all his men, approached Johnny. Sensing danger, Checker positioned himself in front of his master and began to growl, but Johnny stooped down and stroked his neck, speaking in low tones.

"It's okay, boy. They just want to talk. Stay with Lilly, Checker."

Taking her cue, Lilly stroked the dog's head with one hand and held him securely with the other, all the while speaking softly into his ear. Johnny stepped forward to face the chief, who wisely kept some distance so as not to excite the dog. He spoke first to his men, then turned and addressed Johnny with what was quite obviously a question.

"Why have you come into my people's country? Who sent you?" translated Lilly.

Remembering her warning, Johnny looked intently into the fierce brown eyes of the young chief. Yet in those proud eyes, he did not see violence, but curiosity.

"We fell into your world by accident, sir," he replied. "We live in the land of the shining sun by a lake. The lake has a waterfall at one end that hides a watery cave. While exploring the cave, we were carried down a terrible whirlpool and fell into your world. It is there that you found us."

After Lilly had translated, a whisper passed through the crowd. After the chief silenced them, he turned back to Johnny and said, "My men are not happy with this, because you were in one of our most holy places. No one but a priest and his escort may ever enter into that pool."

"We are terribly sorry," responded Johnny. " We truly did not intend to trespass. We were thrown down against our will. We desire only to return to the land of the sun and to our homes and families."

"Tell me more about this land of the sun, as you call it. We have heard of it in our ancient legends and are even told that we came from that land ourselves ages ago. It is also written that we will go there again when a new leader comes from this land to take us away. But we must leave by a path that you have not seen. It is written that we will depart from a very holy place. We have several such places and do not know which one it is. Do you know anything about this?"

"I am sorry. I do not. I would be lying if I said I did, but I do know much about the world of the sun and can tell you of it. I think you would like it there, but I do not know the way out of here."

The chief thought about this for some time, oblivious to the quiet tension among his men, who watched and listened, awaiting some decision. He looked over to the rock wall from where they had emerged, gazing intently at it—almost through it—as if he could see the Crystal

Pool itself and was seeking strange guidance from it. Finally he sighed and, returning his attention to Johnny, spoke again.

"We have been expecting young ones from the land of the sun to lead us back. Many of us have longed for the day. Our holy books say it will happen, but they speak of two young braves, not one, with two maidens. Also, they speak of an elder of the white tribe; one who knows this place himself and has strange guidance of a spirit. You seem to fulfill some of the ancient prophecy but not all. This is very confusing. Many of my men are afraid of the shaman's son, who wished to destroy you. He said you were false beings and a mockery of our holy books. By now, he will have reported this to his father, and there may be trouble when we return."

Johnny knew that their fate depended on his answers. He knew he could not question their holy book, whatever that was, but could he lie? Could he make something up that would satisfy them, at least temporarily, so that they had time to make a plan for escape? Was it wrong to lie when your life was in the balance? He knew his parents always told him to tell the truth in all situations, but would they really say so about this? Clearly the lives of the others also depended on his answer.

Johnny looked into the piercing, yet honest, eyes of the chief. He realized that the chief had told him more than he needed to.

"Sir," began Johnny, "I would like to tell you that we have been sent by a spirit, just as your holy book said. But I will not lie. I know nothing of this. It is true that four of us came here. My cousin was lost when we fell down the water spout into the Crystal Pool. We knew nothing of your people or of this underground world. We knew only that our great-grandfather had gone on perhaps the same journey many years earlier and hoped to discover what had happened to him. We truly have no clue, and we have lost my cousin as well."

A great stir arose among the men after they heard this translation from Lilly. Johnny feared that telling the truth would be their end, since he had admitted they did not fulfill the prophecy. The chief turned to his men and began to speak with much force as well as a hint of concealed excitement.

"What is he saying?" whispered Johnny to Lilly.

"I don't know; he's speaking much too fast, with hard words," replied Lilly. "But don't talk to me anymore. It doesn't look good."

The young chief shouted something to his men and waited, as if for a response to a question. But none said a word. He then repeated it, and again there was no response. He repeated it once more, in a much lower tone, and this time all the men responded with a single word, low in tone. It seemed to be a confirmation of some kind. Johnny was nearly beside himself with curiosity but heeded Lilly's warning to avoid talking to her. Lilly was deep in concentration, trying to pick out something from this strange conversation. Patty paid no heed to the proceedings but simply sat despondently on the ground, occasionally looking over her shoulder at the cliff behind them, still searching for her brother.

The chief then turned to Johnny and began again a slow, deliberate statement within reach of Lilly's ability to translate.

"My men and I have agreed that the prophecy is being fulfilled and that you are part of it."

Johnny could hardly believe his ears and guessed this was also true for Lilly, from the tone of her voice.

Then the chief continued.

"I understand this may confuse you, since you know nothing of this prophecy and you yourselves do not believe you have any part of it. But our holy book speaks of four children, two boys and two girls. One of the girls is to be from our own people of the distant past. The story speaks of these children showing us a way back to our original homeland through a narrow and difficult road. It also speaks of a very old man, lost in this underground world, who is a relative of the children and helps find the way out. It tells also of a strange spirit that guides them in times of trouble. So you fit part of the prophecy. The part that does not yet fit is still to be revealed."

Lilly was quite shaken at the end of her translation. In spite of her reluctance to speak in front of the chief, she interjected, "Johnny, don't you understand? Ben must still be alive! Patty is right—he must be alive, or the prophecy could not be true!"

"Lilly, this is all just a bit much. We cannot trust some old legend."

The chief looked confused at this unexpected dialogue, prompting Johnny to return to a more formal composure.

"Sir," he began, directing himself back to the chief, "we are most interested in this prophecy and must confess our ignorance. It makes us hopeful of finding our lost companion, though we had given him up for dead. But we cannot imagine finding our great-grandfather, whom we have never met, because he went searching for this underground world long before we were born."

The chief replied, "Nevertheless, we believe he is alive and here as well. Our prophecy says that you will be reunited soon. And that becomes our opportunity for escape and return to our beloved homeland. We are not of this world but of another. Our holy book says this. It makes us hope."

All this time Patty, who had been largely ignored, had been listening intently, particularly about the part that involved her brother. But rather than look hopeful, she seemed worried.

"How do they know about Ben?" she mused. But at least for the moment, she neither said nor did anything else.

The chief turned and addressed his men, giving them several instructions. They all prepared to move on, albeit in no great hurry. For the first time, the three children were left unguarded. This was no oversight. The chief soon returned and addressed them.

"You are no longer captives," he said, again using Lilly as translator. "You are now guests of my father's realm. I have taken upon myself responsibility for your behavior. I ask you to come back to the main village with us and meet my father. He is a good man. But there will be trouble waiting for us. Do you have the courage to face an uncertain reception?

Johnny nodded.

"I am glad," he responded. "From now on, please call me by my name. It may seem unusual, but perhaps Lilly can translate it to something that will be familiar to you." He carefully pronounced his name, and Lilly turned to Johnny and explained: "His name is Ojibwan. He wants to know if that has some significance in your language."

Johnny turned to him and replied, "It sounds something like the name of a tribe I heard my father speak of once, but I can't recall anything more about it."

Ojibwan nodded after hearing Lilly's translation. He straightened up and indicated to all that it was time to go. The procession turned, resuming its journey. Lost in thought, Patty continued to stare at the vast cliff that lay behind them. Lilly went to guide her back to the group.

"Lilly," began Patty.

"Yes?"

"Don't you see it?"

"See what?"

"On the cliff, over there in the distance. Something moves every once in a while."

Lilly stared as long as she dared. Nothing was there anymore, though perhaps something had flickered once or twice.

"Patty, we have to go."

Patty shrugged her shoulders and turned to go.

"It's okay—he's following," she said.

They walked in silence for a few moments.

Lilly said, "Yes, Patty, I think so too."

Rediscovery

The group journeyed up the underground valley all day, or at whatever time Ojibwan decided was day. Light emanated from everywhere, but its source remained a mystery. Johnny wondered whether it came from some kind of underground firefly. He had heard of other light-emitting insects, even on beaches, that in sufficient numbers could produce such a suffusing glow. He was grateful for it: it would be a dismal place, indeed, with no light.

Ojibwan was clearly in no hurry to get home. He stopped the group earlier than his men expected, but no one objected, and they made camp for the "night." They soon started a fire—using what for fuel, Johnny had no idea. The men brought up smooth stones for makeshift chairs. *It is almost like camping,* Johnny thought.

They sat together, making whatever small talk possible. Lilly seemed to have tired of translating. Patty decided to go to sleep accompanied by Checker, who had stayed by her side constantly since her escape attempt. But escape was no longer an issue. No one was being held prisoner anymore, and where was there to go anyhow?

Finally, Ojibwan wished all a good night in his own language, or so it seemed. Soon Johnny found himself alone, staring into a slowly dying fire. He was surprised to realize it had been getting continually darker and the notion of "night" did exist, even in this vast underground cave. His mind replayed the previous day's conversation. He wondered at this legend—or prophecy, as they put it. So much of what had happened was truly consistent with it, but that just did not make any sense. Why would Ojibwan want to believe such things about them? Yet it was not just Ojibwan. Clearly, all his men were convinced by the story too.

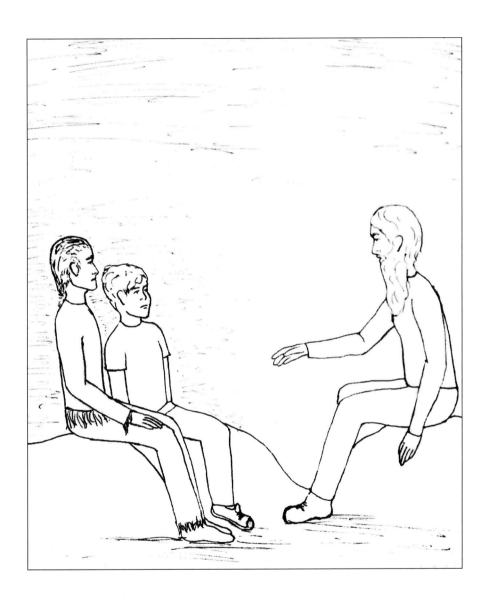

Johnny's mind retuned to Ben.

If the legends are true, he mused, *wouldn't they have to be true in every respect? And if so, what did this mean for Ben? Could he still be alive somewhere? If not, the prophecy could not be true. Who is the old man they mentioned?*

It was too much to think that his great-grandfather could still be alive after all these years under conditions such as these.

"What if I had tried to make up a more believable story?" he wondered, now muttering out loud in a low voice.

He recalled how he had been tempted to lie to the chief's son.

"But if I had lied," he continued, "we would not have built their trust."

"Of course you wouldn't have. Lies never work," said a voice from across the fire. Startled, Johnny looked up, thinking that everyone had gone to bed. The gloom had settled in, and the firelight was low, making it difficult to see who was speaking. It couldn't be one of the Indians, and quite obviously not Patty or Lilly. So who else would know English?

"Who are you?" asked Johnny.

"You don't recognize me? Well, I suppose you ain't to blame entirely for that. You've had quite an experience, but still—I thought by now you'd be gettin' more used to me comin' and goin.'"

"Abraham?" asked Johnny.

"And who else?" came the reply.

"How in the world did you get here?" Johnny asked in amazement.

"Oh, why don't the Master give young'uns any sense? Never did, yet somehow they survive. Must be grace. What do you mean, how did I get here? How did I get *there*—or leave, for that matter, all the other times?"

"I don't know. It's always a kind of shock."

"Well, okay—but maybe you could be gettin' used to shock one of these days. Anyway, we're wastin' a lot of time jawin' about nothin.' Johnny, you need a little jump-start because you've got things to do. "All four o' you kids have a big role down here, and your great-grandfather too.

Johnny stared at him but said nothing.

"Yes, I suppose you may be a bit surprised, though it's hard to understand why. You heard the prophecy; you saw how you all fit in. The tribe here has less trouble believing it than you. But you come from a culture that doesn't believe much of anything unless it practically hits you over the head, so perhaps you can be excused."

Johnny noticed that Abraham's manner of speech had abruptly changed. There was no more of the country twang or the random progression of thought. Abraham was on a serious track and clearly had an objective in mind.

Johnny looked intently at him.

"Who are you?" he asked earnestly.

Abraham returned the intensity of Johnny's gaze but said nothing as his form began to change, along with his apparel. Any sign of age faded away, and his face became brilliant. His body grew in stature and strength, and his appearance became fearsome yet not threatening. Johnny began to shudder uncontrollably until Abraham touched him, after which all fear melted away.

Lifting Johnny to his feet, Abraham pointed to the cavern ceiling and said, "Behold."

There, covering the entire cavern ceiling, they saw the huge silhouette of a lamb wrapped around a cross. The silhouette, both subtle and overwhelming, was almost impossible to take in. It was part of the natural formation of the rock. Awestruck, Johnny wondered why he had not noticed it earlier. But before he could say anything, Abraham moved to Johnny's left and stooped down to lift a shuddering, prostrate man to his feet. It was Ojibwan; unnoticed by Johnny, he had heard their murmurs and come to see the source. He had arrived just as Abraham changed form. But upon his touch, Ojibwan's fear dissolved, and he too saw the silhouette on the ceiling.

"How did that get there?" Johnny asked Ojibwan, forgetting he could not understand English. But much to his amazement, Ojibwan responded fluently.

"I've never seen it before. But look, it's changing with the light!"

He clearly did not notice the impossibility of their newly found direct communication. They both watched as the image became more and more obscure, finally disappearing altogether.

Johnny and Ojibwan looked back at Abraham, who remained in his radiant form. He no longer inspired fear or even awe—but certainly much respect. He then spoke to them both at once.

"You have been chosen, along with Ben, Lilly, Patty, and one whom you will be surprised to meet. I am nothing. You have been chosen by the Lamb. It is now time for you to lead this people to the light. But you yourselves must find the light before you can lead anyone. The path is narrow and difficult, but you will be given guidance."

"This is all confusing to me, but I will trust in what you say," replied Johnny. "But please, Abraham, who are you?"

Abraham smiled.

"Ah, I see you realize that Abraham is not my true name. It is one I borrowed from a friend just for this purpose. You may still call me Abraham because my true name is too difficult for you. Perhaps you have heard of other friends of mine named Michael and Gabriel. We are all of the same order. We are servants of both the Most High and all people. We may appear great, and I suppose we are from your current perspective, but in fact, you are much greater than we are— or at least you will be. This, however, you cannot understand now.

"My allotted time is nearly gone. Furthermore, I have been told by the Master that this is my last visit until the very end. From now on, you are on your own but not without help from friends."

Abraham turned to Ojibwan and addressed him.

"I am about to loan Johnny the most important book ever written. Johnny saw it once before, in his great-grandfather's library. It had been lost near where we are now standing for many years, save for the short time when I took it back. After Johnny read some of it, I returned it to the very spot where his great-grandfather had lost it, and there it lies. This book contains the Master's full message to all people. It is not just a book for Johnny's people, but for yours as well. You must explore it together, though neither of you may understand it right away. It contains the key to life. You must find it. The path is narrow."

Overcome by awe, Ojibwan found these words difficult to understand.

"I will do as you ask, though your words are full of mystery beyond my understanding. And yet, were not we already given books and legends of prophecy?"

"Yes, you were given these gifts to bring you hope during your struggle beneath the surface of the earth. But now that purpose is nearly complete. The book I will show you has no end to its purpose."

Abraham guided Johnny and Ojibwan away from their camp. No one stirred. Everyone else had slept peacefully through their entire conversation. Johnny wondered about that for a moment, but Abraham's ever quickening pace demanded his complete attention as they headed toward the nearest cavern wall. Abraham's agility was remarkable, shown as he began to climb a rough path that zigzagged up the steep slope. It was such a contrast to the old man Johnny once knew. Ojibwan was surprised at the existence of the path, clearly never having seen it before. But there was no time to do anything but try to keep up with the pace set by this powerful being. Soon Abraham stopped, sat down on a rock ledge, and waited for the others to arrive. They did so shortly afterward, quite out of breath. Abraham looked toward a narrow crevasse about three feet deep and asked, "What do you see in there?"

Johnny peered intently, but it was too dark in the crack to see much of anything. Then Ojibwan crouched down and even lay on his stomach, being careful not to cut off much light, and stared for some time.

"I think I see a book, but it is hard to tell for sure."

"It is the book of the lamb," stated Abraham. "You must seek the narrow path. Do not forget that."

"Here," said Johnny, having found two branches that were unusually straight. "Try picking up the book with these."

Ojibwan took one in each hand and reached for the book, grasping it between the branches. Slowly lifting the book up, and with some excitement, he uttered something in his native tongue, which Johnny assumed to be "I've got it."

In a few moments, he succeeded in raising the book out of the crack and gently set it on the rock. Ojibwan dusted off the cover and looked at the title, but he appeared confused. Again he spoke in his native tongue, looking questioningly at Johnny.

"It says *The Holy Bible* on the cover—that's all," said Johnny.

Ojibwan looked more confused but said nothing. Johnny carefully picked up the Bible and turned to Abraham, but he was gone. Both Johnny and Ojibwan looked down the path, back to their camp, where all were still asleep. There was no sign of Abraham.

Johnny sighed. "He's just that way. He suddenly disappears when he's through. It's always like that."

Ojibwan just looked at Johnny. His confusion turned into resignation, and again he said something in his native tongue that Johnny could not understand. Johnny suddenly realized that Abraham had given Ojibwan the ability to speak English but only while he was present. Or perhaps Johnny had been given the ability to speak Ojibwan's language? Or perhaps they could just understand each other—who could say? But that gift was clearly temporary.

Both turned, without need of communication, and proceeded down the narrow path, with Ojibwan in the lead and Johnny holding the Bible. The path, difficult and narrow, was also somewhat dangerous. It reminded Johnny of Abraham's parting words; *What was that again?* He wondered. *Oh yes, I remember what he said: "It is the book of the lamb. You must seek the narrow path. Do not forget that."*

Johnny repeated it over and over to himself, knowing that Abraham had impressed this upon them, and it must be important, though bewildering.

Ojibwan arrived at the bottom of the path and was proceeding back to the camp. Johnny scrambled after him. They sat down and waited for the others to awaken. Lost in thought for some time, Johnny looked back at the book. Near the bottom of the cover, he saw the name John Matheson.

"Yes, this is the same Bible that was in the secret library," Johnny said to himself in a low voice.

He marveled at Abraham's ability to move the book several times from its place in the crevasse, where his great-grandfather must have dropped it so many years ago, to the library, where he was to find it.

I wonder why he just didn't leave it with us in the library, he mused. *But then of course, we probably would not have brought it with us.*

Ojibwan began preparing to break camp, pulling out something to eat from his bag. He offered a portion to Johnny, who gladly accepted the food, having none of his own. The food was like a cross between a mushroom and a cauliflower. His hunger made it palatable, but he imagined that at home he would have turned his nose up at it. Interesting how a lack of food affects the flavor of what *is* available, he thought. The two ate together while others in the camp began to wake up. Ojibwan clearly was in no hurry and allowed the process to work at its own pace.

With nothing else to do, Johnny opened the Bible. Surprised at how thin the pages were, he looked and discovered they numbered almost two thousand.

"How does Abraham expect me to read all that?" he complained out loud.

Ojibwan saw what he was doing and moved closer to Johnny to see the Bible for himself. Johnny handed it to him, and Ojibwan began to turn the pages carefully, feeling them with his fingers and marveling at its construction. He noticed they were white, but when he closed the book, the edges looked gold. He looked questioningly at Johnny, said something Johnny could not understand, and then looked at the cover. The printing was faded, but the leather binding had survived the years and the embossed title fascinated him as he carefully felt the indentation.

Johnny realized that others from the tribe had joined them and were looking over Ojibwan's shoulder. Ojibwan turned to one of them and spoke quietly, handing the Bible to him. Carefully receiving it, he opened it and noticed that thumb indentations opened the book to sections that were clearly titled. A stir arose as increasing numbers of curious onlookers came by, each wanting to hold the Bible and look at the golden edges and the strange, delicate pages in this obviously ancient book. Everyone handled it with great respect and care, always closing it before handing it to another person, finally returning it to Johnny.

The gathering attracted Lilly's attention. She was surprised to see this crowd surrounding Johnny and Ojibwan. She joined the group, waiting for her turn to see over what they were marveling. Ojibwan noticed her, and after speaking to her briefly he motioned to Johnny, clearly wanting Lilly to see the Bible; so Johnny gave it to her. She examined the book, though without the awe displayed by the others, and nodded her head. She spoke to Ojibwan as if answering a question. Nodding his head, he gave the Bible back to Johnny, addressing him with a comment. Johnny wished they could have retained their temporary ability to understand each other. Lilly returned to her role as translator, saying, "Ojibwan is interested in this book. He would like you to read it and tell him what it says."

Johnny looked a bit shocked but kept his wits, saying, "I would be happy to do so, but it may take a very long time." Lilly translated again.

Ojibwan nodded as he listened, then replied through Lilly, "I understand it is very big, but Abraham gave it to us for a reason. Perhaps you can decide what part of it will answer our questions. I am sure you can, or Abraham would not have given it to us."

Although Lilly dutifully translated, she looked confused at what he was saying.

"I'll tell you what happened later," Johnny said to her, apparently no longer concerned about speaking directly to Lilly in front of Ojibwan. She did not seem concerned either.

Johnny addressed him directly.

"I will do my best, and Lilly will help us understand each other. I'm sorry we can no longer talk directly, as we did earlier."

Lilly, noticeably confused at this statement, translated with some hesitation.

"I will read it first myself, and then we will get together when I have something to share." Ojibwan nodded, then began mustering his people to prepare to leave. Lilly went to wake Patty. They shared what food they had, and others were sharing food and water with them freely.

The group was now ready for departure. Ojibwan led the way, setting an easy pace. There were no more guards, and no more attempts at escapes. Patty must have noticed the change as well, for her fear left her. She seemed content to walk with Checker, who had been making a point of staying close to her, sensing the need for a protector. Patty clearly liked this growing relationship with Johnny's dog, and Johnny didn't seem to mind.

They soon crossed a bridge that carried them over the river they had been following. Their route stayed close to a sheer rock wall that quickly separated them from the river. Lilly caught up with Johnny after seeing that Patty was well cared for.

"So what was that all about?" asked Lilly.

"What do you mean?" replied Johnny.

"That bit with the chief's son that you said you would tell me later. Well, it's later now."

Johnny smiled. This was the most casual he had ever heard Lilly speak. She almost sounded like one of his friends at school.

"It's tough to explain, mostly because it is hard to believe myself."

"Try me."

"Well, I woke up early this morning…" Johnny paused mid-sentence. *I don't even remember sleeping at all…almost as if the night got cut short*, he thought before continuing. "Don't know why—just couldn't sleep. Then it happened again: Abraham was sitting in our camp. He really startled me, though he said I ought to be used to it by now. I don't get how he pops in and out."

"Go on," prompted Lilly.

Johnny saw genuine interest on her face, giving him the courage to tell a story that would normally be pretty tough to swallow.

"Okay. So anyway, he shows me a huge silhouette on the ceiling of this cave—of a lamb and a cross."

"Where?" interrupted Lilly, looking up and scanning the vast cavern roof.

"You can't see it now. In fact, we could see it only for a minute, when the light was changing—almost like a strange underground sunrise."

"What do you mean by 'we'? You and Abraham?"

"No, by this time Ojibwan had arrived to see what was going on. At that point, Abraham changed." Johnny paused.

Lilly didn't prompt him again, knowing that something significant had occurred.

"Well," continued Johnny, "he really changed. I mean *really* changed. He went from being a funny old man to being a huge, powerful angel. It was the scariest thing I ever saw. Ojibwan saw it too. We were both paralyzed until he touched us, and then the fear suddenly left."

Both Johnny and Lilly became silent. Johnny was unsure how this was coming across. He almost felt foolish, telling her what must seem to be a fantastic story. But Lilly did not question it at all.

She finally broke the silence and said, "I knew he was an evil spirit."

The Bible

The party enjoyed a leisurely day of travel, quitting early in the mid-"afternoon." They stopped by a pool nestled against the cavern wall. Johnny marveled at this, since there was no source of water—yet the pool was not stagnant and the water was fresh. Johnny, Lilly, and Patty sat down at the pool's edge and dangled their feet into the water.

There was no shore as someone on the earth's surface would think of it. Beyond the edge where the rocky ledge met the pool was a vertical boundary, dropping off to unknown watery depths. One of the chief's men stepped off and disappeared underwater. Then he bobbed to the surface somewhat farther out, swimming in this unusual pool. Patty suddenly pulled her feet out, unnerved by her sudden realization that the water was quite over her head.

Johnny reached into his pack and pulled out his great-grandfather's Bible, deciding that this would be a good time to investigate it. Seeing Johnny occupied, Lilly decided to join the growing number of those wanting to swim, and she dove into the pool. Checker barked at her when she did so, but he shortly retreated to where Patty was, continuing his newfound role of protector.

Where should I start? Johnny mused. *This Bible is so big!*

He leafed through a few pages and found a table of contents, but the chapters (or "books," as they seemed to be called) had titles that made no sense to him. He turned another page and saw a handwritten note, directed to his great-grandfather, which read as follows:

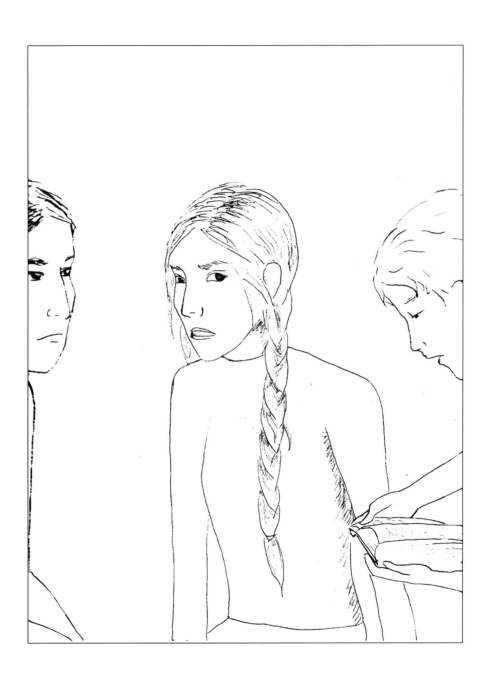

John, the Bible is best read starting from the New Testament. To get a view of the mind of Christ, start with the book of John. God bless. May He guide you in your understanding.

Pastor Nelson.

Well, that was helpful, Johnny thought. The book of John—I wonder where that is?

It was not long before Johnny discovered the section called the "New Testament" and then found the "book of John" in its table of contents. He went to it and wondered why there were numbers next to all the sentences.

No matter, he thought and started to read.

In the beginning was the Word, and the Word was with God, and the Word was God.

The same was in the beginning with God.

Johnny re-read that line two or three times before continuing.

All things were made by him; and without him was not any thing made that was made. In him was life; and the life was the light of men. And the light shineth in darkness; and the darkness comprehended it not.

Johnny put the book back on his lap, somewhat bewildered.

"I don't get it," he confessed out loud.

"You don't get what?" replied Patty, who had come alongside him, unnoticed. Johnny looked over at her while Checker lay next to him. He started to pet his dog's head, looking at him thoughtfully.

"I haven't been paying much attention to you lately, have I?" he apologized. Checker thumped his tail several times, apparently not having taken any offense by this confessed neglect. "We were supposed to have had a great summer, romping around the lake, but it looks like I have gotten us stuck underground."

Patty looked at Johnny, thinking about defending him against himself, but decided otherwise and returned to her original question.

"What is it that you don't get?" she repeated.

"Oh," replied Johnny, "it's this book. It doesn't make any sense at all. I don't understand why Abraham wanted so badly for me to read it."

" Johnny, that's a Bible. It has to make sense. Everyone knows that."

"Okay—you read it and tell me what you think it means."

Patty read the same passage with which Johnny had just been struggling.

She straightened up and said, "Well, I think it's just like what Grandma use to say when she would tell us stories at night. She would always tell us something about the Bible—at least she did for Ben and me. Anyway, I think *the Word* is another name for Jesus, and he was with God, the Father, when the world was made—even before the world was made. It basically says that everything we see was made by them together, even this big cave we're in."

Johnny looked it over again. That did make sense, sort of, except maybe the part about Jesus being there when the world was made.

"But I thought Jesus lived two thousand years ago. Wasn't He born in a manger in the Holy Land? How could he have made the world?"

"Because He existed before He was born on Earth. He was the only one in history like that. His mom was the Virgin Mary. God just sent Jesus from heaven because we needed Him."

Johnny looked back at the words again. He had to admit: in that context, the words did make more sense. But why did Patty know all this and he didn't?

"Maybe he was a good teacher, but I think no one can make the world before being born," interjected Lilly. She had joined them, noticed only by Checker.

"My people have stories of how the world was created. Maybe you don't need that book."

"Oh, I don't think that's why Abraham gave us this book. He said something about a narrow way and the Lamb," Johnny replied.

Lilly didn't look satisfied with that answer, shrugging it off and returning to the main group. Johnny and Patty continued to pore over the book, reading it carefully. Johnny was surprised at Patty's apparent understanding of what was read and by his confusion. After all, he was older than she was. So why could she understand things that he couldn't?

> And the Word was made flesh, and dwelt among us, (and we beheld his glory, the glory as of the only begotten of the Father), full of grace and truth.

"Now, you can't tell me that makes any sense," retorted Johnny. How does a word become flesh?

"Johnny, it does make sense. We know that when the Bible says *the Word*, it is referring to Jesus. *The Word* is used over and over. Besides, it talks next about the Jews coming to Him asking where He came from. What else could it mean?"

"Okay, Patty," said Johnny, controlling his agitation, "I guess it makes sense, but how did you learn all that?"

"Well, Grandma used to tell me a lot of things like this, and she used to read to me parts of her Bible. I don't remember this part, but maybe she read it. I was pretty young then. But it is exciting to see the same things she told me right here in Great-Granddad's old Bible!"

"Hmm, you seem to be better qualified to read this than me," Johnny replied with a shrug. "Come on, Checker. Let's see what Lilly is doing. Maybe we can find out about some of those old Indian stories."

Checker thumped his tail a few times but didn't follow Johnny as he walked off. Instead, he stayed with Patty. After Johnny had taken several steps, he looked back and saw that Checker was not following him.

"Fine. Do what you want," he muttered to Checker and turned to find Lilly.

She had joined the others in the water, and Johnny decided to do the same. He pulled off his shirt and shoes and jumped in. Lilly was glad to see him. Everyone's mood became lighthearted—they were like vacationers near a lake. The tension of the previous days faded as water fights began, and the Indians taught them various games. Johnny looked in vain for Ojibwan, who—to Johnny's surprise—was sitting with Patty, watching her pore over the Bible. A slightly uncomfortable feeling came over him, but he ignored it. Checker was still there, looking relaxed. Everything was okay. But he still felt strange.

"Come on, Johnny; check this out," said Lilly, as she pushed off the ledge that separated the "shore" from the water. It was a short swim to the opposite side, which was bounded by a sheer obsidian wall rising from the water to the cavern roof. Johnny followed her. It was uncomfortable not knowing just how deep this pool was. There was nothing to hold on to for support, so they both treaded water by the rock wall.

"What do you feel against your feet?" asked Lilly.

Now that she mentioned it, Johnny could feel a steady, though not forceful, pressure.

"What is that?" replied Johnny.

"It must be how water gets in here. The wall must have some kind of opening in it."

"But the water has to get out somewhere," observed Johnny.

The two stared at each other for several moments, thinking about what Johnny had said; then, without a word, they swam back to the shore and got out of the water. Neither really wanted to find out where or how the water left the pool.

After the evening meal, Ojibwan lingered around the fire they had made. Johnny noticed that the "logs" burned with mixtures of colors, mostly yellow and green. He wondered what kind of fuel they were using. There were no trees in the cavern, yet the "firewood" they had found looked much like old logs that one might gather in a forest somewhere. As with the previous night, the light changed its hue, becoming dimmer as "evening" approached.

Patty was absorbed in the Bible, which annoyed Johnny. He knew that Abraham had given him the task to find out what it said, and Ojibwan expected that of him as well. It was hard to read. He resented his younger cousin's ability to understand it. He looked up and saw Ojibwan and Lilly talking together, which surprised him. The old protocol did not seem relevant anymore. Lilly talked directly to Ojibwan much more frequently now. The rest of the men ignored them. Johnny slipped next to Patty and saw where she was reading. She was still in the book of John.

"Johnny, you should read this. Grandma used to tell me at bedtime the same stories that are in here. I didn't realize she got them from the Bible. Did she ever tell you Bible stories?"

"I guess so," replied Johnny a little despondently. "I know she told stories, but I didn't always listen to them. Maybe I should have."

"Look here," continued Patty. "This guy's a pretty important ruler who came to Jesus at night."

"Why at night?"

"I think he didn't want his friends to know he was there."

"Why not?"

"I think Jesus wasn't very popular with the rulers. They might have been jealous because he could do miracles and they couldn't. He had turned water into wine at a wedding. He told people things about themselves that they didn't think He could know. But he also chased out of the temple moneychangers who really shouldn't have been there, but the leaders hadn't done their job in chasing them out themselves. So they were getting kind of mad about it, I think—he was making them feel unimportant."

"Okay, so what did this ruler want with Jesus at night?"

"Well, they were just sitting around, sort of like we are around this fire, and he told Jesus that he and some of his friends knew that God had sent him."

"How could they know that?"

"Because of all the miracles. No one else could do them, so they figured it had to be God doing it through Jesus."

"I guess that makes sense. But it seems strange that this guy would come to tell Jesus about it, especially at night."

"Well, I think it was because he wanted something for himself. I think that this ruler felt, well, maybe incomplete."

"What do you mean?"

"Haven't you ever felt like there should be more purpose to life than going to school, coming home, doing chores, doing homework, going to school, coming home, and so forth—on and on?"

Johnny thought about this for some time. She had a point. Did God have some purpose for him besides just the stuff he did every day with his dog and friends? But he said nothing.

"Well," continued Patty, "Jesus didn't even respond to what this guy said. He just told him, 'You must be born again.'"

"What? That doesn't make any sense. How can somebody be born more than once?"

"That's exactly what this ruler said—look here." Johnny looked where Patty was pointing, and he read:

How can a man be born when he was old? Can he enter a second time into his mother's womb and be born?

Johnny was surprised that his thought process mirrored so closely what the ruler had pondered thousands of years ago. But even so, it was confusing.

"Now, this is the part I don't get," said Patty. "Maybe you can figure out the next part." Johnny looked back at the text and read the following passages:

Marvel not that I said unto thee, Ye must be born again. The wind bloweth where it listeth, and thou hearest the sound thereof, but canst not tell whence it cometh, and whither it goeth: so is every one that is born of the Spirit.

Johnny read the passage twice. The words were strange. He wondered how old the Bible actually was.

"I am not sure, Patty, but maybe it means that if God is leading you, you can't guess where He will take you and why. So maybe His purpose is real, but we can't see it until it is over. What do you think?"

Patty's face lit up.

"I think that's it, Johnny! That has to be it! And it makes sense for us too. We don't know why we are here. We don't know where Ben is yet. But it will make sense later. I'm sure that's it."

Johnny was encouraged and also a bit surprised. He wasn't sure what had made him say what he did, but he felt good about it. They both returned to the passage and read on.

"Look at this, Patty," continued Johnny. "This old ruler guy never did get it. All he can say is, 'How can these things be?' And it looks like Jesus got a little annoyed with him for not getting it, especially since he was a teacher of some kind."

"You're right, Johnny. I can see it now. But maybe after he thought about it, he understood. You know, kind of like us. We didn't understand it right away either."

Johnny nodded thoughtfully but said nothing. Could this be part of what Abraham wanted him to know? But Abraham had said something about a lamb and a narrow way. This passage didn't say anything about that. Then Johnny did something impulsive. He looked up to the cavern ceiling and spoke distinctly, as if to someone above him.

"Abraham, if you can hear me, could you show me where the lamb and the narrow way are in this book?" he said out loud.

Patty looked a bit shocked but said nothing, and they both waited.

"Abraham, please tell me. Where do I find out about the lamb and the narrow way?"

The cavern swallowed his words. It suddenly felt stuffy. Johnny almost sensed rejection, and suddenly felt humiliated at this failed effort to call out to Abraham.

"I should have known better. He told me that he wasn't coming back, and we were on our own now."

Patty considered his words.

"But maybe we aren't supposed to ask him for help. It might seem like we were praying to somebody other than God. I remember Grandma saying that we could and should pray directly to Him."

Johnny felt embarrassed and shrugged it off, wanting to be somewhere else. He walked back to the main camp, forgetting about the Bible. Patty placed it carefully into her backpack. Checker nuzzled her hand to encourage her to pay him some attention, which she did, briefly stroking his head. Then she sat down and looked wistfully back to where they had traveled.

"I wish Ben would come," she said to herself.

The next morning, the group rose earlier. Ojibwan was more resolute about getting back than he had been the previous day. He looked grim and spoke little. Lilly didn't try to draw him out either—as if unconcerned about his more sober mood.

After a few hours, they came to a small village. The people looked frightened to see their party, and some stared at Johnny, Patty, and Lilly. Most kept their heads down, focusing on some task. No one spoke a word. No one looked happy. No children were playing anywhere—only working.

Johnny noticed that Ojibwan's expression had changed slightly. He looked a little sadder as he watched the people. Suddenly, a young girl—perhaps five years old—came running up to Ojibwan. Her mother, panicked, tried too late to stop her. As the girl ran toward him, Ojibwan's men poised their spears, aiming them at the girl. Ojibwan stepped forward toward her and held up his hand against his men. He then stooped to her level to receive the flower she held out to him. Ojibwan smiled and took something shiny from his pack, placing it in her hand. Her face lit up—a unique expression in this village. After saying something to him, she ran back to her mother, who picked her up and hurried into a hut. The men looked surprised but not shocked, and they all continued their journey.

"What was that all about?" Johnny asked Lilly, when they were well on their way again.

"No one is allowed to cross the path of the chief or his son, upon pain of death. Not even children," she replied. "He is very unusual. I don't think many leaders here have his mercy."

"But your tribe isn't like that."

"True, but I think many years ago we did the same thing—probably not to children though. Something has gone wrong here over time. I am not sure what, but I know Ojibwan does not like the shaman. I think he expects a problem when we get to the main village."

The rest of the day passed without incident. They crossed through a number of other villages, with much the same response from the residents. Everyone nearby held his head down. Children came nowhere near. Ojibwan ceased to look at them and pressed on.

As "evening" was again approaching, Johnny noticed two changes. First, the path they trod was maintained; second, masks started to appear along their route. At first the masks were mounted on an occasional pole or on the cavern wall. As they marched on, the masks became more frequent and gruesome. The faces followed them as they went by, each having an unnatural expression designed to frighten the observer. Patty stayed closer to Johnny, protected by her cousin on one side and by Checker on the other. Structures appeared, larger than those in the outlying villages but built in the same manner.

After they rounded a corner, a great arch loomed before them, forming an official gate to the main village. On top of the gate stood a row of masks, monstrous in both size and expression. Each had a leer, as if enjoying some great evil it represented. Here Ojibwan halted, paying no attention to the gate or the masks. He turned to his men, giving a number of instructions. Preparing their weapons, several of them moved ahead through the arch and into the city, wary of each step. The remaining sat down outside and hastily constructed a camp.

"So why are we stopping here?" Johnny asked Lilly.

"I have no idea, and I don't think it's a good time to ask. But I imagine that Ojibwan is expecting trouble and is taking precautions."

"So what do you think will happen to the men he sent on?"

"I think those are his best scouts. It may be dangerous. They do better in smaller numbers in a situation like this."

"A situation like what?"

"The shaman is probably very powerful and not too nice. If he's anything like his son, we will have a problem."

"Do you think Ojibwan will turn us over to him?"

"I don't think so. But there still may be trouble. We should be on our best behavior."

At Lilly's lead, the three of them, together with Checker, made seats from more of the plentiful smooth "logs" and sat down. Johnny looked up and surveyed the area. The cavern ceiling now seemed lower than it had previously been—or perhaps the cavern floor had risen up closer to the ceiling. He looked in the direction of the path before them. In the fading light, he thought he could discern a multicolored, flickering glimmer in the distance. He wondered what new marvel might lie ahead.

Patty scooted up to him, putting her head on his shoulder and closing her eyes. He put his arm around her and let her rest.

As she started to drift into sleep, she said, "Johnny, I know Ben will come. But you are like my brother too." She said no more.

Johnny noticed she had made a necklace from grasses she must have found along the way. There was a stone in it, held together by thin grass fibers. It made a nice decoration and dangled around her neck. Johnny wondered about it but was glad his cousin had found something to occupy her instead of thinking about running away. As she slept, he looked closer. *The stone must be very old*, he mused. As he studied it he could see a worn image that resembled the sun and the moon, perhaps even stars. Clearly this was made by man, perhaps ancestors of this underground people. Nevertheless, he had better things to worry about. He gently removed his arm from his sleeping cousin, laying her down in the most comfortable position he could. As he did so the Bible she had been grasping began to slip from her hand. Johnny gently removed it from her fingers, careful not to disturb her, and put it in his lap. He looked at it again, re-membered his responsibility, and opened it. It fell open easily to the third chapter of John, so he re-read the passage they had looked at earlier.

"I should read more of it," Johnny said to himself. "There must be something about a lamb and a cross somewhere in here."

Recollections

Ben and his great-grandfather didn't make camp until after they had succeeded in working their way down the difficult slope to the cavern floor. From the vantage point of the cliff, they had seen the same river the others were following and deliberately made their way toward it. Once on the cavern floor, they worked their way along the river, heading downstream in the same direction that Johnny, Lilly, and Patty were traveling—but with no idea of what had befallen them. They proceeded more doggedly, deliberately trying to avoid people and villages. This was difficult, since most of the villages were built along the river. Upon finding a secluded area, Ben thought it best to give Papa another rest, which was gratefully accepted. A very convenient rock formation bordered the water; it resembled a lounge chair and almost felt like one when they sat on it.

"If only we had the sun, this place would be just like a river at home," said Ben.

"The sun," mused his great-grandfather. "I can almost remember what it felt like, Ben." He thought about that for a few moments and then added, "I have been down here much, much too long. I would so much like to breathe the open air again and feel the sun's rays."

Ben reflected on this for some time. He had regretted coming here from the moment he fell through the whirlpool in the cave behind the layered falls. His great-grandfather's words reminded him how much he longed to be reunited with his sister, friend, and cousin and to find their way out of this forsaken place. Suddenly a feeling of determination came over him.

"Papa, we will find Patty, Lilly, and Johnny, and we'll get out of here. All of us." His great-grandfather smiled in appreciation but said nothing.

After another period of silence, Ben spoke up again.

"Papa, tell me more about yourself, when you were younger. What was life like back then, and what was my great-grandmother like? Why did you come here? What were you looking for?"

Ben's great-grandfather looked at the river. A somber expression had come over his face. Old memories, long suppressed, produced fresh pain, making Ben wish he had not asked. But the moment passed and he shrugged it off.

"I should tell you about it, Ben. It is amazing we ever met each other, and it's a part of your family history that you'd never know if not for this strange but happy circumstance."

Papa closed his eyes and leaned back against the smooth rock. He looked at the water, but his mind reached back many years. Then he started his story.

"When I was young—well, not as young as you, but it seems young to me now—I moved by the lake where you live. There is another story behind that, but we don't have time to go into that. I was twenty and alone in the world. Times were different then, both better and worse. There were a lot of Indians by the lake, and the tribe I imagine your friend Lilly came from was the biggest one in the area."

"They are the only tribe now, Papa."

"Is that so? Well, not then. There were more Indians than whites in those days."

"Wasn't it kind of dangerous? I thought there were wars between Indians and whites."

"No, the Indian wars were in the late eighteen hundreds and mostly south in the United States, but this was the nineteen thirties. We were pretty remote then, and the Indians still lived much like they always had. This particular tribe never had fought against the whites, and the whites didn't mistreat them, so things stayed pretty peaceful. The only real problem was between the main tribe and some other rough Indians, but that had been mostly settled by then."

"That sounds pretty good. It must have been beautiful. With everyone getting along so well, I can see why you wanted to settle there."

"There were other problems though. We might have gotten along well, but there were some unwritten social rules…and I broke one of them."

Ben thought it best not to ask; he just waited patiently for Papa to continue.

"I'll just tell you up front, and I hope you won't think badly of me as everyone else did—at least the other whites—but you should know the truth. The fact is I fell in love with a girl from the tribe."

He paused, waiting for Ben's reaction, but Ben just waited. He was plainly interested in the story as it was unfolding, so his great-grandfather continued.

"She was pretty, Ben—real pretty. I've seen a lot of Indian girls in my time, but none like her. She was the chief's daughter too. She had only one brother and no sisters. She was kind of shy at first, but she knew I liked her. She liked me too but stayed away from me for quite a while. I used to come over often, under the pretense of wanting to trade—which I did, of course—but to be honest, the business was better with the whites."

"So, before long I built a trading post. I specialized in trading goods between the whites and the Indians. I helped the tribe by showing them stuff that was likely to bring in more money from the whites. Of course that helped my relationship with the chief.

Eventually they asked me to join the tribe. I accepted but didn't tell any of my white buddies."

"Papa, what's the big deal? Why would anyone care?"

"People were fine with being friendly but not too friendly. I had to become a blood brother with the chief's son to become part of the tribe."

"That's cool; I did the same thing with Lilly. Now that I think about it, I didn't tell Mom and Dad about that either. They didn't know until my sister told them—but that was because I made her do it too. She was kind of mad, and so was Mom when she found out."

The old man smiled and continued.

"Things were both simpler and more complicated in those days. Eventually, I asked the chief for permission to marry his daughter. That was the complicated part—not for the tribe but for the whites. Being a blood brother was enough to make me acceptable to the tribe, but nothing could make an Indian acceptable to the whites. I didn't care what anybody thought in those days, and we were married. Those were good days, at least at first. She and I made the trading outpost our home. Then we added on and made the store separate. The traders that came by got used to seeing my Indian bride, although they were surprised at first. She did a great job. She could trade with her own people better than I could, and I ran the store, dealing with the whites myself."

"Sounds like it worked out to me," commented Ben.

"Yes it did, for a while. We even had a baby girl. Just as pretty as her mom."

"What was her name?"

"We named the baby after my wife—Little Flower."

Ben raised an eyebrow.

"That's Lilly's name too."

Ben's great-grandfather paused in thought for a few moments, then nodded. "Makes some sense, I think. Yes, it does fit."

"So what made things get complicated?" probed Ben.

"A rumor of gold. We didn't really have any or at least not of any significance. But a little was found in one of the two rivers that feed the lake. A rush of whites came up, all wanting quick riches. Those are not the nicest people to be around."

"What did they do?" inquired Ben.

"At first, they caused a huge increase in my business. I could hardly keep up with the demand. But some people didn't like the fact that I had an Indian wife. They treated her badly. I got mad once when I saw it, and just about—well, there's no point going into that. Anyway, it caused them to turn into a mob. They thought they should be the self-appointed law. It could have turned ugly, but my wife said she wanted to stay with her people until it all blew over. I thought it was a good idea too, mostly for her protection. That was the biggest mistake of my life."

A dark cloud came over Ben's great-grandfather's face. He hung his head and said nothing for some time. Then he collected himself.

"She was gathering wood for her family. Some of the worst of the ruffians found her. It's enough to say she didn't live through it. I have never forgiven myself for not being there."

Ben wished he could think of something to say. Thoughts rushed through his mind, such as: *What happened to those guys; did they get hanged? Don't blame yourself. There was nothing you could do; and I am really, really sorry, Great-Grandpa.*

Nothing felt right, so Ben just waited. Suddenly the old man cast off his depression and his face returned to normal.

"It was a long time ago, Ben, and a lot has happened since. I can't change any of that. It's enough to say that those ruffians got caught, though not by me—which was fortunate for them. They went to jail someplace. They should have been hanged, but in those days killing an Indian didn't have the same weight as killing a white person."

Ben nodded but still said nothing.

"So, I just ran the store for several more years, and Little Flower was raised by her tribe. I visited her a lot, but I never really became the father I should have. She lived with her aunt and uncle. They became her parents, and I became the uncle. It worked out best that way."

Finally Ben spoke up.

"Papa, then your daughter Little Flower must have grown up to become the grandmother of my friend Lilly. She is from that same tribe. I have met her grandmother in her village. Lilly always said she was named after her. So I guess Lilly and I are cousins, right?"

The old man stared hard at Ben while his words slowly sank in.

"Papa," said Ben after some pause, "There were four of us that followed you down here. Didn't Abraham tell you?"

"Well, no, not exactly," he responded. "Abraham can be a bit vague though. What did he say exactly? It was something about some of my kinfolk coming down to see how I was doing. I never dreamed he meant my great-grandchildren, however. So are you saying I've got four great-grandchildren down here somewhere?"

"Well, yes, I suppose you do. You see, Patty, my little sister, came with us, along with our cousin Johnny. He brought Checker too."

"Checker?"

"Checker is Johnny's dog. I wasn't counting him as part of the four. The fourth one is Lilly, just like your Lilly. In fact, her real name is Little Flower too. "

"Now isn't that something?" Papa responded. Ben thought he noticed a little sparkle creep back into his eyes. "What does she look like, Ben? Is she pretty?"

Ben suddenly felt a bit awkward. He hadn't really thought about it much, or least he hadn't tried to think about it too much.

"Well, you know, she looks—well—well, she looks like a girl."

A slight scowl that could have been mistaken for a kind of smile came over Papa' face as he mused over the boy's response.

"What kind of answer is that? Of course she looks like a girl, but what does she look like? Does she have long hair? Is she tall? Is she skinny, or is she chubby? Is she pretty or plain? What do you think?"

Ben rubbed his feet together underwater and wished his great-grandfather could think of a different subject to talk about. Papa may have noticed that the pinkish-colored plants they were sitting next to seemed to take on a more brilliant hue. After a pause, still looking at his feet, Ben responded.

"Oh, I suppose she is kinda pretty…just a little, you know. She does have long, brown hair. She's not fat at all, but I wouldn't say skinny—maybe just slender. She also knows all about her tribe and their ancient customs. We try to follow them closely in the tribe we formed. But please don't tell her I told you about the tribe. She likes to keep that kind of stuff secret."

The old man reflected on this for a moment.

"I never thought about her still being there." He paused and then, with increased passion, continued, "I want to see her again. There are many people I want to see again." He added, "But no, Ben, Lilly wouldn't be your cousin. She would be more like a second cousin. Actually, more like a step-second cousin, if that exists. My daughter, Little Flower, was not your grandmother."

"I remember my grandmother, but she died several years ago. She talked about God and the Bible a lot. I probably should have listened more, but it seemed kind of boring then." Suddenly the memory of his vision on the cliff came back vividly. He realized he had nearly forgotten about it altogether. But his great-grandfather broke his train of thought.

"Yes, she was pretty religious. It was her mom's influence. A couple of years after my wife had been killed, a missionary family moved into the area. It was the best thing that had happened for a long time. They somehow brought the whites back into control. Maybe they were embarrassed to act badly with missionaries there. It wasn't long before a little church was built. Most people went to church in those days, even if they didn't really believe what was preached."

"Did you go too?" Ben asked.

"Of course. As I said, everyone went except the Indians. No one expected them to, and I think it might have been awkward if they had. The missionaries would have been okay with it, however. I was surprised that they went out to visit the tribe so often—but that's another story."

"What did the missionaries have to do with Grandma?" asked Ben, trying to keep his great-grandfather on some sort of track.

"Oh yes, I suppose you might be interested in that," he replied, with a slight twinkle in his eye. "Well, I got to be pretty good friends with them. I guess I went to church not just to hear the preaching but also because the preacher had—well, I guess you're old enough—his daughter was the prettiest girl I had ever seen. I was over twenty-five by then and she was still nineteen, but in those days, age wasn't such a big deal. She was the only thing that made me forget about my Little Flower. So you can probably put it together without me jawin' about all the details. We got married, and she became your great-grandmother. We were very involved with the church. I tried to take it seriously to keep her and her family happy, but I was mostly concerned about the store."

"I think I see what must have happened next," said Ben. "You then had a daughter, who became my grandmother."

"Almost," replied the old man. "We had a son, actually, and he is your grandpa. When he grew up, he married a girl from our church who had been taken in, so to speak, by my wife."

"Was she an orphan?"

"No, but sometimes it seemed like it. Her parents didn't spend much time with her, and they abandoned her before she turned sixteen. We took her in, and she became as religious as your great-grandmother. My son married her. So—I think you probably know the rest of your family history."

Ben reflected on what his great-grandfather had been saying. It was a lot to take in all at once, but he was glad to have heard it. He looked back up at him, realizing that a significant part of the story was yet untold.

"But then why did you leave home and come here?" Ben regretted asking this as soon as the words left his mouth, for he saw that same look of pain come back over his great-grandfather's face. But as before, the cloud was fleeting, and he resumed his composure.

"Ben, the fact is that I lost her too but not due to evil men this time. She got sick. We don't know with what. It happened pretty fast. By the time we realized we needed a doctor, it was too late. Her family prayed for her, but it did no good. After she died, I became pretty bitter and decided that if God did exist, He sure didn't care much; and if he didn't, then what was the point in all that Christianity she believed in so deligently? Either way, it wasn't for me anymore."

Ben didn't reply for some time.

"So is that when you decided to come here?"

"Not right away. Your grandmother and grandfather had been married for a few years and even had had a baby—your dad, in fact. I didn't know this underground world existed then, so I just kept running the store with your grandfather. Eventually he was doing so well that I just took on the role of assistant. As your dad and your uncle, who was born just a year later, started getting older, they really didn't need me there. Of course, they never made me feel unneeded, but I knew it was time for me to withdraw. So I started exploring. I started with my old Indian friend who had adopted my daughter, Little Flower. She had been married for some time and had a family of her own."

"How long ago was this?" interrupted Ben.

"Hmm. You know, I really lose track of time down here. Perhaps your dad was about ten, maybe eleven."

"Well, I just turned fourteen, and my dad is thirty-six."

"Okay, so maybe this was about twenty-five years ago."

The old man paused and then added, "Oh, my—that's too long…much too long."

The old man hesitated for a while as if the years bogged down even the telling of his story. Soon enough he shrugged it off and resumed from where he left off.

"It wasn't too long after that when we discovered the whirlpool you fell down recently."

"Did the same thing happen to you as happened to us?"

"Not exactly. We found that same cave you did, but we noticed that the current was strong inside the cave, and that struck us as being strange. We explored the back of the cave with torches, staying close to the edge and away from the main current, and saw the whirlpool from a distance."

"I wish we had done that. We went back with only the light that came into the mouth of the cave—it was very dim near the whirlpool. We were sucked in before we knew what had hit us."

"Well, I had a few more years on you, and my partner was an expert explorer."

"Your partner?"

"Yes, I think I mentioned I was pretty good friends with the chief's son—you know, the one who took in my daughter. I think I mentioned we had become blood brothers."

"Yeah, but wouldn't he have been chief by that time?"

"Sure, he had been chief for a long time, but his son had grown up by then and had taken over most of the village leadership. So you might say, my friend and I were both retired. It was kind of fun to have an exploring partner, and we were still pretty strong in those days."

Ben's expression changed, as if he were starting to put everything together.

"Papa, was his name by any chance Great Bear?"

The old man looked surprised.

"And how on earth did you know that?" he asked.

"A few days before we came here, we found a hidden library in our house, and it was there that we found your old journal."

"Really!" exclaimed his great-grandfather. "I would like to see that again. Strange things were happening about that time…But what do you mean about a secret library? I didn't have any secret library. I had a number of books, but I kept them in my bedroom, in plain sight for anyone to see."

"I don't think you could have fit them all into your room, Papa, unless you had a different room from the one I thought was yours. It was pretty small. We had Johnny staying there when he came to visit."

"Hmm…I'll bet someone put a wall there. I wonder why? Well, no matter. You found my journal. That is good news. Anyway, getting back to the story: we decided to explore the whirlpool. This took a lot of thought, because we didn't know what we would find. We knew that we would never get out once we got in, unless we found another way. I think we both wanted a change or an adventure and decided to go for it. Pretty stupid, when I think about it now. You fell in by accident, but we did it deliberately."

"Go on, Papa! How did you do it?" urged Ben, growing more and more fascinated by his great-grandfather's story.

"We first wrote notes to our families, telling them we loved them and that we wanted a new adventure and not to look for us. I knew they would, but I had to tell them something. I knew I couldn't say anything before I left, or I'd never get away."

"I think I heard about that. Johnny's dad told him that the family looked for a long time, except the Indians said it was pointless."

"Probably Great Bear could explain it to his people. It would fit their culture better than ours. So one day we thought we had everything ready. We got ourselves food and other supplies that would keep for a long time, and some basic tools. Then we set out. Something happened on the way though that we didn't expect. We met an old man in the woods. He spoke strangely, but we could understand him. He knew all about us and said that our great-grand-children would follow us. We thought he was just crazy, but then he called us by our names. That stopped us short. So we talked to him for a while. We decided not to go that day after all but rather to think about it. I believe I mentioned him in my journal, if you got that far."

"Yeah, we did. Johnny really freaked when he read it. Got me up in the middle of the night to see it, and we got caught by Dad. But he was right: Lilly has to be Great Bear's great-grandchild, and Johnny, Patty, and I are yours."

The old man nodded and grew introspective.

"He said a lot of other stuff about heaven too, but I never want-ed to hear about anything religious in those days. His visit did make us more confident, however, and we departed a few days later."

"So how did you get down here?" Ben tried not to sound impatient.

"Well, we had previously attached ropes to some nearby boul-ders to try to lower ourselves through the whirlpool. That turned out to be pretty futile."

"Why? That seems like a great idea. You could lower yourselves down and pull yourselves back up."

"Don't you remember how hard that whirlpool hit you? Great Bear went first in his canoe, holding the rope. When the current started spinning the canoe, he jumped out, still holding the rope. But he got caught in the current and lost his grip almost immedi-ately. He and the canoe spun around together, making insanely tight circles. It was pure luck the canoe never hit him. An instant later, he and the canoe were sucked down into the swirling water. It was the most horrible thing I had ever seen. I immediately began to grieve, seeing what a ridiculously stupid idea this was and knowing I had almost certainly lost a dear friend.

"The next thing I did was the most frightening thing I have ever done. It would have been easier if I hadn't seen Great Bear go first.

I grabbed the rope, without the canoe, and swam to the whirlpool. I don't know why I even bothered with the rope, because I lost it pretty fast. All I remember is the ever tightening grip of twisting water—and the falling. I was sure I was going to be killed. I couldn't even think about what might lie below, the water was crushing me so. But you probably remember pretty much the same thing from when you fell."

"Yes, but I was in the canoe with Lilly. I remember the twisting and confusion, but then I blacked out. I don't know what happened after that."

"I think I do. I didn't get knocked out, but I hit the pool pretty hard. That is quite a drop, especially under pressure. I went down a long way but struggled back up. When I got to the surface, I saw Great Bear floating toward an opening in the cave where the water exited. He was face down. I was a pretty good swimmer in those days, so I caught him before he got very far, and I drug him to a nearby rock ledge. I had to force the water out of his lungs, but he was still alive and started to breathe again. It was a close call, and we were both very lucky."

"Lucky for sure," replied Ben. But the word *lucky* struck a chord. His mind shifted unexpectedly to the vision of his grandmother that he had when he had nearly fallen over the precipice. *Lucky*—somehow that word didn't sit right. All of this was too much for luck. *Impossible* might be a better word. How could his great-grandfather and Great Bear have survived? How could *he* have survived? How could he meet up with his great-grandfather after getting lost in an underground tunnel with a river rushing who knows where? How could Abraham be involved across four generations of his family? How could he be related to Lilly? Lilly. And Johnny. And Patty. What had happened to them? Had they survived? As he reflected on their fates, his continual sense of fear was suddenly replaced by confidence.

"Papa, this can't be luck. It makes no sense. There has to be purpose. It has to be what Grandma said to me in my vision, when I was knocked out on the cliff. This all couldn't happen without planning."

The old man reflected on his great grandson's words.

"Purpose…yes, purpose. I think you are right, Ben. Maybe I gave up on God too soon. Maybe He didn't give up on me."

The two of them pondered this silently. Again, Ben's thoughts returned to the vision of his grandmother on the cliff where he had nearly perished.

Renewing an Old Acquaintance

Ben's great-grandfather stood up, looked toward their path, and said, "A rest is good, but if we stay much longer, this is going to be a vacation. We'd better move on."

Picking up his backpack, Ben followed his lead, and the two proceeded on their journey.

They continued their strategy of following the river but avoided any signs of people. The river had been getting steadily closer to one side of the cavern. It would not be difficult to ford, but the villages clustered on the opposite side made travel there too risky. Suddenly they were stopped short: the village ahead spanned both sides and was connected by a bridge. In the village, men, women, and children—all with downcast expressions—were each busy, performing some toilsome task.

"They don't look real friendly," said Ben, in a hushed voice, as the two of them crouched behind a tree of sorts.

Ben's great-grandfather studied them for a moment and commented, "I would normally agree, but these people look more beaten down than dangerous. They look nervous. Look how they work—no one's talking except when they have to do some job. No one's smiling. Even the kids are doing the same jobs as the adults. Look how young that one is!"

Ben saw a young boy who could not be older than six. He was picking up stones from the main path and carrying them to a box, returning again and again to repeat the same task. Ben thought about what he would have been doing that age.

Certainly not spending all day carrying rocks, he thought.

Ben surveyed the area. On this side of the river, the village covered both sides of the road. It filled the entire area between the cavern wall and the river. The path they had been following led straight through the middle of the village, crossed the river over a bridge and proceeded through the rest of village on the far side.

Papa slowly shook his head.

"There is simply no way to avoid this town, Ben. No way around on either side. We're going to have to wait until things get less busy and then go straight through, I think."

"Should we wait until dark?" asked Ben.

His great-grandfather thought about this for a moment.

"Maybe," he finally replied. "But I wonder. We might get away with walking through like we own the place. These people look pretty beaten down, and I am not sure they are up to much of a fight. They might even ignore us if we don't run into the wrong person."

"Who would be the wrong person?"

"The local shaman or one of his helpers. There is a nasty religion here, Ben. I wouldn't doubt that these people are being oppressed by someone in that cult. You saw the masks—what did you think of them? They were made by those guys."

"Yeah, they do look pretty scary. These people actually resemble the masks, except they look scared rather than scary."

"Yep, that's exactly right. They pattern the masks' features from their own faces, and their religion keeps them in fear. That's why I wonder if we would be better off just walking through rather than trying to sneak through."

Both of them fell quiet, evaluating the town again and watching all the toilers. They continued their mundane tasks with no sign of joy, hope, or even life in their faces.

"Follow me!" the old man said suddenly. "Keep your head up like you own the place. Don't look at anyone. Just follow me, and we will see if we can't just walk straight through."

The two stepped confidently onto the road at a determined pace but without any appearance of being confronted. Ben's heart began pounding so hard that he was sure the people could hear it. They were well within view and heading straight to the central part of the village. It seemed like a crazy thing to do, but the strategy was working. For the most part, people let them pass without acknowledging their presence. A few, especially the younger ones, looked at them with surprised expressions but quickly averted their eyes and stayed out of their way.

As they arrived at the village center, Ben noticed that one of the huts was much larger than the others.

Probably the village chief, Ben thought.

He noticed that several masks were placed over the doorway, but these were not as gruesome as those he had seen in the cave. For one thing, the eyes of these masks did not follow you, as with the others.

Suddenly a young man emerged from the hut and looked directly at them. He did not have the downtrodden expression worn by the other villagers. He carried himself upright with pride and assurance but mixed with caution and observation. He looked directly at Ben, and the two held each other's gaze for a moment. Ben suddenly realized how dangerous this was and looked away, keeping his eyes fixed on the road ahead of them.

The bridge was not far ahead.

If only we can make it a little farther, we will soon be out of this village and away, Ben thought. They continued their steady and determined pace. People still ignored them, avoiding any glance in their direction. Ben felt that the bridge would prove impossible to reach. Everything inside him screamed out to run and get away, but he held fast to the plan, keeping a steady walk toward their goal. Finally they reached the bridge. No one hindered them as they ascended its gently sloping path upward, over the river. Ben wondered what it could be made of—perhaps these unusual, underground trees that looked and felt more like giant mushrooms?

Ben looked over the side of the bridge and saw the river, lazily passing underneath.

We're nearly at the middle, he thought.

But no sooner did he think it, the sound he dreaded most came to his ears—the sound of running feet and voices from behind. The urge to run was overwhelming, but without warning, his great-grandfather came to a stop and turned to face the intrusion. Ben did the same. His heart went to his throat as he saw the same proud and assured young man, accompanied by several others, running hard toward them. Each carried a spear. Ben and his great-grandfather held their position, watching them as they arrived. The men stopped in front of them and regarded Ben and his great-grandfather with an air more of curiosity than of confrontation.

The first young man, clearly their leader, spoke. There was no doubt that he was asking a question, but there was no hope of understanding him—at least not for Ben. Papa was trying to make out what had been said. Much to Ben's surprise, the old man uttered a one-word reply, and in response the younger man repeated himself—but much more slowly this time. Papa replied briefly, and the young villager nodded, gesturing with his spear to follow him.

"Let's go, Ben. I guess my plan didn't work, but it could be a lot worse."

They followed the young man back down the bridge, returning to the village. The others walked behind, making any hope of escape futile. Ben's heart fell to his stomach as they retraced their steps. Soon they turned from the path and approached the large hut.

If only I hadn't stared at that guy when he came out of the hut, Ben thought. *We might have been long gone.*

Their captor put up his hand, gesturing them to stop. The others motioned them to sit on some nearby stools while their leader ducked inside the hut. Ben watched the villagers, still performing their toilsome routines and occasionally stealing a glance in the direction of these newcomers. Some of the younger children ran up to get a better look, but they were quickly shooed away.

Hardly a minute had passed before their captor emerged from the hut. He gestured to Papa to come in. They both stood, but Ben quickly returned to his stool—only the old man was permitted to enter. Ben looked at his great-grandfather with apprehension.

"Don't worry, Ben. They could've killed us on the bridge if they'd wanted to. I'll be fine." Ben acquiesced but was not happy as Papa disappeared into the hut. For the first time since he had been on the river through the tunnel, Ben was overcome by a feeling of fear, despair, and abandonment. But then he remembered the vision of his grandmother.

"There must be a purpose," he said, half aloud.

The elder John Matheson managed to hide the apprehension he felt. He took a few steps inside and saw an old Indian huddled near a fire, facing away from the opening. The young man approached him with much deference and gently got his attention. The old Indian nodded to him and then turned to face his visitor. Each looked into the other's eyes. John was surprised to see a reaction in the old Indian's face but stunned to see him slowly rise to his feet and say quite clearly, "John—you are alive, after all!"

"Perhaps you will recognize me better if I take off some of this headdress," he continued, as he began to remove it. "Perhaps this will help," he added, bringing forth some worn-out clothes that clearly had not originated from below the surface of the earth.

"Great Bear!" exclaimed John. "I never dreamed of ever seeing you again! How on earth did you get here?"

"I should ask you the same question, along with a million others, but I am afraid it will have to wait. I am the elder chief in this village. This young brave will be chief when I am gone. His name is Light Foot. It is a truly long story, and it will have to wait. I need to tell you something more urgent."

Light Foot brought up stools for the old men, treating them both with great respect. He then began to withdraw, but Great Bear motioned him to stay and nodded, granting him permission to speak. After a moment's delay, Light Foot gathered himself and spoke.

"My father, Great Bear, has taught me some of the new speech. I welcome you to our village."

"Thank you," replied John. "Your speech is very good."

Light Foot looked pleased.

"John," continued Great Bear, "We have little time to lose. Light Foot told me that just yesterday a group of warriors from the head village came through. They had three captives, a boy and two girls. The prisoners were not being mistreated, but they were being taken to the head village, and that is not good. All the villages down here are under the bondage of a wicked shaman and his son. They have many warriors in their home village. The children were being held not by the warriors but by the chief's son, which is a good thing. He is a good man."

"I am traveling with my great-grandson, Ben," John interjected. "I am sure that the others are also my grandchildren, based on what Ben has told me."

"Interesting," replied Great Bear. "No, this is more than interesting—it is very significant. You see, there is a widely held belief that an old man, accompanied by four children, will come in the last days and lead all who will follow him out of this underground world. You fit the part perfectly. Everyone can see it. But there is more to this prophecy that most people don't know: the coming of the four marks the end to an evil leader who holds the people in bondage. Most people don't know this, but the shaman certainly does. So does the main village chief."

"Are they both evil?"

"No, just the shaman and his son. The masks you see everywhere are required to be put up in key locations. We had to have some on our hut, but I tried to make them less gruesome—which would normally have gotten me into trouble, but I still have some influence."

"Why are the masks so important?"

"The people are taught, and they believe, that the shaman and his son see through them. Have you noticed how they seem to look at you as you walk by?"

"Yes, but that's nothing new. I've seen other artwork that does the same thing."

"But it was new to these people. They had never seen anything like that until it was introduced, maybe ten years ago. At first they were told the masks were there to protect the people, but that pretense didn't last long. The masks started seeing people when they broke rules, and they got taken away. At first they were only punished, but lately they have been taken and never seen again."

"So the shaman must have spies that report back to him," John observed.

"Exactly. It is impossible to tell who is working for him, but when they are reported, the people believe they were caught through the masks. That is why I had mine made so that the eyes don't follow you. It does give the people some relief, but still they fear them."

"So why don't you tear them down?"

"I may have influence, but not that much. I would disappear pretty quickly, and one of his henchmen would take over as village chief."

Both men became quiet and introspective. Light Foot approached Great Bear and spoke a few words, to which Great Bear nodded. At this, Light Foot left the hut, only to return with Ben, who looked quite anxious.

"Ben, I'm glad you're here," said his great-grandfather. "Much to my joy, my plan to walk through this village did not succeed, because now I've been reunited with a very old friend. This is my traveling companion and brother-in-law, Great Bear. I spoke of him to you earlier. I am overwhelmed that he is still alive and that we can see each other again."

Ben had trouble taking this in. It all seemed impossible. Yet he kept sensing a feeling of destiny: so many impossible things had already happened, and this was yet another. Destiny? That sounded much the same as *lucky*. Planned? That sounded more like it. His mind raced back to the vision on the cliff and the parting words of Abraham: a *narrow way* and *the lamb*. What did they mean? They just didn't seem to fit anything.

The old man interrupted his thoughts.

"Ben, Great Bear tells me that the shaman and his son in the main village are evil and very dangerous. They are responsible for all these masks and use them to intimidate the people who are convinced that the shaman and his son watch them by using the masks. Probably he uses spies in all the villages to keep him informed about "unacceptable" behavior. People "seen" by these masks are taken away and never return. All the villages live in a state of fear."

"Why would anyone do that?" asked Ben.

"The world has always had power-mad people. This is just another despot wanting to control others. But that's not all. There is a belief among the villagers that an old—well, let's say very mature—individual accompanied by four young people will bring an end to this little dictator and free all the people from their underground world."

"Some of the people," corrected Great Bear. The Indian word actually is best translated as *remnant*. Not all will be rescued."

With these words they fell silent, each pondering the significance of the ancient prophecy. For Ben, something about it felt both right and wrong. The accuracy was unnerving. So was the threat of the evil shaman. But what about Abraham? What about the vision of his grandmother? What about the "lamb" and the "narrow way"?

"Great Bear," said Ben, interrupting the pensive mood that had overtaken them, "does the prophecy say anything about an angel?"

"An angel?" asked Great Bear.

"Well, maybe an unusual man, also old. Or maybe a powerful person who seemed ageless?"

"An ageless, powerful man you say," Great Bear replied thoughtfully. "I am not sure, but I am not an expert on the details of the prophecy."

"He's referring to the man we saw in the woods years ago, before we came here," interjected Papa.

They could see Great Bear straining his mind back to another world, when he lived under the sun. Then he remembered.

"Oh, yes. I had completely forgotten about him. Why does he come into this at all?"

John Matheson told his old friend of all that had transpired, including the various appearances of Abraham. Great Bear looked very sobered, even disturbed, by the account.

"This is not one of our ancestors. He sounds powerful—clearly one of the gods. But I am not familiar with his manner. He is not of our people. I fear he may be one of the shaman's demons.

"No, I'm sure he's not a demon," said Ben. "He's been too much of a guide. I don't think we would be here now if he had not helped. But tell me one more thing: does the prophecy say anything about a 'narrow way'?"

"A narrow way," mused Great Bear. "No, not a narrow way. It does say that the four youths will lead the remnant on an 'unknown way.' It is interesting that you ask, because the prophecy does not use our word for *path* or *road* or *trail*. The word 'way' is used, and it can mean *path* or *manner* or even *philosophy*. It has deeper meaning than just 'path.' One cannot be sure which meaning applies. All three could make sense, and it is hard to tell how to interpret that part of the prophecy. "

"I wonder," reflected Papa. "Could it mean all three?"

With this, Great Bear stood up. "It is time. We must rouse the people," he declared, as he began to move toward the door of the hut.

John reached out, putting his hand on the old chief's shoulder and gently restraining him.

"My old friend, you are certainly right. But let's plan this first. If you rouse the people, you cannot turn back. None of us can. We know the shaman has spies. Once we play our hand, we must move quickly and decisively, or we will not survive."

The old chief sat back down and nodded.

"So, what do you suggest?"

"I have the beginning of an idea, though I doubt any of us can see the end clearly. Do you have any closely trusted friends in the village, ones who would surely not betray us?"

"There are some we suspect we cannot trust. Others are so frightened that they would not be reliable, unless they were sure it was not a trap. However, there is another group."

Great Bear turned to Light Foot, who had been following the conversation intently, though with difficulty. The two spoke briefly, and then Light Foot quickly stood up and left the hut.

"There is a group of young men in this village who are dedicated to him," explained Great Bear, as Light Foot departed. "By rights, Light Foot should be chief now. His father was the chief but was among those who mysteriously disappeared several years ago. However, it would be impossible for Light Foot to take over the village without interference from the shaman. We have only been waiting for an opportunity. In truth, I am merely an advisor."

"Where is he going?" asked Ben.

"He has gone to tell his most trusted friends what has happened. Many villagers saw you, and we have already used up precious time. Light Foot and his friends will set up guards around the village. No one will enter or leave without their knowledge. If someone has already left for the main village, they will know."

"So let's make a plan," interjected John. "I agree, we have little time."

Confrontation

Johnny was getting anxious. They had been camped at the gate of the main village for hours, with no sign of change. Patty had fallen asleep. Lilly was biding her time, being annoyingly patient, and Ojibwan was conferring with his leaders, with little sign of moving on.

"Calm down," said Lilly. "Everything is under control."

"But why do we just sit here? And what happened to those scouts?" Johnny surprised himself at his own impatience.

Ojibwan was roused by his voice and moved toward them. He spoke slowly but deliberately to Lilly and then sat down, waiting for her to translate.

"Ojibwan says there's a rule that no one can enter the village without specific approval by the chief. Since his father *is* the chief, there's not much risk of being refused. The rule also says he's allowed to send only one herald to announce that we're at the gate, and then he must wait for the invitation to enter the city."

"But he must have sent at least three men in there," replied Johnny.

Ojibwan smiled, perceiving Johnny's question, and provided more explanation. Lilly looked momentarily humored but quickly regained her serious composure and translated again.

"You saw three. Well, so did I, for that matter. But there were actually six. The three we saw consisted of his herald and two escorts, who will pretend to hide from view as they enter the village center. They will be caught and disciplined. The other three entered by a different route unknown to the shaman and his son. They will keep an eye on the entire process from a distance."

"I don't get it," reflected Johnny. "Why all this sneaking around, especially since Ojibwan is the chief's son? And why aren't we at risk, staying in plain view? It seems to me we're sitting ducks right here."

"The shaman and his son are dangerous, but they're not completely in control. They can't hurt Ojibwan, at least not yet. They know where we are, and Ojibwan knows that. So by staying here, we cause no alarm. The shaman expects Ojibwan to send someone to spy on the village. The two escorts will make it look believable when they get caught. That will protect the other three. The shaman's son will believe he outsmarted Ojibwan and be proud. He is already too proud. It will be his downfall."

Reflecting on this, Johnny was filled with admiration. He slowly nodded his head.

"I see. I also see this is a very dangerous place."

Johnny looked back at Patty, who was petting Checker's head and talking to him. A renewed sense of responsibility came over him. Ojibwan was their best protection at the moment, but how could he allow his young cousin to enter this trap?

Sensing his thoughts, Lilly responded, "Johnny, I think things are going to be okay. We need to be careful; but even more, we need to follow Ojibwan's leadership. He is our best chance of making it through this."

Johnny nodded. He turned to Ojibwan and gave him a nod too, before sitting down next to Patty and Checker.

"Hey, boy," Johnny said to his dog, stroking the dog's head together with Patty. "I haven't been paying much attention to you lately, have I?"

But Checker seemed completely content, willing to forgive and forget whatever he was presumed to have suffered. Patty joined

Johnny in rubbing Checker's ear. If there *was* tension in this waiting game, Checker did not react to it, being quite content to receive an unprecedented amount of attention.

Without raising her eyes from the dog, Patty spoke deliberately to her cousin.

"Johnny, do you think we'll ever get home?"

Johnny was surprised at the calmness and increased maturity in her tone. She did not sound like the little girl she had been just a few days earlier.

Was it days or weeks? Johnny thought. It was hard to remember a time when they were not in this underground world.

"Johnny?" repeated Patty, wondering at his lack of response.

"Yes, Patty, I do think we'll get out. And I'm also sure we'll see Ben again. There's too much that has been planned for us not to see it to the end."

"Planned?"

"Yes, planned. Too many impossible things have already happened. Abraham made it clear that something is predestined. I don't know what, but I think he's trying to tell us that God has a plan. I don't understand it, but I'm beginning to believe it."

"I believe it too, Johnny," replied Patty.

Lilly said nothing.

Suddenly the camp stirred. Ojibwan had risen and was mobilizing his men. Johnny, Lilly, and Patty joined the group and saw a large procession of armed warriors heading toward them. Two men, their hands tied behind them, were being driven harshly by the leader. A sinking feeling came to Johnny's stomach when he saw that the leader was the shaman's son himself and that the two men were the spies that had been sent in earlier. But then he noticed that there were only two—the other three that Lilly had mentioned were not there.

The shaman's men were all dressed in hideous attire, each having as a symbol on their chest the central mask at the gate. Many took positions at each side of the road, drawing their bows and aiming toward Ojibwan and his men. Ojibwan did not flinch, and his men stood by him. The shaman's son walked up to Ojibwan and recited his memorized speech. After he finished, Ojibwan walked by him without responding and went up to the two captured men, who had been shoved onto the ground. Immediately Ojibwan pulled out his knife, cut their bonds, and helped them to their feet despite a stream of loud objections. Johnny surveyed the area and noticed that Ojibwan's men had taken positions, bows drawn and pointed at the shaman's son.

Ojibwan looked at the opposing men. Johnny followed his gaze and saw confusion and fear in their eyes. Then Ojibwan spoke a single word, quietly but with authority. A tense moment passed. Slowly, each man lowered his bow. The shaman's son was beside himself with rage but clearly did not have the support he expected. Ojibwan spoke again, and his own men lowered their weapons as well. With one more word from Ojibwan, both groups began to walk toward the central village. At first the young shaman stared at the procession in disbelief, rapidly consumed by rage. Running at Ojibwan with his knife extended, he ended up flat on the ground, thanks to a quick strike from the butt end of Ojibwan's spear. The procession moved on, continuing to ignore this enraged false leader. Sprawled on the ground, he shouted an unintelligible venomous threat at Ojibwan, who ignored him altogether and continued to head toward the main village. Soon he was out of view. The shaman's escorts had abandoned him in favor of Ojibwan and they joined Ojibwan's men, together proceeding to the village square.

"I can't believe what I saw," Johnny said to Lilly, after he recovered enough to speak. Lilly said nothing in reply, but her eyes were full of pride and admiration.

The entourage had swelled to twice its original size, thanks to the shaman's men, and soon arrived at the main square. A number of guards protected the central hut, but they looked confused and nervous, remaining motionless. The door of the hut opened, and an old man emerged. He looked across at Ojibwan, and his face lit up. Ojibwan ran up to him and knelt down before him in respect. The guard looked increasingly nervous, as if something were amiss, but did nothing. Father and son were reunited.

The old chief beckoned his son to rise, which he did. As the chief began to move away from the hut, Ojibwan became confused yet followed his father without a word. The two sat at a nearby fire and began to talk quietly.

"Don't look at them," Lilly said to Johnny. "See how everyone looks somewhere else?"

Johnny obeyed. Patty was already sitting down, returning her attention to Checker, who seemed at peace with the world.

"Don't worry Checker," said Patty. "I know this is very tiresome, but it will end soon enough, and then we'll go back home."

Checker thumped his tail in agreement but turned his ear closer to Patty, who had stopped rubbing it while she spoke. Checker didn't stay interested in his ear for long. Instead, he perked up, looking intently at one of the nearby huts. Without making a sound, he got up and trotted toward it. Patty followed him with her eyes but was reluctant to repeat the earlier scene.

"Fine," she said. "If he doesn't like me petting his ear, I guess I won't bother." She returned her attention to Ojibwan and the elderly chief.

All eyes had now turned to the two leaders, despite Lilly's warning. Ojibwan listened without speaking, only occasionally nodding his head in agreement as his father spoke. This went on for what seemed like hours. Finally the old man rose, followed by his son. As soon as they stood up, a commotion of yelling intermixed with growling and barking broke the silence. Ojibwan nodded to several of his men, and they ran to one of the smaller huts to discover the source of the noise. Everyone could see an agitated struggle between a dog and a man. The dog growled threateningly through bared teeth, positioned on top of a man and pinning him helplessly to the ground. To Johnny's horror, he realized it was Checker!

Johnny rushed to the scene, calling to his dog. Checker refused to be coaxed, and he continued threatening the man on the ground. Several men arrived and were prepared to shoot the dog, but they hesitated due to Johnny's plea. When Ojibwan arrived he surveyed the situation, and then burst out laughing. He gave some orders to his men, who looked uncomfortable as they gingerly approached the dog. Perceiving their intent, Johnny stroked his dog's head and was able to coax him away. But as the dog moved, what appeared to be a crossbow fell to the ground between the man and the dog. The man was the shaman's son.

Ojibwan, no longer laughing, picked it up and looked at him. He asked him a question. In response, the shaman's son stood up, scowled, and started to walk away. Then, with a nod from Ojibwan, several men blocked his path. With renewed rage, he shouted at Ojibwan. Lilly, comprehending his retort, winced slightly. The debate going on in Ojibwan's mind could not be perceived from his expression, though the time he spent at it made Johnny nervous. Finally, in carefully measured tones, he uttered one word, and they released the shaman's son. As if freeing himself, he shrugged off his captors and, with a sneer, cast a final insult to Ojibwan and turned to leave. Then, witnessed only by Lilly, Ojibwan glanced up to a nearby hillside and nodded imperceptibly. Following his glance, Lilly thought she saw a slight movement of brush on the hill; but then all was still.

Ojibwan turned back to where he had left his father, hesitating as he spoke momentarily to Lilly. Lilly turned to Johnny and Patty.

"Ojibwan wants us to meet his father," she said. "It is a huge honor. We must go immediately."

"Bring Checker too," she added, turning to go.

Johnny was spent from the tension, but without questioning her, he turned to his dog.

"Come on, Checker. I don't know what this is all about, but at least we survived another close call."

Checker wagged his tail and sprang up.

"Don't look so proud of yourself. I'm surprised you didn't get us all killed."

But perhaps the tone in Johnny's voice didn't match his rebuke, because Checker jumped up to his master, placing his paws squarely on Johnny's chest and attempting to give him a very sloppy lick. Johnny was experienced in getting his face out of the dog's way in time and escaped from his dog, so instead, Checker nudged Patty to her feet, and the three of them followed Lilly.

As they arrived, the old chief studied the dog. Ojibwan reached down and stroked his back, and Checker approved. As Ojibwan found just the right spot, Checker's leg started to scratch his side involuntarily, and he began to make low, grunting sounds in appreciation. The old man burst out laughing and tried it himself. Checker, most diplomatically, continued his obvious doggy appreciation, greatly humoring the old man.

"He has never seen a dog before," commented Lilly in a low voice. The sound of her voice attracted the attention of the old chief, and he turned to Ojibwan, quizzing him about her. Lilly suddenly became quiet, regretting she had stepped out of her expected role.

After some discussion, Ojibwan spoke to her. She responded to him, but he gestured for her to talk directly to his father. Lilly looked surprised—and tense as well—but turned to the old man and began answering a number of questions. After some time, the conversation stopped, and Ojibwan resumed speaking with his father. He then turned to Lilly and gave her some instructions before addressing his men. At his summons, they all stood up, collected their belongings, and got ready to move on.

"So what was that all about?" Johnny asked, once he was safely alone with Lilly.

"The chief surprised me by talking directly to me. I am a woman, and not fully grown at that. It just is not done."

"Well, maybe their culture is a little different from yours," responded Johnny.

"I don't think so. Our tribes are closely related, otherwise I would not be able to understand their language. Their culture seems very much like what I heard from my own grandfather about our tribe long, long ago. My tribe would never allow a woman to speak directly to a man, especially the chief, unless..."

Lilly's voice trailed off as she pondered that thought.

"And?" queried Johnny, after it was clear she was not going to finish her thought.

"And nothing," retorted Lilly. "That's all. It just wouldn't happen."

Johnny decided it was best to let it be.

"It looks like everyone's ready to go. Where are Patty and my dog?"

They both surveyed the area. Patty and Checker sat together, to the side of the group. Lilly ran up to them to make sure that Patty was ready to leave. Johnny continued to survey the area as he made his way to them. He could not help noticing that many of the men were securing their knives inside their belts, out of sight.

Soon the entire group got up and began to assemble. Both chiefs, old and young took the lead together. Johnny, Lilly, and Patty—along with Checker—were escorted to the chief's entourage. Johnny noticed that the group had swollen considerably. Many among them were those who had come with the shaman's son.

The procession moved toward the village center. All three children could not help notice how intently the people they passed were staring. This would have been understandable, considering the size of the group, but their stares froze when they observed the three children and the dog. With each step, the group grew in numbers as many young men joined them. But others drew back in fear.

After a last bend in the path, they came to a wall. It was circular, with a diameter of perhaps seventy-five yards, and towered above them at least twenty feet. A single gate allowed entry, but it was guarded by fifty heavily armed soldiers, all dressed in red. A red eye was painted on each soldier's chest, much like those on the engraved faces they had seen many times. The guards blocked the gate, somewhat ritualistically. They appeared tense and nervous but would not move.

Ojibwan spoke to the leader of the guard—not in an unkindly way, but sternly. The head guard responded with a single word and did not move. Ojibwan spoke again, this time in a more cadenced tone, yet without raising his voice. The guard, clearly nervous, held his ground and said nothing. The old chief stepped forward and put his hand on the guard's spear, gently forcing it down. The guard hung his head and did not resist. The other guards followed his example, and the group began to enter, unobstructed. Before passing by, Ojibwan privately spoke a few words to the head guard, at which he brightened and stood at attention.

"I am sure we are entering a holy place," whispered Lilly to Johnny. "I think it is normally reserved only for the shaman, his son, and specially appointed people. This is a big thing we're doing."

Although the surrounding light was now failing, as was typical of this underworld's "evenings," a sparkling illumination continued to emanate from the center of the ring. When they got further in, getting a clear view, they saw water falling from a hole in the center of the roof. Light passed through the falling water, refracted into a million rainbows by ever moving prisms of watery drops. It fell into a basin, collected itself, and flowed under the floor to some unknown cavern.

A Turn for the Worse

The old chief led his entourage directly to the fountain, where he assembled his warriors, and they quickly took up a defensive posture. Calmly, the chief called to Lilly, motioning to Johnny and Patty as well. Without objection, Checker allowed himself to remain in the custody of one of the younger warriors, who was no older than Johnny himself. The old man, escorted by his son and the three children, stepped up to a dais. He seated himself, flanked by his son and Lilly. Just at this moment, hundreds of warriors dressed in red, each having a gruesome face painted on his chest stepped into view on a high ledge surrounding the waterfall. Each one fitted an arrow into his bow, and aimed at a specific target. Many arrows were directed toward the chief and his son as well as at Johnny, Lilly, and Patty. In turn, the chief's men had arrows trained on the menacing warriors as well. The ensuing silence was deafening.

The old chief was undisturbed. He simply sat, looking out over the fountain, consumed in thought. Johnny was amazed at his calmness, each of them moments from certain death. Ojibwan remained motionless, save to survey the men on the ledge and his own as well.

Lilly reached for Patty's hand, whispering, "Please do not make a sound. We will be okay."

Remarkably, Patty remained calm, dropping her head and silently praying.

Then someone moved on the ledge. It was another very old man, hideously painted and dressed entirely in red. The face on his chest was the most terrifying of all. The old man seated himself in an ornately decorated chair. From behind, a younger man came alongside him and stood on his right. It was the shaman's son.

The two old men looked at each other for some time but said nothing. The shaman's son broke the silence. His words were foreign to Johnny and Patty, but no one could mistake the sinister tone and threatening manner. Ojibwan spoke quickly to Lilly and then turned to his father, requesting to represent them—to which the old chief nodded in consent.

"Ojibwan has asked me translate for you what they say. He wants you to understand everything. But he stresses how important it is that we do not move and that we say absolutely nothing," explained Lilly.

Both Johnny and Patty nodded.

The shaman's son took a steady breath and started his speech. Clearly, he had rehearsed his oratory well.

"My people," he began, "you all know how the gods gave us this world and the protection from outside enemies. Our holy writings tell how our people were led here by the god of the under earth, promising deliverance from those who wished to kill us. Look anywhere in our kingdom, and you will see the good things Morgothus provided: water, food, ability to make shelter and protection from evil. He gave us all we need and asked only that we follow his law— a law designed to protect us. But he also demanded our respect and made places of worship that cannot be defiled. Accordingly, he made two most holy places where only certain worshipers may go. One is where you now stand. Every one of you is breaking our law by bringing weapons where only my father and the defenders of the holy place are allowed. This passage you now defile is a forbidden path from our world to the overland. We use this place to honor Morgothus with our worship. It is he who protects us from the overlanders. The other holy place was the entry used by our forefathers when Morgothus first led them here. Both are forbidden to all except his priests.

"Several days ago, we were following our law by worshiping Morgothus in the holy entrance. This was in celebration of our holy day of beginning. We made the long trek to the crystal door and brought with us all preparations for our sacrifice, as required by our law. Following our ancient custom, the chief's son, who stands before you, was also present. But as we arrived, we discovered to our surprise, heathens, sons and daughters of our ancient enemies. They had discovered our holy door, so we sought to have them destroyed as our law requires. To my shock, the son of our chief forbade their death and commanded that we bring them here. Out of respect, we reluctantly obeyed him until an animal, clearly a spirit from the evil gods attacked us. These heathens, appearing as children, arranged this through hidden promptings forbidden by Morgothus. Do not be deceived by their disguise. Even now, they show themselves in the form of innocent children. I had no choice but to slay them before they could call down an evil spell upon us. But our own chief's son, bewitched by their enchantments, not only forbade it but attacked me as well, as can be seen by my injured hand."

He paused, showing his hand to his father, who removed the bandage and exposed an ugly wound. A murmur through the crowd interrupted what had been deathly silence during his speech. Ojibwan said nothing, and no change came over his face. He simply watched the shaman's son, who looked satisfied with his introduction and pleased with the response of the crowd.

"Faithful worshipers of Morgothus," he continued, energized by his apparent control over the people, "through no fault of your own you stand here today, defying the will of our great god and savior. Morgothus understands the deception that has occurred and will not punish even those of you who have set your face against him by opposing his priests. But now he will test your devotion to him by judging what you do next."

The shaman's son paused, gauging the effect of his words.

"This is not going well," whispered Lilly to Johnny.

"What should we do?" asked Johnny.

"Nothing—if you value your life. It is up to Ojibwan. Our fate rests with him. If he can sway the people, we have a chance. If not—well…I think I know of this Morgothus. We have teachings of good and evil. The Great Spirit is good, but an evil angel became bad and rebelled. We don't have the name Morgothus in our tradition, but he sounds more like the evil angel than the Great Spirit. If so, this people has been led by deception and fear. I don't understand how this could have happened."

Johnny could see a look of disappointment, almost disillusionment, as she expressed her thoughts. They all looked toward Ojibwan, who remained expressionless and said nothing—as if waiting for a call. But they quickly turned their attention back to the shaman's son as he resumed his monologue.

"My people," he continued. "*My people*," he repeated. For the first time, Ojibwan's expression darkened, as if a line had been crossed; but he said nothing. "My people, it is now time for action. Our chief and his son cannot violate our faith. By their action they forfeit their leadership of Morgothus's people. But in his mercy and forgiveness, he has offered them a path back to our fold. He has told me that if Ojibwan will show his loyalty and leadership by a single act, all will be restored to our previous order."

He turned and faced Ojibwan and spoke directly to him. "From Morgothus's own mouth, through me his mouthpiece, he offers this opportunity for your restitution and cleansing."

Pausing, he turned and pointed his staff at Johnny, Patty, Lilly and Checker.

"Kill these demons who falsely disguise themselves as children and as an animal. Kill them by your own hand in the presence of Morgothus's people. He will accept this as atonement for your sin and the sin of your father. Then, and only then, will our order be restored."

Johnny was stunned. Lilly remained unmoved. Patty looked confused.

Johnny could see that the effect of his words on the listeners was just what the shaman and his son had hoped for. The people looked relieved. All eyes turned to Ojibwan with looks of anticipation and hope that he might accept this offer of redemption from Morgothus by way of his priest.

Ojibwan stepped into the middle of the assembly but spoke directly to his rival.

"And how is it that you, while your father still lives, speak against our holy writings and claim to be the mouthpiece of Morgothus?"

Hearing this, the crowd seemed uncertain and murmured in hushed tones. But, as if on cue, the shaman's son turned and looked up at his father. The old man rose, drew out his staff, and held it as an offering to his son, who walked up to him and accepted it.

"So what's all that about?" Johnny whispered to Lilly.

"We have no such custom as this, but I think the shaman has just made a permanent transition, passing spiritual leadership to his son. This is unusual, since this generally occurs only at or near the death of a shaman."

Johnny looked at Ojibwan, who was watching the process with a steely gaze. His father had dropped his eyes, refusing to watch the process.

The young shaman held the staff above his head and addressed Ojibwan, as well as the entire assembly.

"I am the mouthpiece of Morgothus," he declared.

Another hush went through the assembly. The new shaman turned slowly to Ojibwan, and Johnny could see a wild glint in his eyes. His expression reminded Johnny of the many masks that surrounded the city. This was his hour, and with evil authority, he addressed Ojibwan once more.

"You try the patience of our god!" he shouted. "He gives you one last chance. Slay the demons now, or forfeit your place with Morgothus and his people!"

Johnny felt like a truck had slammed into him. His every nerve begged to flee, yet he was held in a kind of paralysis, helplessly waiting for what might befall them. He couldn't even look to see what Lilly was doing, though he sensed that she also seemed paralyzed. Patty alone was able to move, and she drew close to her cousin for protection, sensing things were becoming truly perilous.

Time stood still. No one spoke. All eyes moved between Ojibwan and the children, but the chief looked at no one. The tension was electrifying, but oddly enough, Ojibwan seemed immune. He looked somewhat sad yet mostly resolute. The young shaman allowed Ojibwan his time and said nothing, though he was eager to move to the next step. He was confident that he would prevail. After all, he was not the "young" shaman: he was the shaman. His father had passed the staff to him even though the elder man was in no danger of dying, something that had never occurred within the memory of the tribe. Clearly, he held their fate in the palm of his hand, and he would revel in the ultimate doom of his opponent. But that opponent showed no sign of fear. Contempt for the shaman and admiration for Ojibwan began to well up inside of Lilly.

Finally Ojibwan stirred and began to address the people.

"My people," he began, refusing even to acknowledge the shaman, "the prophecies speak of an event to come, which now has. Our holy writings tell us that we are not always to live in this world. It speaks of the coming of people from the outside, particularly children, who will guide us through a difficult and narrow path to a better life. It speaks of this happening during a time of great fear and oppression. It speaks of the need for courage in all the people, to resist the evil that would have them live in slavery with no hope. We all know that the faith promoted by this evil man has done just that."

The shaman's face flushed as he shouted, "Away with the blasphemer! He speaks blasphemies about our sacred writings! Do not listen!"

"Silence!" commanded Ojibwan with surprising strength. The new shaman was taken aback.

"Our law forbids you to interrupt the chief of this people."

This stopped him cold, for he had temporarily forgotten that Ojibwan was not yet the chief—his father had not ceded that position. But Ojibwan had regained control and continued.

"My people," he resumed. "Our new shaman has failed to reveal the rest of what the prophecies foretell. Our ancient writings do speak to us of these children, who will lead us to a new land. Now the prophecies are about to be fulfilled. We cannot destroy this gift that has come to us."

With this statement he stopped, giving the shaman an opportunity, which he quickly seized.

"The chief's son speaks falsely," he began. "He must necessarily speak falsely, since he represents himself as the chief when he is not. His father has not given up that position. Therefore, Morgothus does not give him wisdom or clear understanding of our holy writings. I will tell you what the prophecies say. Remember, our holy writings are always true; no part is false. So when they are fulfilled, they will come true in full and not just in part.

"Our ancient writings speak of four children, not three. They say nothing about a creature they would bring with them. More importantly, they speak of a very old man who comes with them. This old man, who has lived much longer than most men do, and the four children are guided by a spirit, holy and powerful. So, I ask this false leader: Where is this old man? Where is the fourth child? Most importantly, where is the guiding spirit?"

Ojibwan again spoke in reply. He still had the look of towering strength and confidence, but Lilly could see a hint of doubt and confusion in his expression.

"My people: what you have just heard is true. But because we do not see them all at this moment does not mean that the others are not on the way. I have been told through one of the three children here that another boy was with them and has been separated from the group. We all know of the rumor that a very old man lurks somewhere in our caves. He may be waiting for the right moment to appear. And last of all"—here he hesitated, choosing his words carefully but perhaps revealing a trace of doubt—"last of all," he repeated, "I have seen this guiding spirit myself."

A great murmur arose among the people. Ojibwan's speech had gone well but now took an unexpected turn. The shaman contained his elation as he again took control of the debate.

"As you can see, our self-styled chief is presenting a transparent lie. We all know that the ancient writings make it very clear that only the people's spiritual leader can see and commune with Morgothus. Praise to Morgothus, who put a stumbling block into the mouth of this pretender so that we would not be deceived!"

"I did not see Morgothus!" Ojibwan shouted. "It was not Morgothus who showed himself as the guiding spirit."

Another murmur rose from the crowd, this one even more alarming than before. The shaman lost no time in turning to Ojibwan and addressing him directly.

"This is enough! By your own mouth, you have been communing with demons! You may have spoken your last words, yet for reasons beyond my understanding, Morgothus is patient and forgiving. He has told me he will yet restore you if you show your adoration for him by performing his sacrifice. Kill the demons before us! Do it now, and show the people and Morgothus himself that you are still one of us!"

Most of the crowd looked hopeful. Even though they loved their chief's son, such words could not be tolerated. A sense of gratitude came over them as they saw their new shaman as merciful, reflecting the apparent mercy of Morgothus. Certainly Ojibwan would recognize their god's truth, wisdom, and mercy. Certainly he would re-join his people and destroy these demons in disguise. Yet, some of the crowd looked doubtful, as if something behind the words of their new shaman did not ring true. He detected this division and knew that the drama must soon come to an end.

Ojibwan spoke again, with steady determination in his voice.

"I will not slay these children—children that are part of the prophecy. I forbid anyone to do so. Anyone who so much as threatens them puts his own life in jeopardy. I will wait for the prophecy to be fulfilled. I will await the coming of the other boy and the old sojourner from among our caves. I will trust the true guiding spirit and not Morgothus, whom I now see as evil."

The old chief, who had remained silent and expressionless throughout the debate, now groaned. His head sank and his shoulders sagged. But few noticed him as the crowd rose with one accord, shouting angrily, and could not be calmed until, after a significant pause, the young shaman held up his staff and silence was restored. With perfect timing, so as to maximize the intensity of the event, he turned to Ojibwan and stared at him for several moments. Then he turned to his private guards and addressed them.

"If Ojibwan has chosen the path of blasphemy, then we must fulfill his duty. I command you now. Slay these demons in my presence."

To the continued shock of Johnny, Lilly, and Patty, three of his guards fitted arrows to their bows and aimed squarely at their hearts. But before they could release their arrows, the guards suddenly collapsed, each of them felled by an arrow through the chest. Their own arrows streaked through the air, wildly off target. The entire assembly, including the shaman and his father, looked for the source of the attack. Positioned in a rock formation high above the crowd, three soldiers were rapidly fitting new arrows into their bows. They took aim at the shaman himself but held their fire, waiting for Ojibwan's command.

"I think I recognize those men," Johnny managed to whisper to Lilly, even though his heart had leaped into his throat. "They were in our party, I'm sure."

"Yes," replied Lilly. "Those were the three scouts that Ojibwan sent ahead in secret. Remember, he sent three to observe, with two pretending to go in secret. But these three are his best scouts and most loyal subjects."

The crowd was now in an uproar. The shaman recognized his peril. Nevertheless, he again raised his staff to calm the people. Others rushed to help the wounded guards. As the crowd became quiet, he turned to Ojibwan with suppressed rage in his eyes.

"You continue to show your betrayal of your people. You not only protect demons; you blaspheme Morgothus. And you now attempt to kill the loyal and faithful of our people. Morgothus has told me you have refused his last offer. No more forgiveness may be extended to you; you have sealed your own fate. You may have archers in place, but three cannot stand up against a united people. You may kill some, but you cannot kill all. You have a debt to this people. Since you will not obey, we must do this for you. The children's lives are forfeit. The law forbids us from killing you ourselves, but Morgothus will see that justice is done.

"Morgothus has commanded me to seize these demons now. It may be my last command, but either upon my death or upon my word, I will command the faithful with one accord to seize the demons and kill them. You can only add to your sin by resisting and killing your own people. Or you can obey. The choice is yours."

A tense and silent standoff resulted. Fifty of the shaman's faithful now stood poised, ready to attack Ojibwan's archers. The shaman continued to stare condescendingly at Ojibwan, who surveyed his men and the crowd at large—certainly there would be a horrible bloodbath in a few moments. But then he spoke, and what he said shocked all.

"I invoke my right for substitution!" he cried.

He sat down silently in the center of the assembly. All looked confused, except for the old shaman and Ojibwan's father, who kept his head down. The elder shaman called for his son and spoke to him in a low tone for some time. Then he straightened up and addressed the assembly himself.

"The son of our chief has exercised his right to substitution," the old shaman declared. "Our holy writings allow a member of our tribe to substitute himself in the punishment of another. This act results in his death. The sacred writings say that he who chooses to do this is given three days of consideration. At the end of that period, if he chooses to exercise his right, he will be shot with a dozen arrows in place of these foreigners."

Lilly had ceased translating, so Johnny and Patty did not understand what had just transpired, but they were surprised to see both the shaman and Ojibwan motion to their own followers, and the standoff quickly dissipated. Lilly turned her head suddenly and moved away. The old chief sat where he was, staring into the distance. No one disturbed him. It was Ojibwan himself who came up to Johnny and Patty, motioning them to follow. He took them to the central hut of the village, which belonged to the chief and his family.

The hut had many rooms. One was given to Johnny, who was allowed to keep Checker with him and another to Lilly and Patty. Checker was the only one of the party that seemed to be in a bright mood, interested in exploring every nook and cranny of this unusual residence. Johnny sat down, and Checker came to him quickly—expecting his ear to be scratched. Johnny obliged.

"I don't get it, Checker. I thought we were about to be killed. Ojibwan makes one last statement, and everything calms down like there was never any problem at all. But our side looks a lot sadder than the shaman's side, so something was agreed to that was not good. Lilly knows what's happening, but it seems like she's not ready to talk about it."

It wasn't clear whether Checker was following all this, but he did think it was time to flip over on his back and continue this attention to his stomach. Johnny cooperated, much to the satisfaction of the dog.

Darkness before Dawn

Johnny found himself alone in his quarters, lost in thought. Everything was a mess. Ojibwan was unapproachable except by Lilly, who was no longer sharing anything. Patty was asleep, and so was Checker. Johnny felt entirely alone. He looked out a window and saw the land surrounding the village. It offered such a contradiction between beauty and oppression. The fields were full of strange plants resembling oversized vegetables of unknown origin. The natural architecture surrounding the fields surpassed that of the castles and cathedrals of Europe, yet the village inhabitants were a forlorn people without hope or purpose—enslaved. Johnny wondered how, with such abundant resources, the people could have created a prison for themselves and their descendants. But then, was it so different from his own world?

Turning away from this view, he saw Lilly studying him. He wondered how long she had been in his room, but before he could inquire, she broke the silence.

"I'm sorry to disturb you, but I thought you should know what has happened," she offered.

Johnny nodded, offering her his full attention.

Lilly paused for a moment, clearly struggling with her emotions and showing a side of herself that Johnny had not yet witnessed. Then, finding it easier to move her gaze to Checker, she gathered herself together and began to speak.

"This people…my people…have strong beliefs. I think they are good beliefs, but they can be bent. Part of my people's belief is that there are two main forces in the world and in the heavens. Both forces are powerful beings. One is good and one is not. The good one made all we see and feel and touch. He made us and also the heavenly beings. But one of those heavenly beings rebelled and became evil.

"The people who live in this great underworld kingdom became separated from our people many years ago—maybe two hundred years ago, but I'm not sure. While they lived here, their beliefs changed; they confused the good one with the evil one, whom they call Morgothus. I had never heard of that name, but I am sure from what I've heard that he is the evil one, even though the people here think he is the creator. They worship him and fear him greatly. The shaman and his son have used this to their advantage, and they are believed to be priests who connect the people to Morgothus.

"Ojibwan broke the law when he brought us to this city, and bringing us to one of the holy places was unforgivable. The shaman made that clear to everyone, and all are fearful of Morgothus's wrath. Only Ojibwan's most loyal soldiers will stay with him if the people believe he has committed blasphemy.

"The shaman's son was very shrewd and offered forgiveness, supposedly from Morgothus, only if Ojibwan would kill us. This brought hope to the people, because they do love their chief and Ojibwan. But he refused. He went even further than that. The only way he can protect our lives is by offering his own, which is what he has done. He has three days to prepare himself, and after that he will be brought back to where we were earlier and will be killed by a dozen archers.

Lilly suddenly burst into tears.

Johnny hung his head, unsure how to console her, but then slowly took her hand as Lilly brought herself back under control.

"He thinks this will save us, but the shaman is not trustworthy. I know he will find a way to kill us too."

"But why?" asked Johnny. "What have we done that is so terrible?"

"It's the prophecy. The shaman feels threatened by the prophecy, which says that four young people from a land on the earth's surface will meet an old man in the sacred city and in its holy place. When this happens, the people will be freed from this underground world and from an evil tyrant; they will then return to the surface. He's not sure whether there really is a fourth one of us, but if there is, he sees that as a threat to his power. He has fallen in love with power."

"But Lilly, I don't see how that can work. We might find Ben, but what about the old man? It seems like people would believe the prophecy had been fulfilled only if the entire prediction had come true."

"Yes, that's true," responded Lilly. "But what about that old man you said you saw several times? I think you called him Abraham. What about him?"

"That's definitely a long shot," he replied.

Johnny looked down at the Bible, thinking silently to himself, *The Bible has prophecies. The Indians have prophecies. Which are true? How could I possibly be part of a prophecy? And Abraham? That is pushing things.*

"I don't know," Johnny continued. "Somehow I don't think Abraham fits the prophecy very well."

Johnny paused, becoming more introspective.

"Lilly?"

She regarded him with silent anticipation.

"Patty and I have been talking and remembering things our grandmother taught us. She was very sure that God is really the one in charge. God is the One that did the creating, not this Morgothus. Patty and I have been reading some of Great-Grandpa's Bible, and it talks about Him—how He created everything and everything was good. It also talks about an evil one who rebelled against God and started all the human misery. I don't know much about your history, but it seems to me that God would love all people. Perhaps He provided for your people and mine as well—until we might find the truth that's the same for all people. Lilly, this Bible is not really mine. It was not written by white people at all. But I am sure God provided it so we might know Him the way He wants to be known."

Johnny was surprised at what he had said, since he had felt pretty confused, but Lilly was silent and reflective. They sat together for some time, saying nothing, until Lilly finally broke the silence with a sigh.

"Johnny, we really need to do something. We can't just let them kill us. We must find Ojibwan. Lilly jumped up suddenly and departed. Johnny started out after her, calling for her to wait. She turned only once, saying, "Let me talk to him alone for a while. Please stay here. I'll come back later."

Johnny stared after her as Lilly disappeared out of the house, and an overwhelming sense of hopelessness came over him. There was nothing—absolutely nothing—he could do to change anything.

"I wish I had never come here," he murmured to himself. "What were we thinking, going into that cave under the waterfall? There's nothing good about this place. Everything has gone wrong. Ben is lost, most likely forever. We've solved no mystery. We've upset the entire culture of this underground world, and we'll probably cause the death of the chief's son as well as our own."

Johnny felt despair take hold of him, which was unusual. He generally tried to solve his own problems. His thoughts drifted back to his grandmother—how had she put it? Something about trusting God for the big and little. He had always assumed that was just what grandmothers say, but what if…?

His eye caught sight of the Bible once again. He recalled the unusual manner in that he had obtained it and Ojibwan's interest in it. He thought how Patty simply trusted everything their grandmother had told her; but of course, she was too young to know anything, really. He opened the Bible, intending to return to the passage in John that he had read when Abraham first gave it to him. Suddenly, a previously unnoticed bookmark guided him instead to the seventh chapter of Matthew. Much to his wonder, he saw the following underlined verse:

Enter ye in by the narrow gate: for wide is the gate, and broad is the way, that leadeth to destruction, and many are they that enter in thereby. For narrow is the gate, and straitened the way, that leadeth unto life, and few are they that find it.

Didn't Abraham say something about that? But what does it mean? He read further but could not make sense of the following passages. Leaving the bookmark where he had found it, he turned back to John.

Johnny read and read and read, unable to stop. He read of Jesus's teachings to disciples—how they often had trouble understanding what he had said and yet would make tremendous statements of faith. He was astounded at the miracles—from making wine to calming the sea to raising the dead. How could this be?

He was appalled by the friend's betrayal, which led to Jesus's arrest, and by the denial of Peter, who had promised with such passion that he would never do such a thing. And then the darkness of the execution of this One, sent from God: the humiliation, the beatings, and the cruel crucifixion. Johnny paused. That darkness was greater than anything he was currently experiencing. The unfairness far exceeded any cruelty this underground world could bring.

Johnny read of the grief of Jesus' friends after His body was taken down from the cross and placed into another man's tomb. He felt the hopelessness of the disciples as they gathered together without the One in whom they had put all hope. Even Peter had just wanted to go back to fishing. He had no other hope.

But then women had gone to the tomb and found angels instead of Roman guards. The tomb was empty. Peter and another disciple raced to the tomb and found the same thing. Later, Jesus appeared to them several times—even once to Thomas, who had been unable to believe the testimony of his friends and who was humbled when Jesus showed him his wounds as proof of who He was. Finally there was a special appearance of Jesus before Peter, restoring him from his denial by having him declare his love for his master the same number of times he had denied Him.

Johnny paused and wondered. Would he be like Thomas, who could not believe the testimony of others, or would he be one of the "more blessed" ones that Jesus spoke of—who would believe without seeing? Glancing at the Bible, he saw faint writing that simply said, "Romans 10:9-10." Johnny searched hard, wondering where this might be, finding it finally:

> ...*if thou shalt confess with thy mouth the Lord Jesus, and shalt believe in thine heart that God hath raised him from the dead, thou shalt be saved. For with the heart man believeth unto righteousness; and with the mouth confession is made unto salvation.*

With sudden determination fused with a sense of humility, Johnny bowed his head and started to pray.

"Dear God, I am not sure how to approach you. I know my grandmother could, but it seems hard for me. I would ask that I could also be one of your disciples. I believe you did send your Son, Jesus, to save me by dying on a cross for the things I have done wrong and that you did raise Him from the dead, as it says in the Bible. Jesus, thank you for sacrificing yourself for me too, just like you did for Peter and Thomas and all others that believed in You. I ask you, Jesus, to be my Lord and Savior."

There he stopped. A quiet sense of peace began to fill him. All his dread of this situation was replaced with a sense of purpose and confidence that a bigger plan, not of his own making, was at work. Johnny jumped to his feet. There was work to do—he must find Lilly and Ojibwan. Ojibwan could not become a sacrifice for them. That was absurd! Only Jesus could do that—and in fact, He already did! No—they must not go through with that plan at all.

A Better Plan

Johnny searched the entire house without success. Lilly and Ojibwan were nowhere to be found. Patty was sleeping, with Checker curled up next to her.

Good, Johnny thought, *she is protected as well as anyone can be for now.*

He carefully left the house, knowing he was in much greater danger moving about on his own. Surveying the area, he noticed another house, much grander than the others, and decided to check there first. A few people were in nearby gardens. He would be in plain sight if he walked to the house, but he had to risk it.

"Grant me safety, God," he prayed without thinking, and proceeded to the other house.

Once, he had to pass within ten feet of a worker but escaped notice, for the worker toiled aimlessly with an expression of purposelessness. Johnny proceeded to the main door and entered the house without incident.

He heard a long, moaning chant coming from an inner room. The voice sounded like Lilly's but had a very odd quality. Following the sound, he peered into the room and saw a sight that made his spine shiver. Lilly was performing a ritual of some kind, and Ojibwan was sitting still. Johnny watched from the threshold, hoping for Lilly's acknowledgment, but she was too caught up in it to notice anything. Suddenly Ojibwan sighed, took off an elaborate headdress and turned away. Lilly paused, concerned, and spoke gently to him. But Ojibwan looked up and saw Johnny. Surprised at first, he beckoned him in. Lilly looked upset but said nothing.

"What's happening?" asked Johnny. She explained in English and then translated for Ojibwan what she thought he needed to hear.

"Ojibwan is preparing himself for death, and the ritual requires assistance from the shaman. But Ojibwan refuses assistance from him or anyone associated with him. I know the ritual from my own tribe, and I am helping. I am sure it's the same, or almost the same, as what the shaman would do.

Then Ojibwan spoke, clearly distressed. As Lilly listened, a cloud came over her face, but she translated for Johnny.

"Ojibwan is sure that I cannot do this ritual. I do not have authority, even though I know what should be done. But he is sure that the shaman is evil, and he will have no part of him. Ojibwan is forlorn because he sees no hope for himself."

"I don't understand why Ojibwan is offering himself to be killed at all, especially if we are sure that the shaman and his son will have us killed regardless. Why don't we at least try to escape or fight or something? It seems a lot better than just giving up."

"Because Ojibwan is hopeful that the people's belief is strong enough that they will rise up to defend us if he truly follows the rules of the faith with this sacrifice. You must see that he is willing to die for us, in our place. But without this ritual, it will be for nothing. Our greatest of all spirits must be with him when he dies, and we are trying in this way to gain his blessing."

Johnny was thoughtful for some time.

"May I speak to Ojibwan?"

Ojibwan was looking directly at Johnny, seeming to understand this conversation, though Lilly had paused in translating. He continued.

" I see in your eyes that you have new knowledge. "

Johnny glanced at Lilly, who looked defeated but was willing to continue her translation. He looked back at Ojibwan and met his gaze for a few moments. Then he held the Bible out to Lilly and Ojibwan, and in the process the pages fell open to a painting of Christ being crucified. Johnny, surprised, did not recall seeing the painting earlier, but then he had been very engrossed in the story.

"Ojibwan," began Johnny, "this book is a very special gift to all the people of the world, given by the one God who created everything. I did not accept this gift until recently, but I know it is true."

Johnny glanced at Lilly, who translated with a somewhat broken spirit.

"This book belonged to my great-grandfather, who was lost in these caves many, many years ago. Do you remember when Abraham came to us and gave me the book several days ago, before we came here?"

Ojibwan nodded after Lilly translated, his interest being clearly piqued.

"All people on Earth do wrong things. God calls those wrong things sin, and even one separates us from Him because God is perfect. This book tells us that God does not want us to be separated from Him, because He loves all people. God knew that we could not avoid sin, no matter how hard we tried. So He sent His own Son to come to Earth, teach people truth, and then suffer and die in our place for the wrong things we have done. He himself had done nothing wrong, not even once, but he was willing to take our place in punishment for our sin. When He did this, we were offered complete forgiveness and a promise to live with God in heaven forever, if only we accept His Son, Jesus, and put our trust in His sacrifice. But that is not the end. There was yet another miracle, without which we would have nothing.

Johnny then had an idea. Quickly turning the pages, he found another picture of an empty tomb and one of Jesus rising from the dead.

"Jesus was dead for only three days. On the third day, He came back to life. His followers could not believe the reports that He was alive. But Jesus kept appearing to them in many different situations. It took a little while, but once His followers really understood that He had risen from the dead, they knew that He was the firstborn of an entirely new people—those who believed Jesus was Lord, accepted Him as their Savior, and believed in His coming back to life. These believers will all live forever with Him in heaven. People all over the world are still coming to Him."

"Ojibwan, you cannot substitute your life for us or for anyone else. I know you can feel this is true. You may accept Jesus as the One who already did that for us. Do you want to do this now?"

Lilly was stunned. She failed to translate Johnny's last question, but Ojibwan obviously understood. He suddenly fell prostrate on the floor and began praying loudly in his own tongue. Although Johnny could not understand the words, he knew that Ojibwan was offering the same prayer as he had earlier. Lilly, however, turned away and buried her face in her hands, unwilling to translate Ojibwan's prayer.

Ojibwan stopped and lifted himself to his feet, his face radiant with hope. When he saw Lilly turned away, still with her face in her hands, he gently turned her around to face him and removed her hands from her face. She looked through her tears at him, visibly startled by the change in his expression. Ojibwan spoke to her gently. She did not respond, so he repeated himself and she nodded submissively. Then he spoke quietly into her ear—hardly necessary since Johnny could understand none of this. As he spoke to her, she brightened. Looking into his eyes, she nodded hopefully but was still too emotional to speak.

Ojibwan regained Johnny's attention, and all three sat down on the floor, facing each other. Johnny was clearly no longer in charge, and Lilly was mostly recovered. Ojibwan was ready to make a plan and started to speak, giving Lilly time to translate.

"Ojibwan says that he can face death now if he must, but he realizes we must try to serve God alive if possible. Johnny, you must understand that Ojibwan has believed your story of the White Man's faith and has accepted your God. I have not, but I will support Ojibwan in whatever he wants me to do."

Ojibwan continued explaining his plan.

"I am certain that the God of the Bible is really the One I have tried to believe in for many years. I did not understand how to make peace with Him until you explained this to me, for which I am grateful. He is so clearly seen in all that He has made, that no one can be excused for failing to at least seek Him. I also think that God brought you here for a reason and that our legends are true also. I believe this lost cousin of yours is not dead and that God will bring him here. I also wonder if your grandfather is not still alive and will come also. If this happens—no, when this happens—it will be a miracle all my people can understand. Anyone not following us then would have rejected what he already believes. I think we must pray for them to come and to come soon."

Johnny was not sure what to do with this. It was one thing to believe in the miracle of Jesus's resurrection, but to pray for and believe in something not promised in the Bible—and yet so necessary to their own survival—was difficult. Ojibwan could sense Johnny's confused hesitation, but he ignored it and began to pray, this time not translated by Lilly. When he was finished, Johnny prayed as well, asking for the quick arrival of his cousin Ben and his great-grandfather. This Lilly did translate, and Ojibwan looked satisfied.

"We will now wait," Ojibwan said in English.

They did not wait long, however, before a scuffle was heard outside. They hurried out to see what was happening. Ojibwan, alarmed, shouted at soldiers loyal to the shaman who were abusing three men. Lilly gasped.

"They are Ojibwan's three spies. It's unbelievable! They've been captured, and now we truly have no hope. They are his best men—

no one should have been able to capture even one of them, and certainly not all three."

Ojibwan walked up to the soldiers, shoving away the guard, who then let him go—he dared not cross him. Ojibwan continued to shout at the soldiers and by sheer force of will caused them to back away, releasing the three spies. They all withdrew to Ojibwan's home. Lilly rushed to get water and bandages for their wounds. Ojibwan began to grill them for information, and Lilly again translated.

"Why did you come into the village? I clearly told you to stay hidden and watch for signs. No one could have caught you unless you permitted it," Ojibwan said sternly.

"We saw signs that we knew you needed to know about. We tried to get to you without being seen, and we almost made it here—until we had the misfortune of getting caught between two patrols. There was no escape. This house is heavily guarded. We were caught just before you came out."

A brief look of pride came over Ojibwan's face as he recognized the skill and loyalty that allowed the three of them to get as far as they did.

"Ojibwan," said one of the men. "There is more."

He looked at Lilly, Johnny, and Patty and hesitated, knowing that Lilly was translating.

"Speak on," replied Ojibwan. "They are friends."

Returning his attention to Ojibwan, he continued.

"Before we were captured, we overheard a plot to kill you when you leave this house. I am glad we stayed outside briefly, for we saw archers in the bluffs. I fear that the shaman would rather explain your death than allow you to speak again to the people."

Ojibwan looked incredulous and then paused, realizing that his men were not the only ones who were skilled archers, but he shrugged it off, saying, "So tell us: what is this sign you saw which was important enough to risk your lives to tell me?"

Again, Ojibwan's men looked at Lilly, Johnny, and Patty, but this time with a hint of wonder, which they quickly suppressed.

"There are others like these," said one of the men. "We saw them when we watched over the city. They have a large escort—there must be all the men from a number of our villages coming with them. They will be at the main gate in less than an hour."

"What did he say?" asked Johnny.

Visibly surprised, Lilly translated what she heard.

"Could it be Ben?" asked Johnny with cautious hope.

Lilly was now too absorbed in the conversation to effectively translate, leaving both Johnny and Patty frustrated. Patty's unrelenting hope for her brother's survival surged, but even that was overshadowed by Ojibwan's reaction. He obviously had heard more than Lilly had translated. Johnny and Patty would now learn a big lesson in patience, for Lilly refused to translate further and focused her entire concentration on the conversation between Ojibwan and his three spies.

After they had finished and Ojibwan was satisfied he had heard the entire story, he thanked and dismissed his men, directing them to a place they could rest. Lost in thought, Ojibwan said nothing while Lilly waited for a signal from him. But he was too preoccupied to notice.

"So what was that all about, Lilly?" Johnny asked.

Lilly was noticeably excited, well beyond her usual demeanor.

"I think Ben is alive. What's more, he may be with a most unusual escort. Ojibwan's men know secret places from where they can see not only what happens within the village but also for several miles around it. A large group of men from outlying villages is approaching, and they are dressed for war. Among them is the chief of one of our villages. This chief is just as well respected as Ojibwan's father, and, in fact, they are friends. Even the shaman would think twice of opposing him. If this chief and Ojibwan's father meet, that could be the end of the shaman. He will try to prevent this, I am sure."

"But what has this got to do with Ben?" interrupted Patty, who had joined Lilly and Johnny when she heard her brother's name.

"A white boy was reported to be part of the group and walking with this chief. Who else could it be?"

Patty stared at her for a moment, then burst into tears.

"I knew he was okay, I knew it! I prayed for him all the time." Johnny hugged his cousin.

"There's more," continued Lilly. "There is another white man with them. They cannot be sure, but they think he is old by the way he walks."

"Abraham!" exclaimed Johnny. "It must be Abraham! We may get out of this pickle after all!"

"Did Abraham seem old to you when you saw him?" asked Lilly.

"Yes, I think he must have been very old. He "talked old," if you know what I mean. In fact, he used a lot of strange expressions that people don't say anymore."

"But did he *act* old?" persisted Lilly. "You must remember that although Ojibwan's men are excellent spies, they're looking from a considerable distance at people moving. They cannot make out faces, but they deduce things from people's movements. The party of men is moving much more slowly than they normally would, even more slowly than they would need to, considering they have their old chief with them. The white man seems to require frequent rests, and the men are respecting that. The whole thing is very unusual."

"Okay, so maybe that *is* a bit strange, but what does it matter?" asked Johnny.

"The group is dressed for war. No one brings an old man and a boy, particularly a foreigner, to war. The whole thing makes no sense at all, unless…"

Lilly paused. Johnny and Patty just stared at her, so she continued.

"…unless these two—the old man and the boy—fit our prophecy."

Johnny let out a sigh.

"Okay, I guess you better fill us in on the details."

Lilly straightened up. Her expression became that of a story-teller, one with a fierce pride in her people.

"This underground people and my own people have common ancestors. We were divided perhaps two hundred years ago, when some of my tribe ventured to this place. The original leader who brought them here was one of Ojibwan's ancestors. He was young and courageous, and he was looking for a safe and fruitful land. One day he fell asleep in a cave. When he awoke, he saw a spirit in front of him. He was very afraid but kept his composure, asking this spirit if he was the Great Spirit. The spirit replied saying he was a messenger of the one true holy spirit. He said our people would be divided for many generations until we learned that there is only One whom we should worship. He said there was only one way to Him, and the way was narrow.

"But then he warned of a time to come when evil men would want to rule the people for their own selfish reasons. He foretold a crisis that would end in great loss, unless the people showed courage and faith. Now this is the oddest part of the prophecy: this messenger said the time of decision for our people would occur when five visitors from the outside world would arrive and they would enter the underground kingdom through a crystal pool. They could be recognized in two ways. First, there would be four youths and one very old man. All would be related to each other. Second, they would bring two gifts. The first would be an ancient amulet of a previous era, and the second would be the message of hope.

"He warned us that the evil men would oppose them and their message of hope and they would desire the amulet even though its power had long been emptied. But those who believed their message would follow them out of the underground kingdom and be reunited with those of their people who were still on the earth's surface. The way would be narrow and difficult. Those who doubted would never leave."

Johnny remained silent for some time, reflecting on what he had heard. The silence was interrupted by suppressed growls and whimpers from Checker, but clearly he preferred the company of some doggish dream rather than the ancient stories being retold.

"So," began Patty, "it's certainly creepy to hear about all this, but it can't be about us, even if it does sound that way. Only four of us came through that awful waterfall that forms the crystal pool. We certainly did not have an old man with us. Furthermore, we aren't related! Well, Johnny, Ben, and I are but not Lilly. I say a prophecy is a prophecy—it's either all true or not true at all. That's what Grandma used to tell me."

"And also," continued Johnny, "what's all this about an amulet? What in the world is an amulet anyway? What does it mean to be 'emptied of its power'?"

"I'm not sure," conceded Lilly, "but I thought it was a kind of necklace, perhaps with a gem or precious stone with magical qualities. In any case, we don't have one."

Patty slipped her hand in her pocket and slowly rolled the stone around in her palm.

I don't think they need to know about this—not yet anyway, she thought. *Amulet…so that is what my pretty rock is called. But they might not give it back if I show it to them, and besides—it's none of Lilly's business.*

Patty and Johnny found a place to sleep and entered into a realm of uncomfortable dreams.

Johnny awoke to the sight of men moving in the weak light. Fear gripped him. Patty was asleep next to him, but Lilly was gone. The men were speaking in low whispers, barely audible, but even if he had been able to hear them, he could not understand their language. Johnny remained as still as stone. Then he heard Checker next to him, growling low as he stared at the figures in the dim light. Johnny reached over to pet his head, hoping to calm him. Checker looked over at Johnny and wagged his tail slightly, but Johnny could feel the tension in his dog. Checker continued to growl quietly, attracting the attention of the figures in the room. From their midst came a slightly built woman heading toward Johnny. Checker did not react other than to wag his tail harder. As she came closer, Johnny recognized her as Lilly. He wondered why he hadn't recognized her earlier, and he marveled that she now appeared older than she was.

"Please be very quiet," whispered Lilly.

"What's going on?"

"Ojibwan's men are going out. It's dark, and they should be able to get out without being seen. They are very skilled," she replied. But even in the weak light, Johnny could see that she was not convinced by her own words.

"They're going to try to disable the archers," Lilly continued. "The archers hidden in the rocks above this house have strict orders to kill as many of us as possible when we are escorted out this morning. They will aim for Ojibwan first, but we will be next."

Johnny saw the men slink through the opening one at a time, each turning in a different direction and disappearing almost immediately into the darkness. Ojibwan spoke briefly to Lilly and retired to his room.

"We are to go back to bed. We'll need rest, for tomorrow will be a big day," she explained. Johnny realized that this was the third day—the day that Ojibwan must choose his fate and theirs.

Impasse

It was well after dawn when a hard knock was heard at the door. No one needed to answer, for soldiers came in immediately, followed by the young shaman. They ordered Ojibwan, Johnny, Lilly, and Patty into the center of the room and looked for the other men. Johnny held Checker tightly, knowing the dog would attack if it felt threatened. When Ojibwan's men could not be found, the shaman demanded information from Ojibwan, who ignored him. He gestured threateningly to his men, who looked uncomfortable. Ojibwan continued to ignore him and proceeded to the door.

"Come on!" commanded Lilly to Johnny and Patty. "We mustn't get separated!"

Convinced that his legs would buckle under the certainty of his imminent death, Johnny obeyed, with Patty gripping his hand. As they crossed the threshold, Johnny's mind focused on two things: the certainty of arrows instantly piercing his back and his wonderment at how the plant and mineral life could so effectively mimic morning light so far from any source of sunlight.

Ojibwan led the group at a fast pace, much to the shaman's frustration and the humiliation of his soldiers. The young shaman's anger quickly transformed itself into anticipation, and anticipation into confusion, as they made their way toward the same place they had been three days earlier. Before long, confusion turned to silent rage as he scanned the bluffs, clearly dissatisfied with what he saw—or didn't see.

They quickly arrived at the gate to the holy place, where their previous drama had gone so badly three days earlier. Ojibwan headed directly for the silver pool, walking so fast he was nearly running. His adversary screamed a futile command in protest. Waiting for them was a small party including Ojibwan's father and another elder chief of whom they had not previously seen. With them was a very old man clearly not descended of this tribe. To everyone's amazement, Ben stood there too.

Lilly and Johnny stopped short, but nothing could prevent Patty from running to her brother with Checker bounding at her side.

"I knew you would be okay! I knew it, I knew it, I knew it! I prayed just as Grandma taught us," Patty kept repeating. Most uncharacteristically, Ben gave her a huge hug, picking her up off the ground, twirling her in circles, and holding her so tightly she could hardly breathe. But she didn't complain.

"Ouch!" Ben suddenly exclaimed and set her back on her feet. "What in the world is in your pocket?"

"Oh …I'll show you later."

Ben was satisfied with that and turned to Johnny while Lilly looked curiously at Patty. Patty chose to ignore her.

"Johnny, you wouldn't believe what's happened. I can barely believe it myself, even though I've had a lot of time to take it in."

The chit-chat ended suddenly as the elder shaman joined his son in an attempt to regain control of the situation. He signaled to their archers, each of whom loaded an arrow into his bow, but another group loyal to Ojibwan strategically positioned on the bluff above them did likewise, resulting in a stalemate.

The elder shaman spoke with a voice quivering from age and anger. Ojibwan and his father waited, as if some rehearsed drama were unfolding. Lilly regarded the situation stoically, and Ben suddenly realized he had not recognized her. Lilly looked much older than when he had seen her last. Stepping up to her, he gripped both her hands and then hugged her. Johnny noticed that her reaction alternated between joy and reservation, but she smiled.

"We were so worried about you—but we cannot greet each other properly yet," she whispered, for the elder shaman was addressing the people.

His son looked impatient, but there was no stopping this. Ojibwan glanced at Lilly, turned his eyes toward Ben, Johnny, and Patty, and nodded quickly before returning his attention to the Shaman's speech. Lilly translated.

"He says this is the last chance for the people to obey Morgothus. The punishment for entering this holy place is death, and Ojibwan must now decide if he still wishes to exercise his right to substitution—meaning he dies instead of us. He says the prophecy cannot be partially fulfilled to be valid. Although we seem to fit the prophecy, including the presence of the old man, without the amulet and the spirit guide, there is no true fulfillment."

All eyes turned to Ojibwan. The silence was oppressive, and the younger shaman could barely contain his excitement. He stepped forward and pointed his staff toward Ojibwan.

"It is now time for you to choose. Do you obey and serve Morgothus by slaying these demons who have entered our holy place, or do you substitute yourself and take their crime upon your own person and suffer eternal separation from our god?"

At first Ojibwan made no reply, but then he called out to his people.

"This is the fulfillment we have been promised. We have the visitors that we were told would come. This is our time. I will not lead our people against our destiny. In a few moments, we will see the proof we need. But in the meantime, I will not offend our visitors by preventing them from reuniting, for they have been separated until now."

He turned back to his father and greeted both him and his old friend. Then he greeted the elderly white man and spoke with him.

The young shaman spluttered objections, but a number of Ojibwan's skilled archers trained their arrows on him, convincing him to bide his time. *What proof can he show?* he thought.

"Come on!" Ben urged the others. "This is the chance we've been waiting for!"

Confused, Johnny, Lilly, and Patty walked up to Ojibwan and the others in Ben's party. They stared curiously at the old white man. All eyes turned to Ben.

"Johnny, Patty, and Lilly, I want you to meet your great-grandfather."

Johnny was stunned at Ben's words. Patty had no difficulty believing them, and she threw her arms around her great-grandfather. Lilly looked confused and appealed questioningly to Ben.

"Great-Grandpa, I'm Patty. I've heard all about you. I hoped and hoped that we would find you, but the family gave you up for lost long before I was born. Please tell me about everything that's happened to you."

Johnny stepped in and shook his hand.

"Grandpa—I mean Great-Grandpa—I'm Johnny, Ben and Patty's cousin. I read your journal, and I know I should have asked your permission. I'm so glad to finally meet you."

"I cannot think of a happier fate for my journal than that it might be read by you all, my great-grandchildren," he replied.

"And who is this?" he asked, reaching down to pet Checker, who regarded this entire turn of events as quite acceptable.

"Checker," replied Johnny. "He's my dog."

"I could have used a dog like you during the many years I was here," he told Checker, who was willing to keep wagging his tail so long as his ear was being scratched.

Then he turned to Lilly, who was keeping some distance from this happy reunion. He walked up to her and greeted her in a way that the others could not understand—both in form and in words.

"Lilly, you are also my great-granddaughter. I took a bride from your tribe—I mean *our* tribe, for I was accepted into your tribe as a member, and you are my great-grandchild. You are one-eighth white."

Lilly was visibly shocked by this news but recovered quickly, greeting him in return in the manner of her tribe.

"I want you to tell us everything, Great-Grandfather. I want to know everything that has happened to you since you first arrived. I will tell you our adventures too," said Lilly in a most respectful manner.

Ojibwan spoke to Lilly and motioned them to sit down. He and his father, as well as the chief of the outlying villages, proceeded to sit on the ground while Lilly urged the others to do the same.

"We still have a pretty big problem here," commented Lilly. "Ojibwan has promised proof that we were authentic, that we are fulfilling their prophecy. We have to come up with something."

Ojibwan started to speak to his guests privately as Lilly translated.

"I am convinced that you are the fulfillment of our prophecy. The four of you and our old friend match our ancient writings perfectly. There are significant problems that must be addressed before we can be safe, but first, I need to give you some history of the ancient past."

"Many, many years ago, when times were more magical, people knew God by a different name. They called Him Abba."

"That's a name for God in the Bible," Patty interrupted. "Grandma showed me once."

"Shh," said Lilly. "We must listen now."

"As with all times, there was a struggle between good and evil. There were kingdoms of men, but there were many other creatures— which, we think, have left the earth altogether. In these times, an evil force corrupted men and spun his lies in order to control the earth. This evil being became prideful and jealous of even Abba Himself.

"To protect His created beings against this evil, Abba captured much of it, trapping it into a special magical stone called an amulet. While this amulet existed, the world was not safe. But through many battles, heroism, and personal sacrifice, the power of the amulet was destroyed and the stone itself was cracked. For many years, our people kept this broken amulet as a reminder of the danger in opposing Abba, but it became lost when our people first arrived in this underground world."

"So," he continued, "that has become part of our problem. The same prophecy that describes you also says that one of the youths who arrive will present the amulet to our chief. Without this, I do not think I can master this situation."

Johnny noticed that Patty was looking uncomfortable. Her hand was fiddling with something in her pocket. He stepped closer to her and whispered, "What's wrong, Patty? You look like you've seen a ghost!"

Patty looked back and forth between Johnny and Ojibwan.

"Well—I'm not sure. It may be nothing, but—well, I found this buried near the crystal pool."

She pulled out a smooth stone, very dark and translucent, yet with a mysterious quality that seemed to speak of an inner light long since extinguished. On one side it had a very deep crack as if it had been violently struck.

"I thought it was pretty and wanted to keep it, but I wonder if maybe I should have told someone."

Patty held out her hand containing the gem, still the centerpiece of the grass necklace she had made. Ojibwan came closer and looked at the nearly circular stone, seeing ancient and well-worn inscriptions on it. Some were still legible. He looked at Lilly, beckoning her to come closer. Lilly complied, also carefully studying the rock and its inscriptions as Patty continued to hold it in her outstretched hand.

"What does it say?" Johnny asked Lilly.

"I don't think it says anything," she responded. "There are markings on it, but they aren't even similar to anything my ancestors would have used."

Patty grasped Ojibwan's hand and placed her treasure in it. Awe, fear and hope could be seen in Ojibwan's eyes.

"Look at those symbols." said Johnny. "I think they are the sun and the moon, with some stars. Nothing else is written on it—or if so, it was obscured over the years. It must be very old. I wonder… how did it get down here? Did the villagers make it?"

"I don't think so," Lilly replied slowly. "There is *nothing* like this in my culture or my tribe's history. No, this is much older." Then Lilly burst out in a most uncharacteristic manner.

"It is the amulet! Patty actually found the amulet! The prophecy is fulfilled. I can't believe it! And we've been part of its fulfillment!"

Ben nudged Johnny, nodding toward the crowd. They saw that this event had captured the full attention of everyone present.

"I'm no prophet, but I can tell you that now we have a brief opportunity," said Ben. "Look at these people! We'd better leap at this chance to seize control of the moment."

His warning was not necessary however, for Ojibwan suddenly turned upon the younger shaman. He walked directly up to him, his face revealing a mixture of anger, excitement, and authority. Looking squarely into the shaman's eyes, he held up the amulet for all to see, then turned to the crowd and spoke in a loud, commanding tone that no one could ignore.

Lilly translated, telling them that Ojibwan had boldly announced the finding of the amulet and the complete fulfillment of the prophecy.

"He said that we are now entering a new dawn, an age of light and hope." Then Lilly stopped short, and there was a corresponding hush in the audience.

"What happened?" asked Patty.

"He just said there was no need for shamans anymore. He said that the Creator, Abba Himself, had revealed to him a new order—an order of forgiveness and redemption through Abba's one and only Son. He said he had read Abba's book that was sent to him by one of His servants. Johnny, he's talking about you and your Bible. He said we shall soon be given a new direction, a new purpose, and a new home."

Suddenly, a scream of rage burst from the shaman. All eyes turned to him. He began to chant, and his face was contorted. Shocked, Ben realized that the shaman had become just like one of the masks he had seen on that dark journey down the underground stream only a few days earlier. Or was it weeks? But the shaman continued to rave and jump, screaming hideous curses, until he finally pointed his staff at Ojibwan's heart. He screamed at several of his men. The men were clearly afraid of what was happening, but one jumped forward and fitted an arrow to his bow. He drew the arrow back, pointing it at Ojibwan's heart, but the arrow misfired and flew wide. The would-be assassin himself was struck by three arrows coming down from above.

Ojibwan walked over to the still raging shaman took his staff, broke it in view of all, and then threw it to the ground. With this, those loyal to Ojibwan fitted arrows into their bows, preparing to defend their leader against a likely attack, but it was unnecessary—all of the shaman's guards had lost their spirit and dropped their weapons.

Ojibwan addressed the crowd once more.

"I say again," he continued, "we have a new era before us. We will soon have a new hope and a new home. We now wait for a sign."

"What kind of sign does he expect?" asked Ben. "What'll we do when nothing happens?"

Everyone waited. Ojibwan bowed his head and said nothing.

"What is he doing?" continued Ben. "We can't just stand here."

"Shh," rebuked Patty. "Can't you see he's praying?"

"Praying? Praying?" said Ben. "We shouldn't be praying! We have only a moment to take advantage of this!" but then something did happen.

The Reckoning

Intense light suddenly added a brightness never before seen by any of the villagers. They all covered their eyes until they could adjust to the intensity. Ojibwan was the first to brave looking toward the source of the light streaming from the vast shaft directly above them. As he continued to look upward, his expression changed from one of initial bewilderment to one of hope and excitement and then, finally, a resigned peace. He raised both hands, palms up, over his head and then called to his people to do the same.

Most of the people were dazzled by the rapidly growing radiance coming straight down the immense shaft. Its intensity increased to a near blinding level. Then, for all to see, an angelic form descended in blazing splendor. Johnny looked into the angel's face, staring in disbelief. Was it possible? The face resembled that of Abraham. But Johnny rejected the notion almost as quickly as it entered his mind.

The angel settled on the pool before them and began to walk across its surface as if it were firm ground. A great gasp came over the multitude as they observed this feat. He moved toward Ojibwan and handed him a beautifully decorated silver staff that contained a light of its own. In exchange, he requested the amulet—clearly void of any power it once may have contained. As Ojibwan relinquished it, a sense of such awe came over him that he fell prostrate to the ground and began to worship the angel. The onlookers followed his example and even Johnny felt an urge to worship him too, but inwardly he knew he should not.

The angel immediately raised Ojibwan to his feet and said, "No, brother, for we are both servants of the Most High. And you are much beloved and have found the narrow way that leads to eternal life. You have now been given the task of leading your people through this narrow way and rescuing them from the domain of darkness."

The angel gathered together the old chief, his son, and the children; in the presence of all and in a language Johnny could not understand, he declared the people freed from this domain and restored as children of the light. He announced that he had a great message and that all should heed it. Turning to Johnny and Ben, he congratulated them for their bravery.

The angel addressed the people: "All who have courage should follow the lead of the chief's son and follow him upward through the shaft of light. But first, one of your guests—whom I have sent to you—will share with you the most important message you can hear."

He then turned to Johnny, saying, "It is time for you to share what you have learned from your great-grandfather's Bible." To Ojibwan he added, "Only one opportunity will be given, and those who do not follow will forever live in the darkness of this realm. Make sure they understand."

Johnny nodded his head in submission, quite frightened of what he knew he must do. He reached for his great-grand father's Bible and opened it to the book of John.

How appropriate, he thought, *to explain the gospel through the book that has the same name as my great-grandfather.*

Johnny turned to Lilly to get her help in translating this message, but the angel stopped him, looking straight into his face.

"You do it alone there, young fella."

Stunned, Johnny realized now there could be no mistake. He was looking straight into the face of Abraham. The cherub then guided Johnny to face the people and motioned him to begin.

Trembling, Johnny looked down at God's Word and began to speak. He told of Jesus and his early ministry. He told of how the Romans and the self-serving leaders oppressed the people. He described the miracles that He had done, from making new wine to raising the dead. He spoke of choosing the disciples and of how much difficulty they had in understanding Jesus's teachings. Johnny also described His love and patience for all, no matter how much they may have sinned, and His willingness to forgive if simply asked.

Johnny paused and took in his surroundings. Ben and Papa looked thoughtful, reflecting on what they were hearing. Patty beamed with pride in her cousin. Lilly's head was turned away. Johnny surveyed his audience and saw that many had the look of hope while others looked angry, but no one looked confused. It dawned on him that everyone could understand his speech—each person heard him in his own language, whether their native Indian tongue or English. Johnny was staggered, and he faltered for a moment, but seeing an encouraging look from Abraham, he proceeded with the message. Suddenly a wind rose up from nowhere, stopping him short. It alarmed the people, who had never experienced wind in their lifetime. The pages in the Bible fluttered, and Johnny quickly placed his hand over them to keep them from turning, but he realized he had lost his place. Then his eye caught the verse on the page in front of him, and he felt compelled to read it out loud:

> *The wind bloweth where it listeth, and thou hearest the sound thereof, but canst not tell whence it cometh, and whither it goeth: so is every one that is born of the Spirit. John 3:8*

As if this were his cue, Ojibwan joined Johnny and spoke.

"This breath of air on your face is a sign that we must go. Join me, and I will lead you all to a new home. We will follow the light and be children of this underground world no longer."

Having given this invitation, Ojibwan moved to an open place, where all who would follow could gather. The people looked confused and uncertain. But with a look of pride in his eyes, the old chief followed his son immediately. Father and son embraced and stood together. Lilly was next and stood with the two of them, quickly joined by all of Ojibwan's loyal men.

The shamans, father and son, and their closest servants had been slowly slinking away from the angel, making a place for their followers to gather. Some, although not all, of their soldiers stood with them.

Johnny, now standing near Abraham and joined by Ben, Patty, and their great-grandfather, turned to the angel and said, "Who are you really? I always thought you were just a nice, maybe eccentric, old man. Is your name really Abraham?"

Abraham smiled.

"I borrowed my name from a good friend of mine. His life is described in the first book of that Bible you're holding. But as for me, I am one of the Almighty's many angels. We spend our time worshiping before the Father, praising Him and declaring His mighty works. It is a great honor and privilege for us."

"But why didn't you tell me who you really were?" Johnny persisted. "I would've had nothing to fear had I known you'd be here to protect us!"

"No, I'm not allowed to take from you the privilege of learning to depend on God in faith. I would certainly be doing you a disservice. In fact, this is a most unusual event—that any angelic being should have such a role as I have taken. There are times when God uses angels to intervene in the affairs of men but not many. And even now, my role must soon come to an end. It is up to men to share their faith with men."

Then Abraham turned to Ben.

"Ah, but why are you so quiet? Is there not a message you have been given as well?"

At first Ben looked confused, and then a flood of memories came upon him, and he realized that he too had a role in the plan ahead of them. Fear gripped him, and he felt he could not stand up. Johnny, seeing that Ben was about to collapse, supported his cousin. He almost dropped the old Bible, but Patty rescued it.

"What's the matter, Ben?" asked Johnny anxiously.

But Ben could not respond—it was as if his tongue had become stuck to the roof of his mouth.

Abraham continued, "Ben knows the path to the light through both experience and vision, but he has not started that journey in his heart. You cannot succeed without him, nor can he without you. But he must be obedient to what has been revealed to him."

Confused, Johnny turned to his cousin.

"What is he saying, Ben? What does this mean?" Abraham nudged Patty. "Tell us, young princess, what do you see in the book?"

Patty glanced down at the Bible in her hands and saw a verse that struck her as being bigger than all the others, so she read it.

"It says here in Matthew 7:13:

Enter ye in at the strait gate: for wide is the gate, and broad is the way, that leadeth to destruction, and many there be which go in thereat:

Because strait is the gate, and narrow is the way, which leadeth unto life, and few there be that find it.

Beware of false prophets, which come to you in sheep's clothing, but inwardly they are ravening wolves.

Ye shall know them by their fruits. Do men gather grapes of thorns, or figs of thistles?"

"Ben, what is this saying?" she asked.

Ben's tongue suddenly became free, and he said, "I can't do it! I am a thorn bush. I have never followed the Bible. I have never asked Jesus to be part of my life. How can I have any message to share?"

"Ben," replied Johnny, "neither had I, but we need only to confess the things we have done wrong to God, ask His forgiveness, and then ask His Son to be our Lord and Savior. The Bible says, 'if we confess with our mouths that Jesus is Lord and believe in our hearts that God raised him from the dead, we will be saved.'"

Ben looked at Johnny sheepishly and said, "You mean I can do that now?"

"I think that Jesus would say there is no better time."

So, one cousin introduced the other to His God and Savior, and with that simple step, Ben's countenance changed. He freed himself from Johnny's support, looked at Abraham, and said, "I know what I must do."

He then proceeded to join Ojibwan and Lilly, followed closely by Johnny, Patty, their great-grandfather, his old Indian friend, and the entire entourage that had come from the outlying villages.

"Good people," began Ben, "when I first came to your world, I thought I did so pursuing my own self-made adventure. I came to see if we could follow the path of my great-grandfather and to do something that I could tell my friends about for many years to come. Right from the beginning, my self-made plans turned to disaster. I became separated from my family and friends. I fell down into your crystal pool from above, with no knowledge of its existence or the peril it brought to my very life. I was lost in one of your caverns in which the light was extinguished. I could not see even my own hand immediately in front of my face."

Johnny observed the situation as his cousin continued to relate the story of his trip down the path to hell (as Ben called it). He saw everyone, regardless of his native language, listening intently with total comprehension, yet no one was translating. He also saw Lilly, whose emotions ranged from astonishment to grief as she heard of the horrors that Ben had suffered and the hallucinations that nearly drove away his reason.

"They all can understand him," Johnny marveled in his mind. "They understood me too. It's a miracle, for sure."

Johnny's gaze moved to his great-grandfather, who had survived such an amazingly long time in this place and then to Patty—who simply looked proud as she watched her brother and held on tightly to Checker. Then Johnny tuned back in, realizing that he was missing much of his cousin's story.

"After my great-grandfather and I escaped from the men who wanted to harm us, I nearly fell off a great cliff," continued Ben. "I was knocked out and had a vision while asleep. In the vision, people were climbing up a narrow, rocky path. They were going higher and higher, risking challenges that seemed too great for them. Others, far below them, stayed on an easy and broad path with no apparent dangers but led only into deeper and darker areas. As I watched the group climbing the narrow way, great storms came up; the winds were fierce and falling stones threatened to crush them, but no one was hurt. Their journey was slow and steady, and they passed by without seeing me—because it was a vision. As each person reached the top, his expression changed from solemn and determined to radiantly joyful. Then one by one they entered a gate, and after everyone had passed through, the gate was shut. I was struck with an overwhelming desire to go after them, to try to get in through the shut gate or even go over the wall that now separated them from me, but I was confronted by a new vision of my own grandmother. In life, her faith had been everything to her, but I had never paid attention to that part of her while she was alive. She told me to return to my journey, and to 'take the narrow way and put your trust in the Lamb.' I had no idea what she meant, but even as my vision of her faded and I returned to the waking world, she continued to repeat, 'Take the narrow way and put your trust in the Lamb.'

"My new friends," Ben continued, "that lamb, I now know, is found in the scripture that my cousin, Johnny, read. The path before us will be difficult and narrow. Many will try to talk us out of it, but we now must follow our leader, Ojibwan. We must take the narrow way and put our trust in the Lamb."

Ben concluded his speech.

Johnny turned to speak to the angel. "So now, Abraham, what should we do?"

But Abraham was gone, never to be seen again by any of those present.

Traveling on the Narrow Way

Abraham had left, taking only the defunct amulet and, with it, an inexplicable mystery worthy of its own story. An awkward silence followed. Johnny clutched his great-grandfather's Bible and went to stand by him, followed by Ben, Patty, and Checker. Lilly walked up to Ojibwan and stood beside him. With that, a new look of boldness came over him. He raised the silver staff he had traded for the mysterious amulet, and shouted in a commanding voice to his people. Johnny suddenly realized he could no longer understand Ojibwan's language, but his meaning could not be missed. It was time to enter what had always been forbidden to all but the shaman and his son— the stairway leading up through the opening from which Abraham had descended. Ojibwan headed that way, joined by Lilly, his father, the old chief of the outlying villages and his closest friends and soldiers.

"Well, come on!" said Papa, winking at his grandchildren. "What are you waiting for?"

Feeling startled as if by a cold splash of water on the face, Ben and Patty ran off together to join the procession, with Johnny and his dog following suit.

Others also began to follow—some with confidence and joy, some leaping and dancing, some cautiously, some confidently. Many joined in the exhortations they had just heard, preaching to others with great confidence and authority. Others quietly joined the group.

From somewhere in the shadows, the young shaman watched the turn of events. He observed how some small groups of people gradually overcame their fear and stepped out in faith, following the growing group proceeding toward the once forbidden stairway. Others began to follow from fear of being left behind. He saw several others who he knew to have the same black heart as his own join in—hypocrites who outwardly displayed a joy that seemed to deceive even those who followed their leader with genuine trust and faith. But for whatever cause, the multitude was melting away, heading for a destination that once would have brought them an instant death.

Summoning his closest servants, the shaman leapt out from the shadows and ran to the body of people who were defecting from his ranks and were leaving him with only a small core group. Even some of his most trusted servants wavered in their resolution to stay in this underground world. He approached his former loyalists, imploring them to leave the line. Others he threatened, playing on their superstitions. With some he succeeded, but others remained strong and proceeded upward on the narrowing path.

Suddenly, a large boulder tumbled from somewhere above, narrowly missing a number of people on the path near the middle of the procession. Part of the path fell away, leaving a gap—and, consequently, a potentially fatal fall for those yet to cross it. Seeing his opportunity, the young shaman shouted to those above, asserting that Morgothus was giving them one last warning of their doom should they did not obey him and exhorting them all to come down.

A hush went over the entire group. Some of those nearest the gap studied it to determine whether they could leap across it. Others were sure it could be done, but death was the certain result if the leap were misgauged. Yet others shook their heads and turned back, making their way past fellow villagers in an especially narrow portion of the path. Confusion and arguing quickly resulted, and some of the villagers began to scuffle with each other.

A shout from above stopped what could have been a disaster. Ojibwan called for attention; as soon as all eyes were upon him, he leapt back across the gap himself. Then, taking a child from his mother's arms, he spoke to them both softly in view of all. The mother nodded, and Ojibwan picked up the boy. One of Ojibwan's soldiers was positioned on the other side of the gap, and Ojibwan threw the boy to him with little difficulty. He then looked to the mother took her hand and helped her leap across the gap. She easily made the jump.

Many began to follow this example, but the fainthearted shook their heads and proceeded downward, back to the land and faith they knew. Johnny was surprised to see many of who had initially reacted with joy to the possibility of seeking a new life had quickly rejected it. Others who initially had been wary continued upward, now more resolute.

"Let's go," repeated Great-Granddad. "I sure don't want to get left behind."

Johnny, Ben, Patty, and Checker followed their great-grandfather, heading toward the departing crowd. Ben could not help noticing the faces of those who had turned back, now looking hopeless, having lost the joy they had had just moments earlier.

As they arrived at the gap in the pathway, they paused. It was wider than it had looked from below. Ojibwan had already left and moved up to the front of the procession, but several of his trusted men remained to help others cross over.

"You kids go first," said Papa. "And then don't look back or wait for me. Keep on moving ahead, and I'll catch up. I just need to get my concentration up before I jump."

Johnny clenched his teeth, then took off in a sprint toward the gap and leapt across it, easily making the mark. Then he turned and called Checker, who looked unhappy; the dog walked up to the edge and sniffed it, wagging his tail nervously.

"Come on, Checker!" shouted Johnny. "You've jumped farther than this before! You can do it!"

Checker started to whine, nervously approaching and backing away from the edge.

Patty stroked the dog's head and whispered into his ear.

"You can do it, Checker! Watch me!"

She looked to the two men waiting there to assist, and she held out her arms. Each man held one of her hands and placed the other under her thighs; together, they threw her to safety. Two men on the other side caught her before she even touched the ground.

Checker just continued to wag his tail and whine. One of the men attempted to pick him up, but some angry growls convinced him otherwise. Ben called Checker.

"Come on, Checker, come chase me!"

Ben started to race toward the edge of the precipice. Checker obeyed, but as Ben made his leap, Checker stopped short, nearly falling over the ledge, avoiding death only through the quick reflexes of one of Ojibwan's men. Checker was now very unhappy and started to bark at his master across the gap. Johnny began to worry.

The man who had saved Checker from his fall tried to console the dog by petting his head, much to the amazement of all the villagers watching this spectacle. As he stroked the dog, he spoke to him in his own language, which Checker understood as well as the words he was used to hearing from his master. But somehow the man was able to calm the dog enough to pick him up and throw him to his fellow soldier across the gap, who caught the unhappy dog and set him before Johnny. Immediately, all three children embraced him, forgetting that there was still one more person in their party, far more important than Checker, who had yet to cross this formidable gap. Papa was most unsure of his ability to make the leap, but part of his plan was to try when his great-grandchildren were not looking. He looked toward the two soldiers, who nodded at him. Taking that as a cue, he mustered all his waning strength to make the best run and leap he could. He dashed to the crevasse and, assisted by the two men, jumped across. He barely cleared the gap just as Johnny turned and saw his successful landing. Only then did he realize how much peril this journey might be for his great-grandfather. From here on, Johnny took special care to stay close to him. Checker did too, always staying at the elderly man's side, protecting him from any possible fall down what had become a sheer edge along the upwardly spiraling path. It continued to rise in large circles, working its way up along the great cylindrical cut into the earth.

"Why is this shaft even here? I've never heard of such a place," Johnny said. It seems as though someone had taken a huge cookie cutter and made a giant cutout in the ground.

"Oh, there are other places such as this," replied the old man. "The Yucatan Peninsula in Mexico has what are called 'cenotes.' Usually they're filled with water. But I must admit, I've never heard of one quite this big—well, perhaps Cenote Azul near Chetumal is this large, but it's filled with water. People still don't know how deep it is. It's like a small lake with no shore. You step into it, and you're immediately way over your head, with no bottom in sight."

Johnny marveled at that as they continued to climb, step-by-step, higher and higher, but with no change in view. The village below had disappeared. The shaman's ranting had faded into obscurity. The column of people came to a halt. Ojibwan ordered a rest—and just in time too, judging from the fatigue that was apparent on the face of Papa. The location for the break was wide enough for Ben, Patty, Johnny, and their great-grandfather—as well as Checker—to gather. Lilly was at the head of the procession, by Ojibwan's side.

They were quiet for some time, but then Ben spoke.

"I saw this before," he declared.

They were all quiet, wondering what he might have meant, but he did not explain himself.

"What are you talking about?" said Patty. "We've never been here before."

"I know," continued Ben. "But I tell you, I've seen it all before. It was in my dream, or vision, or whatever you want to call it. I saw a long column of people going up a rugged and dangerous path. The people were haggard and exhausted but kept moving. When they came to the top and leaned over the edge so they could see, they were faced with a city of wonder—a paradise, I think. As each of them cleared the edge and saw the city, their weariness was replaced with joy, and they all entered the city. After the last person had entered, the door was shut. I tried to go too, but Grandma was there and said it was not yet my time. I think everyone must have been dying and going to heaven. And here we are. This is exactly what I saw. Are we dead?"

"No," replied Papa, "We are not dead. But didn't you say that she said something else before the vision ended?"

"Yes, she kept repeating that the way was narrow, but we must enter by the narrow way."

"And we have," interjected Johnny. "We have entered that narrow way. Maybe this path is a symbol. Yes—it is our escape from the underground world, but it is also a symbol of the life choice we must make. We have all become Christians now. Christ-ones, we could call ourselves. And if He has given us such a great gift of knowing Him, and knowing him forever, then we should follow the path He gives us, even though it may be tough like this one. It may be rocky and narrow, and it might even seem impossible."

They all fell quiet for a few moments, each pondering this. Then Patty broke the silence and asked, "Ben, how many of the people in your vision fell off the path?"

"Not one," replied Ben. "Although it looked like most of them should have been blown off by a violent wind. Somehow everyone made it to the ledge, and they all went inside the door before it was shut."

"Of course, that makes complete sense!" exclaimed Patty. "Grandma used to tell me that all the time. When I prayed with her to ask Jesus into my life, she told me that He would never leave me or forsake me. She told me over and over how He would be with me always, even when times were hard. She was telling you this again, Ben, probably because you never listened very well when she was alive."

This would normally have turned into an argument causing Patty to run off in tears, but a display of unprecedented maturity came over Ben, and he nodded in assent. This in turn introduced a new sensation of humility within Patty. Ojibwan signaled to continue their upward-spiraling trek, and the procession once again started to move on. From here on, Ben, Patty, Johnny, and even Checker paid much closer attention to what was clearly a very stout but elderly loved one.

The climb continued in slow, small bursts. Ojibwan was sensitive to the wide age range and capabilities of his flock. The rugged path often looked impassable in places, yet at each challenge, the group found a way to proceed. Ojibwan did not share his fears about the fading light. They had long since left the natural lighting of the cavern and were dependent on the light from above. Although they had been able to overcome obstacles in their path, it would be impossible to proceed in the dark. Furthermore, there was no way that the group could make camp on such a narrow trail.

Then, to everyone's dismay, there came a rumbling noise. Johnny suddenly felt dizzy and could not keep his footing. He looked at others around him and saw that they were also having trouble with their balance. Then he noticed stones were falling from the cliffs, one narrowly missing Ben.

"Sit down!" shouted Papa. "This is an earthquake! Sit down and hold on, or you'll fall! Back up to the wall as best as you can!"

At that, all three children sat where they were, with the others following their example. In terror, Johnny watched large boulders break loose and careen down into the depths from where they had just been. The light was too weak to see what wreckage resulted, but the noise was deafening as the crashes continued relentlessly.

The quake seemed to last forever, though Johnny figured later that it was only a minute. Dust and debris were everywhere. No one dared move. The dust suspended in the air deepened the growing gloom. Johnny came to the same realization that Ojibwan had earlier—they did not have much time left, and now travel was even more difficult.

Suddenly Checker began to whine and cock his head to one side. Then he lay back down and whimpered.

"Hey, boy—it's okay!" reassured Johnny.

Checker thumped his tail but continued to look unhappy.

"What is that noise?" asked Patty.

"What noise?" responded Ben.

"It's in the wall."

Patty had pressed her ear to the cavern wall. Ben did likewise and listened.

"She's right; there's a low, rumbling noise."

"Another earthquake?" asked Johnny.

"Not likely," responded Papa. "I suppose aftershocks are possible but not usually this quickly."

"Well, whatever it is, it's getting louder," replied Patty.

"Now I can hear it too," said Johnny, who did not have his ear pressed against the walls as his cousins did.

But the investigation came to a sudden halt with a signal passed down from the top of the procession—it was time to move and to move quickly. Clearly Ojibwan was concerned about the cavern's instability as well as the fading light, and he wanted to make haste.

The group moved on, now having to negotiate some boulders that had landed on the path during the earthquake. Damage to the trail made it almost impassable in places. But the group found ways to ensure that everyone would make it—the small, the elderly, and those with other frailties.

"This is a miracle in the making," said Ben. "No one has been hurt, and the fact that we're even making it up this path has to be God's work."

"Yes, Ben," responded Patty. "Just like your vision."

Now this was perhaps a first for Patty, for in the past her responses were tainted with some criticism or correction, but this time there was nothing but sincerity and respect in both her words and her tone.

Johnny did not want to say anything, but being closest to the wall, he could hear the growing rumbling that was coming from somewhere within it. Keeping this quiet was pointless, because it soon became loud enough to be apparent to everyone.

"Don't stop climbing, even for a moment," came the command down the line.

This was difficult to obey, as the light continued to fade. But they were motivated by what was obvious to all—the low rumbling within the wall had become a dull roar. Johnny touched the cavern wall as he walked up the trail; to his horror, he could feel the wall shuddering.

Suddenly an explosion sounded somewhere below them. Looking down, Johnny saw huge jets of spray spurting from the wall and falling into the depths below. The procession instinctively stopped to watch this latest phenomenon. It was below them, but not by much.

The pause was momentary, with panicked people from below pressing upward and Ojibwan urgently summoning everyone to proceed. The vibration caused by the jets of water loosened other stones, even some above them, increasing the panic and urgency to escape. Yet no one was hurt.

"Look at that," Ben suddenly said.

Water was starting to ooze from the cavern wall as they passed. As they continued climbing, the entire wall began to slowly leak rivulets that formed into puddles running down the path under their feet.

"Keep going," commanded Ben, "but be careful. It may get slippery."

And indeed it did, for Papa nearly lost his footing in one place. Then, as if this had all been preplanned, the path widened enough for Johnny to come alongside him and provide a needed source of stability for the old man.

Grace persisted for the crowd as they consistently made headway, slowly spiraling upward in this great cylindrical shaft. Ben noticed the water had ceased oozing through the walls, and the rumbling noises continued below them. Suddenly, a shout came from above. They all looked up, and Johnny saw that the head of the procession had disappeared. In the poor light, he could barely see what was happening above him, but as he watched, he was sure he could discern people climbing over a ridge and disappearing into the gloom.

"We're almost there," Johnny exclaimed. "I can see people going over the top."

"I just need to avoid tripping," panted Papa. "It's getting hard to see."

Johnny realized again that this climb was hard for the old man. It was amazing that he was doing as well as he was. After all, he was in his late nineties.

Ben scrambled ahead with great excitement.

"I can see it—I can see the ridge!" he shouted and soon scampered over it.

Johnny and Patty stayed close to their great-grandfather, working their way upward until they saw the ledge above them. The path came abruptly to an end, so they would have to scramble up a four-foot incline to reach the ridge.

Papa stopped, looking discouraged.

"I don't think I can do that," he confessed.

But out of nowhere, Ojibwan jumped down from above and back to the pathway, motioning to Johnny to help lift his great-grandfather. They did so, and others reached down from above to help the old man over the ledge. They helped Patty up in a similar manner before Ojibwan jumped back up. Johnny heard a whimper and looked back to see Checker whining softly and wagging his tail, unsure how to follow the others.

"I'm sorry, boy," said Johnny. "I forgot you were there. Come on, we can do this."

Johnny scooped up his dog and set him on top, where to Checker's relief he found level ground, and the scent of all things familiar. After Johnny reached the top, he caught up with his cousins and his great-grandfather, who had been reunited with Lilly. Ojibwan continued to help his people clear the rim of the shaft.

"This is just like my vision," Ben suddenly exclaimed. "Look at everyone!" As people came over the top, their faces were haggard and worn with fear; but as they arrived and looked around, their expressions changed to wonder and joy.

"This is just what I saw happen. The people became radiant as they saw their new home."

"But where is "home"?" asked Patty.

"I know this place—at least I think I do," interjected Lilly. "I've seen it only from a distance. It's a holy place. We've always been told no one can come here—it's sacred."

"What do you mean?" asked Johnny. "Where are we?"

"We're not far from my village. Something happened here, long before any of us were born. As far as I know, none of my people has ever set foot in this place. We should not be here."

Lilly seemed deeply shaken. Johnny looked back over the rim and saw that there were only about fifty more people still to complete their journey. He noticed that sections of the path below appeared to be damaged or missing, but the growing gloom made it hard to tell for sure. Crashing sounds and rushing water could be heard unmistakably from far below. The underground world they had so recently departed was being sealed off forever by water and rock.

Finally, the last person cleared the rim. Ojibwan ushered them all away from the shaft into the surrounding woods and motioned for Johnny to do the same. Johnny also noticed the look of joy that came across each individual's face.

Reunited

Ojibwan permitted them only a very brief break. Now that they had surfaced from the cavern, the light had improved, but clearly it would not last for long. He first spoke to Lilly, who responded in words unintelligible to Ben, Johnny, or Patty. If their great-grandfather understood their language, he did not show it. Ojibwan listened and nodded his head slowly. He then called out to his people to move on.

Lilly looked uncomfortable and said, "We really need to get out of this place."

"Where are we going?" asked Johnny.

"To my village," she replied, unwilling to say more. She ran off and caught up with Ojibwan. Together they led the procession.

"Papa—how much farther do we have to go?" interrupted Patty.

"Not much—the village is very close by. The real question is: what are all the villagers going to think when this big group of people converges upon them? I hope there isn't any trouble."

Their great-grandfather was right about how close they were, for in ten minutes the group came within sight of Lilly's village. Ojibwan stopped and asked the group to sit down. He called Lilly, his father, a few of his most trusted braves, the great-grandfather and Great Bear. After he spoke a few words to them, the braves put down their weapons. They walked toward the village where its inhabitants were already gathering who were startled at seeing this mass of people just outside their dwellings.

Some of villagers ran back and returned with their chief. Ojibwan stepped forward, accompanied by Lilly. His hands were stretched out in a gesture of peace.

Suddenly, one woman from the village gasped and ran straight to Lilly and hugged her lovingly. Recognizing her mother, Lilly returned her embrace.

The meeting of these two closely related peoples exploded into enthusiasm. It soon became clear that they were members of a common tribe. The village chief made a loud proclamation, after which Ojibwan's father gestured to the rest of the people to follow. Everyone understood that they were at the brink of a most joyous reunion, one that neither side had ever thought possible.

Orders were given. Tents were set up everywhere. A huge feast was quickly prepared. And as all sat down to eat, the four elders— Ojibwan's father, the village chief, Papa, and his old friend began to converse. In the middle of the dialogue, Lilly was summoned, and she in turn called Johnny, Ben, and Patty with Checker following. She explained to them that the entire white community had been in great turmoil as soon as it discovered they were missing. Search parties had been looking for them ever since they were reported as lost.

"How long have we been gone?" asked Johnny.

Lilly spoke to the village chief and then replied, "We've been gone for ten days. The rescue parties have almost given up, and only the closest friends of your parents are continuing to search. There was a big earthquake today, and most of those people had to go home to attend to their families. The village chief feels you should go home as soon as possible to end your family's fear and grieving. Johnny, your mother and father are here too. They've been searching the whole time, along with the others."

A mixed sense of gratitude and shame came over Johnny at once. He was humbled and grieved to think of the stress he had brought upon his family but also overwhelmed by their love for him.

"Yes, we must go at once," he said.

"Let's go now," agreed Patty. "I want to go home as soon as possible."

"It's a long walk still," said Lilly. "It would take hours on foot, especially through the forest in the dark. The village chief has commanded his men to bring a large canoe that could hold a dozen men. He says you can go by canoe. His men are strong and will take you there. There is enough moonlight, and with several of his men paddling, you will get there quickly."

They followed as the men carried the canoe to the lake. Johnny, Ben, and Patty got into the boat. Checker started whining on the shore, chasing up and down at the water's edge.

"Come on, Checker! You're always such a big chicken when it comes to canoes!"

"I can't really blame him," said Ben.

Johnny got back out, picked up his dog, and placed him into the canoe before getting back in himself.

"Papa, let's go!" said Patty, who noticed her great-grandfather was hanging back.

"Not yet," he replied. "Tell them I'm here. I'll come soon enough, but this night I want to spend with my friends. I'll see the family soon enough. You tell them everything, and then they'll be more prepared to see me—at least I hope so."

They shoved off. Six of the village men paddled in a manner that seemed choreographed. The canoe quickly sped away, following the reflected moonbeam that pointed perfectly in the direction they needed to head.

Patty was troubled.

"Why did he say 'I hope so'?" she asked Johnny. "Of *course* everyone will want to see him!" she exclaimed. "Wasn't that the main reason we went on this journey in the first place? I don't think we should have left him behind."

"Patty, he needed to rest, that's all," commented Ben. "Think about it. He's in his nineties, and he just climbed up out of the cavern. I doubt any other ninety-year-old could have done that! He just needs a rest."

Patty looked unsatisfied.

"Well, maybe," she said softly.

Lilly returned to the village after her friends had paddled out of sight, and for the first time, she felt alone. She saw Ojibwan conversing with the elders. Even though he showed deference toward them, he was undisputedly in charge. She knew she could not interrupt their meeting. Looking back to the people, she saw that they looked uncertain as to what they should be doing. Her mother spoke to her and suggested that they help the people find a place to bed down for the night. The two of them returned to the new arrivals and began organizing the families, helping them each find a tent.

"There will be many problems," she said to her mother. "This village cannot support so many new people all at once. We will need to think of some way to involve everyone in the feeding and care of our restored tribe."

Meanwhile, the paddlers made short work of the journey across the lake to Ben and Patty's home. They silently glided up to the dock from which they had set out only ten days earlier. There was no one on the shore, and the cabin seemed quiet. The porch was lighted and a lamp was shining from behind closed curtains.

"I wonder what they'll say?" asked Ben nervously.

"I just want to see Mom and Dad now," said Patty, hopping out of the boat and running toward the cabin.

"Wait!" said Johnny. "Let's go together!" Ben turned to thank the men who had escorted them home. They smiled and departed.

"I almost feel like we're about to wake up from a dream," said Johnny.

"Or a nightmare," added Ben.

"Maybe, but there was a reason for this adventure, and it's amazing we got back alive, all of us—and we're not even hurt."

"We even found our great-grandfather and brought him back," added Ben.

"Come on, you guys! I want to see Mom and Dad," protested Patty.

So together they walked to the door, though not fast enough for Patty. Ben opened it, and they stepped into the living room. The fire burned low. No one was there. A newspaper lay on the footstool. Johnny looked at the headlines and read them aloud: "*Search continues for tenth day: children still missing.*"

"Mom!" shouted Patty. "We're back!" Patty called repeatedly, but no answer came. Ben ran upstairs and called for his parents and his grandfather. Johnny sat on the couch and waited. Ben returned downstairs and said, "Where could they all have gone?" But before he could say anything more they heard barking outside. Checker had run around the outside of the cabin. He heard a car coming up the drive and chased off as a bolt of lightning to greet it.

"They just can't give up!" cried Gail as she, Jim and Johnny's parents, turned up their long drive. "*I'm* not giving up," she asserted.

Johnny's mother and father were sitting in the back, quietly absorbed in their grief.

"What in the world is *that?*" exclaimed Jim, slowing the car. It was too dark to tell what kind of animal was racing toward them, but the car's headlights soon revealed it to be a dog.

"That dog—" stammered Johnny's Dad, "it's impossible, but I swear that dog is Johnny's! It looks like Checker! It *is* Checker!" He proceeded to open the door, even before the car had come to a complete stop. Checker recognized him and jumped up to his chest, almost knocking him over.

"Checker! Where are the kids? Where did you come from?" shouted Johnny's father. Checker, knowing instinctively what was being asked, continued to bark and started running back to the cabin, pursued on foot by Johnny's father.

"Get in the car!" shouted Jim, who had pulled up alongside him. "We can follow Checker more quickly by car!" And so they did—to find all their children standing in front of the cabin, waiting for them. The parents stopped the car, rushed out, and embraced their children. No one said anything for some time; they just held each other, and many tears were shed.

Then Patty started to unload.

"Mom and Dad, you wouldn't believe it! We took the canoes to our secret place behind the—oops, I'm not supposed to say where— but we took them there, and everything was fine, except Ben and Lilly—well, I guess we all agreed to go explore the back of the cave. Anyway, the water started going in circles, and it was sucking us down and down, and we couldn't get out, no matter how hard we paddled—"

"Patty," interrupted her father, "we want to hear it all, but let's get inside first."

They all headed into their home.

"Dad, we'll tell you everything, but it's going to take a while," said Ben. "Before we do, I want to say I'm sorry for all this. We didn't mean to get lost; in fact, I never dreamed that the place we went could even exist. I'm even more surprised that we got out. The story of what happened to us could fill a book. But there's something much more important we need to tell you first."

The parents all sat motionless and expectant.

"We found our great-grandfather—the one who left home long before we were born. He's with the local Indian tribe right now. We wanted him to come home, but he seemed nervous about it, so he asked us to tell you he's okay and would like to see you tomorrow."

The parents were stunned. Johnny's father and Uncle Jim looked at each other and then back to their children. Johnny's father spoke first.

"Johnny, you must have met someone else. Your great-grandfather passed away many years ago, when we were very young."

"No, it really is him, Dad," Johnny offered.

Ben and Patty nodded in agreement.

"We'd better go see who this is," said Uncle Jim.

"Not until tomorrow," objected Patty. "I don't know why, but he seems nervous."

"That's because he's an impostor, Patty. He couldn't possibly have survived this long."

"Look at this," interjected Johnny, producing his great-grandfather's Bible. "You'll have to tell us whether you think this is genuine. It's his Bible, and it's very old."

The two men studied it carefully, turning each page and scrutinizing the contents. After some time, Uncle Jim leaned back in his chair.

"It's genuine!" he exclaimed. "I have no idea how you kids got this, but I'm sure that's his old Bible. But just because someone found his Bible doesn't make the man your great-grandfather."

"He knew too much about us, Dad," objected Ben. "Tomorrow we'll see him, and you can judge for yourself."

"I know it's him," Patty whispered to her mother.

"Yes, I'm sure too," she replied.

If her tone was directed perhaps too much to the little girl she knew, she would find out soon enough that Patty had matured through the experiences of the past ten days—more than she could imagine. But for now she noticed only that her daughter was looking exhausted.

"I think we can answer these questions tomorrow," suggested Aunt Gail. "It's long past time that we all got some sleep."

Johnny suddenly realized how spent he was. With little more discussion, and with some help from Aunt Gail, they all found a place to crash. Ben and Patty were fast asleep within seconds.

Aunt Gail returned to her bedroom and found her husband silently praying at his bed, a sight she had not seen for some time. She joined him, and with more tears than words, they thanked their God for His mercy and the safe return of their children.

Johnny, unlike his cousins, stayed awake for a bit longer, thinking about all that had happened over the past ten days.

"I wonder what Papa will feel like when he sees his family again," Johnny mused. "It would be very strange—his son has become old and his grandchildren have become adults. No wonder he felt a bit shy about coming back. It's a whole new world for him."

As sleep was starting to overtake him, he realized that they had all changed a lot.

Patty doesn't seem like the little girl she was when we started this adventure, and Ben has found his faith, he thought.

Johnny suddenly remembered that he was a changed person too, having found faith in His Savior as well. He realized that their salvation from the underground prison was just a symbol of his real salvation, the release from his own domain of darkness. Then he noticed a shadow on his wall. The moonlight streamed through his window, obstructed by a broken part of the window frame, and formed the shadow of a rugged cross.

Such amazing grace, Johnny thought, losing the battle for consciousness. *Tomorrow we start fresh. Tomorrow is the beginning of the rest of my life!*

He would forever appreciate this thought in a way that most of us never understand.

The End

Epilogue

Although this story has come to an end, the lives of Johnny, Ben, Patty, Lilly, their great-grandfather, Ojibwan, and all the others—yes, even Checker—went on. The Matheson family, together with its newly found eldest member, was reunited. It might have been awkward, had it not been for Patty. As they approached the village the next morning, she ran to her great-grandfather and enthusiastically introduced him to everyone, talking incessantly until her mother had to settle her down so that they all could rest. The old man returned home with them that very day, and he lived another five years until he died at the ripe old age of 103. It took that long to tell and re-tell his story, not only to everyone in the community but also to scores of reporters and even a few government representatives who wanted to hear it all over again. But Papa did not seem to mind the attention, especially when he found himself on the front page of a major newspaper.

Checker became very attached to the elder Matheson. The dog proved to be quite a help to him, somehow able to anticipate his wishes and fetch things for him at appropriate times. When it was time for Johnny and his parents to leave, Johnny offered to let Checker stay. Checker seemed to understand. It was an act of unselfishness on Johnny's part that his parents proudly saw as a new step in maturity for him.

Patty also became attached to her great-grandfather. Although being at school made it impossible for her to spend the kind of time with him that Checker did, she remained most devoted to him for the rest of his life. By the time she finished high school, she was on her way to becoming an accomplished artist. After attending a fine arts college in Seattle Washington, she moved to Italy where she took up painting Frescos—where, to the best of our knowledge, she still lives today.

It is probably no big surprise that Lilly and Ojibwan became close. He was immediately accepted as an elder of their village, something unheard of for a twenty-three-year-old. As soon as the old chief passed away, Ojibwan was recognized as the new chief. He had the foresight to visit nearby cities and could see that the village was living almost as if it had been lost in the previous century. He worked slowly and deliberately to get the village incorporated as a town, and he organized the elders into a town council. The council elected him mayor.

Ojibwan encouraged Lilly, who was only fifteen at the time of their return, to finish high school, which she did in two more years. Then, to her dismay, Ojibwan asked her to attend the University of Manitoba, many hundreds of miles away. Although reluctant, she did not argue and set out to study business administration and political science. She not only became the top student in her class but also acquired a graduate degree in business management. During the time in Manitoba, she became close friends with another young woman, who eventually persuaded her to become a Christian, as Ojibwan had done. During her student years, Lilly returned home only occasionally, so when the time came for her to return permanently, she found herself fearful of what might await her. But her fears subsided as soon as she discovered that, despite his popularity with the young women, Ojibwan was still single. Only six months later, they married. The two of them transformed what had been a nineteenth-century Indian tribe into a successful, self-sufficient community.

Ben and Johnny both joined local youth groups—different ones, of course, since they lived quite a distance from each other. And both became successful in their chosen professions. Ben found he was good at mathematics and went on to become a much sought after aeronautical engineer. He finally settled in Seattle, Washington, where he worked for a large airplane company. Johnny, however, attended

Whitworth College in Spokane, Washington, where he prepared to enter the ministry. After graduation, he attended Dallas Theological Seminary and ultimately became a respected Biblical scholar.

But what about the crystal pool itself? For that matter, what about the entire lake? And what of the mystery surrounding the return of a great number of people from the depths of the earth? This, of course, had not gone unnoticed by local and regional governments and by anthropologists, geologists, and all kinds of reporters. Once the rumor of what had happened got out, the area was overrun by people with various agendas. At first, this was great for local businesses, especially the inns and restaurants, which were usually overbooked. Ojibwan revealed himself as an entrepreneur, employing the villagers to make all sorts of arts and crafts that ended up selling for very good prices. Eventually things got out of control, and Ojibwan requested help from nearby authorities to regulate the visitors. They were happy to comply.

After the initial commercial rush subsided, the scientists and government functionaries came and took an intense interest in the lake. They interviewed people—especially Ben, Patty, Lilly, Ojibwan (who had mastered English very quickly), and (of course) Papa—repeatedly. They inspected the top of the cylindrical shaft many times, sending well-equipped climbers back down the hole. After multiple attempts, they learned only that the hole was filled with debris and large stones well beneath the rim. Finally, the authorities fenced off the area and posted no trespassing signs around it.

They were not done, however. Geologists were troubled that the lake had two sources of fresh water: the layered falls, where the entire adventure had originated, and a small creek on the opposite side of the lake. They could not get enough of the story that the children (now in their mid-teens) kept telling them. The scientists thought their story implausible, but the fact that the story was so consistent, plus the very troublesome fact that there was no river or creek leading out of the lake was very thought-provoking. Granted, the lake was large and the sources of the water small in comparison; still, the lake could not keep filling without getting bigger. Evaporation could not be the explanation, since with enough time the lake would get salty, and the lake water was fresh.

Much to Patty's dismay, divers were sent in behind the waterfall. They were equipped with ropes in case they needed to be pulled out, but nothing of the sort happened. They found no whirlpool, although on one of their trips they discovered an area near the back of the cave that showed signs of recent rock movement in the floor. It looked as though it had a funnel-like shape with new rock jammed into it.

Geologists discovered in government archives that a survey of the lake had been performed ten years earlier that included specific measurements of the lake's elevation. Apparently a team of geologists had noted that the lake had inlets but no outlets; they were curious whether the lake would rise. So these measurements were repeated at the same locations, and—oddly enough—the lake was a full two feet lower than it had been a decade before. Eventually, the geologists gave up on the puzzle, documented everything in a new government report, and left their markers at the locations established in the earlier report. These markers were etched with a very fine scale so future measurements could be made. However, as with so many such studies, later scientists had different interests, so the lake reverted to its original state of remoteness and disappeared from the public eye.

Not so for Ojibwan. He was quite interested in the puzzle and had his people put a fence with a locked gate around each marker. Every year, he recorded the height of the lake and discovered that it was rising. He then decided to move the village to higher ground. Fortunately, they found a site where, if the lake rose another four feet, water would find an exit. Within five years, the lake reached that height and the runoff formed a new creek joining a tributary to a larger river that made its way to Lake Superior.

And now, with the telling of all these adventures and wonders, the story must end. All the characters in our story lived meaningful lives and lived happily ever after.

Afterword

The Crystal Pool was motivated as a means to preserve an era of the Bingham family culture, that of storytelling particularly at bedtime. The stories were intended to be fun, sometimes a little scary, frequently with some underlying moral, and also a means to convey Biblical principles at strategic times.

Although the book began in 1985 targeted to elementary school age children, the business of life and significant periods of writer's block slowed its creation so that it is now dedicated to my children's children. Perhaps due to the time over which the story was created (nearly a quarter of a century), the characters aged in sophistication, perhaps as my own children also grew.

Consequently, early versions of the first eight or so chapters had to be modified to bring up the maturity of the main characters to be more consistent with the main story line as developed in later chapters. Now the target audience is late elementary through middle school.

At first the Crystal Pool was primarily an adventure involving four children, a dog, and some interactions with some family members. It was to be a book parents could trust, having solid ethics and a "safe" story line. As the plot developed, it became increasingly important to me to include a spiritual underpinning, making it more than just an adventure, but an adventure with a purpose and some insight into The Bible's presentation of God, reaching to all people as Savior.

I trust the reader will find this a story an almost possible, though highly unlikely scenario. One where a person could imagine the world this story reveals as perhaps really there.

e|LIVE

listen|imagine|view|experience

AUDIO BOOK DOWNLOAD INCLUDED WITH THIS BOOK!

In your hands you hold a complete digital entertainment package. In addition to the paper version, you receive a free download of the audio version of this book. Simply use the code listed below when visiting our website. Once downloaded to your computer, you can listen to the book through your computer's speakers, burn it to an audio CD or save the file to your portable music device (such as Apple's popular iPod) and listen on the go!

How to get your free audio book digital download:

1. Visit www.tatepublishing.com and click on the e|LIVE logo on the home page.
2. Enter the following coupon code:
   add4-022c-da2e-6d6e-8f49-5a0f-2d4a-8275
3. Download the audio book from your e|LIVE digital locker and begin enjoying your new digital entertainment package today!